From The Red Bench

From The Red Bench

ALEX HENRY

———

Dedicated to Emma, Rita, and Allen.
Who each said at least one word when it was needed most.

———

PART ONE

Prologue

Seventeen years I have been a prisoner. Of my captors I know not, nor do I wish to know. To find a method of escape in the far reaches of myself would be a pain too immense to deal, so in this prison I curse God as my gaoler and ruminate his intentions. The conclusion I come to is thus: a man cannot be freed without first being condemned and so it is in my imprisonment that my liberator is identified. She comes to me as often as the moon and with as much vividness. I wake and recall the most intimate features: her hair the sandy gold of heavens shores reaching just down to delicate shoulders, her strides climax in the subtle bounce of a dancer, and her eyes.. I dare not look into her eyes for it is too obviously a dream when I do. She has shown me the freedom for which my heart yearns and has renewed my creator God as benevolent. A beauty such as hers was no doubt sculpted by a majestic hand and it is through such beauty that I can attempt to comprehend my melancholy fate thus far. I weep with joy that I have been touched by such grace, and I weep in solitude that I cannot conceive of a more perfect creature. I am a dreamer and yet I can dream of nothing but her, for as real as she is, she is concurrently the expression of my inner desires, and the culmination of my being.

The prompting of my endeavor of such expression is the result of a chance encounter. Fate produced a mild event that led to a discovery that has defined my humanhood, has revealed to me my captivity, and has presented me the means of ascension from such imprisonment. I concede that I could not speak, for true beauty pierces the soul, and with a shortness of breath I peered only at the back of my eyelids and was thus lost in her voice. To speak back to her would be to confess my deepest sins and secrets so that she may take me back to heaven with her. I so desperately wanted to proclaim her piety to the world and shout, "I know, I know where it is you reside!" But alas, upon our first meeting I was too cowardly and far too disoriented, as if glimpsing the sun for the first time, to establish anything less substantial than my absolute undying devotion…

ONE

_____

GRACING THE OTHERWISE BLAND CENTER OF THE COUNTRY THE town of Wilheimer Falls initially attracted only the most solitary and introverted travelers. The region in terms of geography was mundane and only the most obsessive fantasizers could attribute any grandiose origin to the town. Like most towns in America some dumb drunk passed out long enough for a town to be erected around him and stirring from a long slumber they conclude themselves the founder. The new townsfolk being too humble to make such proclamations for themselves allow the downtrodden man his triumph. Wilheimer Falls was named after the drunk Alfred Wilheimer, and sure enough he did fall often. A loyalist, his life consisted of a meager enlistment in the royal army and produced nothing of note. Upon the surrender of General Cornwallis, Alfred returned to a destroyed home that was just as he had left it and decided to travel west where the mentioned settlement was inevitably constructed around one of his favorite resting spots. The current condition of the settlement was impressive for its origin and had been growing exponentially over the years. Many people detesting city life, in which everyone was a stranger, had moved to less crowded areas where only the majority of the population were strangers. Wilheimer Falls boasted a cobblestone road and a town square with family owned boutiques sprawled in every direction. The boring, consistently grey weather allowed the well-lit store fronts to glow in contrast. At dusk each shop acted to imitate the setting sun and every establishment, being distinct in some way, drew the eyes of each inhabitant that was still detained by business and like the emerald quality of a rainstorm the town, with its unique hue, managed to intoxicate any participant who would stop to appreciate it.

Of the inhabitants that were primarily enigmatic to each other, some were less unrecognizable than others. There was a boy of considerable wealth who lived in an estate just outside of town. His particular quality was not of personal note but rather he was inclined to attention due to his absence from any affair at all. He had studied in any den that would not pester him with even the most innocent inquiry and he had thus acquired an impressive resume that was entirely empty.

As he entered the town of Wilheimer Falls he maintained a certain quickness to his stride, as if in a hurry.

"Alexander!.." a shrewd voice yelled. A solemn defeat appeared in the boy's decorum.

"Alexander Climicus!" an elderly woman sprang from a boutique situated behind the now quickening boy and exclaimed again. Forced to stop by the etiquette that was drilled into him since before he could remember, Alexander turned. Never being fond of smiling he kept his face neutral.

"Hello Macey." the boy said, running his fingers anxiously through his short black hair.

Macey owned one of the successful shops in the area called "Macey and Mills" that specialized in antiques. In his braver days the young boy had ventured in while searching for old books. He learned quickly that the overwhelming dialogue demanded by Macey made shopping there an impossibility. He felt a mild sense of correctness in his analysis due to the fact that he had only spoken to Macey a few times in the course of years and she still presented such an extravagant welcome.

"Alexander Climicus." she repeated surely. "It has been so long! How long?.. Oh it doesn't matter! How have you been? Oh it doesn't matter! You look well enough, why have you not visited me?"

The rate of the succession of questions startled him and he could not decide which to pretend to answer first. At one point in his life he had attempted to study conversational etiquette in an effort to relieve this clear problem but decided that it was folly. It wasn't worth the time and his plan was to actively not converse with anybody anyway. He conceded to being uncomfortable in such situations and saw it as a fair sacrifice for his true learning. He could maneuver amongst the most aggressive conversationalists but found that those like Macey would often answer their own questions and required only minimal input from him. This was the small joy he saw extractable from conversation.

"How are you?" he said, deciding not to answer any of the inquiries presented.

"I'm good, I'm good! Thank you, you really must come in and look around, it's been so long but that doesn't matter. Come in and look I'm sure we have something that would interest you. We have no books unfortunately but come, come, we can chat more inside."

"I can't Macey." Every conversation went through the same process with Alexander Climicus: first a feeling of dread at the onset followed by confusion at how to answer then climaxed in even more confusion about how to end it. He always made a mental note to have an excuse prepared beforehand, some adaptable story so that if any unforeseen dialogue were to arise he could quickly stifle it and escape. He had no such excuse prepared.

"But Alexander! Why not? Come give an old lady some company. Oh never mind, it doesn't matter. It was good seeing you, take care." Macey turned and waved goodbye as she reentered the boutique and again Alexander was astonished at how little he got away with saying. He was glad when people seemed to understand him

and therefore let him refrain from speaking. It was a certain understanding that he had nothing noteworthy to say; whether this was
insulting or not he debated internally but remembered that no one
else had anything noteworthy to say either and so it was merely his
refusal to state such things that enabled this understanding.

He continued on, glad that one interaction was behind him.
The probability of him being noticed by anyone else was slim and
he could loosen himself a bit. Alexander loved long walks but
stayed mainly in the woods enjoying the orchestra of nature in
which each tiny participant was essential to the masterpiece; the
shades of color excited in him a deep appreciation for the artistry
of the universe. He had spent most of his life in small rooms studying and staring at nothingness while lost in thought, it wasn't until recently that he had begun to understand how compelling the
natural world was. Every shade shown to him here would remain
with the absence of man, the orchestra would still play and be just
as enchanting whether he was in the vicinity or not. There is a
certain gravity to the thought of one not being where one is, the
idea of nonexistence. Alexander felt vividly non-existent on such
nature walks and so they tended to captivate his time. Venturing
into Wilheimer Falls, he didn't expect anything other than fright
but felt a strange energy that was absent all the previous times he
roamed the town. The population had been substantially increasing in his absence and being a busy day, everyone seemed to be
moving much quicker than he understood. This was the feeling
of nonexistence, only intensified. Alexander felt more nonexistent
than he had ever before.

Meandering slowly, he was forced to the outskirts of the walkway by the clearly purpose driven men and women of the town.
He observed with dismay that there was nowhere to sit, no crude
bench or even slight curb where he could bask in the feeling he
was feeling. Alexander noticed that even the most minute multi-

tasking deteriorated everything, even his nature walks would be better described as nature lays. The walking itself tended to be more of a means of seeking a location and the health benefits were substantial, making it a worthy trade. Health is necessary to life, and so some concessions are necessary in order to maintain life. None the less, Alexander remained walking and did his best to think and observe in addition to such an annoying task of moving. He took great lengths to look into the eyes of the oncoming traffic of civilians, the return of such an intimate gesture seemed like a rarity in the current environment. The dynamic of the town usually demanded that his eyes stay planted in a reserved manner a few inches in front of his steps, he felt as if this was no longer a requirement and for the first time was free to enjoy the town and its inhabitants as he had nature. Like nature, there was an intoxicatingly distinct composition of what could only be described as music, the rustling of feet, the small chatter of people talking under their breath to themselves, the clanging of doors, a distant carriage all blurred together and sounds that would alone be agony together were medicine.

Looking into the eyes of the townsfolk Alexander couldn't help but remove the humanity from the individuals he viewed. He noticed that they didn't notice him, if they did, it didn't matter. Like ant colonies that he had observed so many times, the workers kept working and the orchestra kept playing whether he was or was not present. He had always fantasized about finding one ant who was not like the rest, a sort of dreamer ant that was destined for larger things, a hero ant of some kind that would change the world of ants forever. Alexander knew he would not find such an ant. The analogy his mind made of the town to an ant colony made him sick, if he was in an ant colony then he would have to define himself as an ant as well. If he had to define himself as an ant, he would with great hubris call himself a dreamer ant. Dreamer ants do not exist. Observing Wilheimer Falls as an ant colony, from a higher vantage point, he would seem like an incompetent worker ant, unable to obtain a mate, less than the rest, not worthy of survival, not pulling his weight. Alexander redirected his eyes to a few feet in front of him and quickened his pace.

TWO

ANGELICA HAMILTON WAS NOT ORIGINALLY FROM WILHEIMER FALLS, after her parents separated she chose to live with her aunt and uncle rather than pick between them, a decision that perplexed all parties. She was perfectly rural and impressively inviting with intelligent penetrating azure eyes, shoulder length blonde hair usually kept in a ponytail, and she seemed to be unaware of how attractive most people found her. She had spent her youth engaged in ballet and had developed a certain flexible grit that showed spectacularly in her halfcocked grin. Her movements seemed flamboyant upon first impression but closer inspection revealed a determined grace that curved the resolution of every action, softening it. Her first impression of Wilheimer Falls was excitement, eager to be in a new environment Angelica took to her new caregivers instantly and was refreshed by the bond of her aunt and uncle.

The condition that Angelica had accepted as a term of living with her relatives was working at their restaurant situated in town. Always fond of people she had no problem and was optimistic at the prospect. Being trained in every position she quickly became the fondest of bartending and waitressing, the two positions that yielded the highest rate of social interaction. Noticing this and in a fruitless attempt to shield her from the occasional drunkard, Angelica's uncle Wilbur allowed her to waitress most of the time while he attended to the bar.

Wilbur was a stout man shaped by hard work. He wore a smile that was obviously labored, and in moments of thought one couldn't help but notice his fatigue.

"You've been quite the help darling, since you came to live with us." he said, placing a hand on Angelica's shoulder. She instinctually placed her hand on top of his in an equally comforting manner.

"I'm so grateful Uncle.. The way Mom and Dad fought.. It wasn't good for me.. I'm so happy that you and Auntie were willing to let me come."

"Of course darling! We all love you, whatever you think is best for yourself we are willing to help in any way possible. You're doing great here, the charm of Wilheimer Falls is something special." he said with a distinct air of pride and a reassuring smile.

"Thanks Uncle. I'm so glad I came."

"So how's business been today? Are you enjoying the position? There haven't been any drunks have there? I would kick the scoundrels out but they pay so damn well."

"There hasn't been a morning free of alcohol in years, you said so yourself." Angelica reminded him with a grin. "Although.. I rather enjoy the company, they claim to be aristocrats and I the princess."

"You are a princess indeed Angelica, but would you really call them aristocrats?"

"Aristocrats on hard times maybe, the difference between a noble and a commoner is only the vintage."

"Aha!" Wilbur chortled, "What wise words, and have the poor noblemen tipped well this morning?"

"So they have Uncle!" she exclaimed, "The noblemen have attempted to dry our stores and have tipped me a dollar with each drink, although I admit I am afraid to count." She reached into her pocket and displayed to Wilbur a collection of coins and papers. His eyes widened and he embraced her with a loving warmness.

"My princess!" he laughed and added a bow.

As the topic shifted, a lean black-haired boy strode in, his strides noticeably long almost as if intentional. His eyes firmly planted on the ground in front of him, he nearly bumped into a guest that had stopped to look at the menu displayed on a chalkboard near the entryway. He jerked back startled and riveted his eyes to a well-lit booth across the restaurant and made his way, making sure to avoid intruding on anyone's dining space. He sat down and began making small changes to the order of utensils.

Angelica eyed the boy as he entered and found his franticness laughable. His near collision with the patron made her chuckle under her breath.

"Who is that boy, Uncle?" she asked, interjecting into one of his sentences.

"Ah, that's Alexander Climicus I believe. A sad story really.. I hadn't heard he was back in town. I wonder if Macey knows, you remember Macey don't you? She was a family friend to the boy before.. uh.. the accident. Never mind.. Yes, he is a good fellow, always polite. He has an inclination towards silence though, I'll go tell the chef that he's here, excuse me darling."

"But.. you don't know his order yet Uncle.."

"Ah yes.. I forgot to mention, he has become accustomed to a specific order, has gotten nothing but that order since he was a young boy. The funny thing is, it actually isn't on our menu anymore.. I don't think he's looked at our menu since the very first time." Wilbur said with a chuckle.

"Oh please uncle, he looks interesting, may I make sure? Let me take his order Uncle, please please please" she said, her pearl white teeth accentuating every syllable.

"I don't see why not.. You know I can't say no to you. Very well, go take his order, I'll have the chef begin preparation anyway, I have a feeling he won't have changed it"

"Okay uncle, I'll go wait on him," she curtseyed and made her way across the restaurant.

Angelica had never had a boyfriend or even been asked on a date. Lying in bed she often pondered why this must be. Depending on her mood she came to one of two conclusions; the first being that she was too dumb and ugly in which case she would reminisce on all the conversations in which she had intended to be humorous or sarcastic and received concerned or serious responses. She thought long about how unconcerned she was with her appearance; her blonde hair usually banded lazily upwards in a ponytail, or off to the side. She noticed that other girls had evenly toned skin, while hers normally climaxed with a darker nose and cheeks from sun exposure, and a clear farmer's tan from her lackadaisical explorations of Wilheimer Falls where she wore whatever attire suited her whim. The second and much more realistic conclusion, although she would never admit it, is that she is so pretty and intelligent that men are intimidated. She would tuck herself in tight and think back to all the wonderfully sarcastic and jovial things she had said to customers in which they were too intimidated and shy to laugh back and would default to a stern response. She would smile and assert that her blasé', lazy appearance gave her a charm that most perceived as foreign. Both conclusions were concocted in the pre-sleep haze and thus forgotten, but the final thought before her slumber was always, "someday."

THREE

———

ALEXANDER'S MAIN CRITERION FOR DECISION-MAKING WAS FAMIL-
iarity. Familiarity, he noticed, was the best method for quickness,
a word here and there eventually left no more words to be said
and one could continue their thoughts. His proclivity to explore,
it seemed, only operated in an observational capacity, leaving
him with no desire to participate. He had always been this way,
an eternal observer, therefore when stricken with hunger and
thirst while eagerly perceiving the world, he chose one of the few
remaining familiarities from his childhood for sustenance. Alexander recalled his mother bringing him into town when he was
just a fledgling and they would share a sandwich at The Dancing
Sheep Grill & Tap. Although he generally disliked going into
town, even as a child The Dancing Sheep was sometimes a welcome consolation. He was in awe of detail and noted with enthusiasm the systematic and efficient order that the utensils were
placed in. A napkin, dinner fork, and salad fork were placed on
the left side of the plate, shining and sturdy. The plate was always
centered perfectly with small dancing sheep silhouettes gracing
the outer edge and a large one in the middle. On the right were
the dinner knife, butter knife, and soup spoon; everything was
perfectly leveled and edged. The young Alexander was impressed
knowing that the placement surely immigrated and managed
to thrive.

Although The Dancing Sheep was not as meticulous as he remembered it, Alexander was relieved to be somewhere familiar, and more importantly in a place where he was unlikely to run into any old acquaintances. The owner Wilbur had struck Alexander as an intelligent man, first because of the presentation of the restaurant itself and again with the way he responded to his own solitary nature. Wilbur had been careful not to engage in idle chit chat and had memorized Alexander's order and would prepare and serve it with nothing but a nod. With his eyes fixated on the sheep silhouette centered on the plate in front of him Alexander began contemplating the order of utensils through history and how the evolution may have occurred.

He was jolted out of contemplation by a splendid curiosity which originated in his peripherals. The energetic cadence he observed excited in his imagination the notion of an angel, which he felt unable to repel. Each step demanded from him more attention than the previous and he was persuaded almost instantly of some divine characteristic. His heart beat with a deafening, deep thud. The gravity of one being where one is was too much for him to handle and closing his eyes briefly, he expected to wake up the next instant. As she drew nearer, he felt his face redden. He looked at her and their eyes met, he couldn't help but smile.

"I'm Angelica.. how are you..? My uncle Wilbur.. owns this restaurant. I moved here.. three months ago." she said, taken aback by his emerald eyes which she did not notice upon his initial entry. They were soft but welcoming. They both refrained from speaking for what felt to each like an eternity. Angelica's legs felt weak, she wondered if she should sit down. Both refused to blink and risk being denied the view of the others eyes.

"I'm Alexander.. Your uncle Wilbur.. He's a good man, I've been coming here since I was a little boy.. With my mother." he replied, struggling to talk over the sound of his heart pounding, he was convinced that she could hear it too.

"Yes.. yes! My uncle told me. Let me get your order.. a jambon-beurre, right?" Angelica smiled, "A French sandwich?"

"Yes." Alexander said after a thoughtful pause. He wondered briefly if he should ask her to sit down with him but dismissed the thought as unreasonable.

Alexander remained fixated on her eyes. Angelica, blushing, nodded and began walking back to the kitchen. After a few paces she paused and took a hairband she had around her wrist and adjusted her hair the same as it was, off to the side, only tighter. It was a habit she formed in her younger years that still comforted her. Angelica was never overly concerned with her appearance but it was mainly because she was beautiful without effort. Her classmates throughout primary school pained to imitate what Angelica did by mere accident, and her manners came just as naturally and fluid. She was loved by everyone and one day in a hurry she banded her hair to the side and looking at herself in the mirror, laughed and conceded that it did accurately reflect her carefree attitude. Within a week the entirety of her class had replicated it, but as time passed none could perfect it. Soon all except a few stragglers had completely stopped attempting it and Angelica grew to love the style even more. Every time she banded her hair in such a way, it brought memories flooding back, and reinforced in her own spirit, her uniqueness. She felt beautiful.

As Angelica walked across the restaurant towards the kitchen, she felt Alexander's eyes follow her. Time remained suspended and she thought of how desperately she wanted it to be true, she debated glancing back toward him to check but the idea of it not being as she hoped frightened her. Her legs felt heavy and she labored to walk normally. Finally turning the corner and freeing herself from his perceived gaze she clenched her chest. Tears welled in her eyes as she struggled to catch her breath, but Angelica could not decide why. Wilbur, leaving his office just across the kitchen, saw her and began to approach.

"Angelica..? Are you okay darling.. what's the matter?" he said in a compassionate tone that he was clearly unprepared, at the moment, to use.

"Yes Uncle." Angelica said, wiping the corner of her eye and smiling. "I.. I don't know what's come over me.. I'm fine.. I'm okay." she restated, with a regained composure.

"Very well." Wilbur sighed, "I'm sorry but I have a terribly important errand. I have an old friend Benjamin Mills whom I've written a letter to. He only visits Wilheimer Falls occasionally and so I want to be sure he gets it. Darling.. Would you mind running it over to him? He should be at that store Macey and Mills, across town, do you remember it?"

"Of course Uncle." Angelica said, in a relieved air.

"Good! Thank you darling, you're such a blessing. Send Macey my best but remember that the letter must be given to Benjamin." he handed her the letter, bowed, and returned to his office.

As Angelica prepared to leave she felt her heaviness return and was unsure whether she could survive the black haired boy's gaze or not. She took several minutes attempting to calm herself down but to no avail. She decided that the best course of action was to avoid acknowledging him at all and walk straight to the door. She formulated such a plan and immediately agreed to it mentally, taking the first step into view of the restaurant patrons including Alexander. Without hesitation, and to her dismay, she looked directly to him and her heart throbbed. He was lost in thought looking directly ahead but quickly noticed her and peered in her direction. Their gazes locked and she could feel her eyes welling back up. There was no intensity in the eye contact, but a sort of acceptance, as if they were lovers in another life who had been reunited. She fantasized that he was as close to crying as she was and that he could tell her why such a thing was occurring. She felt herself nodding to him, answering a question that his eyes asked imploringly, but remained on her path to the door. She exited finally and was relieved by a large gust of wind. Angelica took a deep breath, looked back at the door, then started in the direction of Macey and Mills, across town.

FOUR

BENJAMIN MILLS WAS AN INTELLIGENT INDIVIDUAL AND PRESENT-ed an untraditionally intimidating decorum. He had deep set green eyes with tiredness embedded underneath, his long face and thin lips managed to exude confidence with minimal effort, and his consciously proper posture made everyone around him instant-ly aware of their own poor posture as they hurried to emulate him. He was as social as one needed to be to ascend the ranks into high society and was warmly welcomed into the upper circles of the literary intellectual scene. His sentences were formulated in a man-ner that produced a prolific effect and made the listener yearn for more, he was notorious for making the most boring occurrences seem prophetic and revelatory. The middle-aged, although graying, man had grown up in Wilheimer Falls and watched it explode in population before his eyes. He was undoubtedly the most nota-ble figure from the town and thus felt it necessary to revisit every so often.

When Benjamin was a young man his ambition had first ac-quired for him an education paid for in full by a famous lawyer by the name of Albus Livingston who noticed the poor boy carrying a worn copy of Plutarch's "Lives." He had attained the copy several months beforehand from an antique store in town called Antique de Macey by promising the owner Macey that he would repay her when he was inevitably rich. She laughed of course but could not deny the boys vigor and thus the book was his. He studied it to its depths and when the lawyer, his future benefactor and mentor, questioned the young Benjamin to his understanding, Benjamin began narrating with enthusiasm each of the lives starting with his favorite, Cicero, until finally halted by the dumbstruck Albus. He was twelve at the time with a widowed mother at home who struggled to find work. She was immediately contacted by the philanthropic Livingston and Benjamin was sent off to boarding school under the condition, set by Benjamin, that his mother be allowed to move in to the Livingston estate. Benjamin excelled and after two years was invited to attend Columbia University, the same institution that Livingston had attended. Benjamin graduated at the age of eighteen and published his first book shortly after.

As Angelica continued her task, she found that the further she got from "The Dancing Sheep", the more vivid her distress was. Every step she took felt like it had the potential to be the step that sent her running back to Alexander. Her internal squabbling forced her to the outskirts of the walkway and she noted the commotion of everyday life, where everyone moved with a sense of urgency. She paused, closed her eyes, and took a deep breath. She found that in the last hour she had become very fond of deep breaths, the air seemed richer and her heart seemed to demand much more attention. She opened her eyes and continued walking, reassuring herself that her newly found enigma would be explorable in due time. She smiled with excitement, wiping her eyes as she went.

Angelica had examined most of the shops in town and was very taken by the immense quantity of conversation demanded by Macey, of Macey and Mills. She enjoyed thoroughly the old woman and made an effort to visit her whenever nearby. Despite Macey's white hair, she had aged very well. Time had been generous and for the most part her face was free of wrinkles, blue eyes illuminated in one's imagination the beauty she had possessed in her youth. Short but erect she moved and talked at a speed that surprised anyone previously unacquainted with her. She had a magniloquent but rambling mode of speaking which produced an endearing effect, and her attention to conversational etiquette enabled her to traverse linguistics without offending anyone.

As Angelica entered she saw Macey entangled in a conversation with another customer, despite this Macey noticed her and waved excitedly, managing not to impede her current detainment in the slightest. Angelica nodded back and decided to wait and inquire to Macey about where to find this Mr. Mills. She began browsing the various artifacts that Macey had acquired over the years. The first thing that caught her eye was a metal crucifix. It was worn but ornate, a vine pattern graced the outer edges and the ends of the cross each had the profile of three apostles etched into a template and fixed behind the cross itself. The metal that situated the apostles was dilapidated but managed to gleam with vigor in the dim light of the shop. The cross itself was wooden and gave way to the figure of Christ that was masterfully carved from what appeared to be the same block of material. The character lacked excessive detail but managed to convey an intense suffering perhaps, Angelica thought, by the juxtaposition of the worn natural figure and vibrant silver. Angelica ran her fingers over it and absorbed the craftsmanship. She then continued to a stone bust of someone who escaped her learning. Angelica was by all means uneducated, she could read and write but other than her fascination with the Bible, her knowledge was primarily practical. She could traverse the world and society better than most and had a wit that projected a higher education than she actually possessed. After admiring the bust of who she knew not, she moved on to an arachnid marionette. The legs were separated into sets of two and each set had its own string attaching it to a wooden control and thus mobilizing it at the puppeteers will. Angelica noticed that as well as being high quality, it was also newer than most of the items Macey was selling.

"She is the famous weaver Arachne. Challenged by Athena to a weaving competition and turned to a spider."

Startled out of contemplation, Angelica blushed and turned to the gentleman who spoke.

"Is that so? Arachne... Why was she turned into a spider sir?"

"She failed to respect the gods." the man said, with a smile growing on his face.

"I wonder.. Is there a worse crime?" Angelica returned, with a grin.

"I suppose not, but Lady Arachne's crime is against Athena and Zeus. I imagine you and I share a similar crime. Or do you entreat the older gods as well as the newer?"

"I'll make a great spider sir, that is, if the Lord I worship wills it." She picked up the handle of the marionette and began motioning it lazily, "See!" she exclaimed.

"I believe it!" the gentleman laughed, "I was the one who brought this piece here. I simply couldn't pass it up.. Last week I was visited in the night by a spider who startled me from my slumber. When I pursued a tool to exact my detest upon the creature, she had vanished. My wrath was escaped.. I was startled then by a lone clump of dirt near my front entryway. And again when I laid down and a breeze rolled across my hair, I was convinced that the beast was trying to get to my ears or nostrils and eventually consume my brain. The thought frightened me to such an extreme that everything I see now is spiders. I nearly wept in terror when I saw this puppet in the gallery of a coffee shop."

"And do you still see spiders?" Angelica inquired earnestly.

"I'm afraid I do.. Everywhere I look. That damned spider torments me.." the man said with a grave countenance.

Angelica reached for the crucifix and handed it to the man with a warm smile.

"Learn to love your enemy sir and you will be free."

The man's expression softened and he looked fondly at the cross, admiring every detail. He placed it in his pocket and extended his hand.

"The name is Benjamin Mills."

Angelica placed her hand in his and he kissed it with a bow.

"Oh! Mr. Mills, sir. My name is Angelica Hamilton, I have a letter from my uncle Wilbur, he claims it's important, if it wouldn't trouble you…" Angelica paused and smiled.

"No trouble at all."

Angelica handed him a white envelope sealed with a wax sheep head stamp of crimson. Benjamin pulled from his jacket a small letter opener and gracefully sliced the envelope in one motion. Angelica watched his eyes intently as he began to skim the letter and noticed that he paused and restarted at a much slower pace. His face looked tired as he read but she could not tell whether it was solely from concentration or if it was the letter's doing. When he finally finished, he looked up at Angelica and smiled, but the tiredness remained.

"One moment please. I must retire to my office and write a response.. I'm terribly sorry but would you mind waiting? I'm going to be leaving town rather abruptly and would hate to keep my dear friend Wilbur waiting."

"Of course."

FIVE

———

ALEXANDER SAT STILL, HIS EYES PLANTED FIRMLY ON THE DOOR. HE had not taken notice of the tear that had ventured toward his jaw, leaving a lonely trail down his cheek, and his hunger was completely forgotten. Alexander had never even entertained the thought of falling in love and grasped for a parallel explanation to the weight that now apprehended his chest. His heart had not slowed and he watched the door intently. As his gaze tightened, the distance separating him from it widened. The other patrons vanished and everything but the door itself dimmed. It was a well-constructed door of oak, unpainted and coated in varnish to give the wood itself a liberating shine with four separated glass windows on it at about eye level. The windows were immaculate, without a smudge on them and had a vibrant red trim accentuating them. Just below the windows was a sheep head silhouette in black. Alexander rushed to the door, nearly knocking down a chair in the process; his breathing was heavy and his strides less calculated than normal.

Disoriented, Alexander catapulted from the restaurant doors and looked in every direction. The walkways were still ripe with people and the sky was grey as usual but Alexander couldn't help but acknowledge the beauty of the town, however briefly. With a franticness he began walking in the first direction available and was accepted into the crowd of individuals, also moving at a frantic pace. There was no sight of her. Back and forth he went, trying to decide where she may have gone, never questioning why she may have left. He was convinced that she felt what he did, her eyes had told him everything. An energetic sapphire set in the white of an angel's robe. Alexander longed to look into them again, wished for nothing more, and as he walked he resolved to devote his life to exploring such eyes. He walked in every direction without the slightest clue or instinct about where she may have gone. In his pacing he had re-crossed The Dancing Sheep several times and always peered in to no avail. He was tempted to continue his search until he achieved the results he wanted but, calming himself, resigned to the next day.

When he finally arrived home he immediately laid down, exhausted, in his bed. An immense bed with white silk sheets and a heavy feather blanket. One of his favorite places, he let his feather pillow with a matching silk cover ease the weight of his head. As a thought entered his mind it was effortlessly pushed away. Not by any other thought in particular, but by the pounding of his heart. His blanket hugged him with an unusual warmness, his bed felt softer, and his eyes heavier. He fell asleep quickly.

MACEY WAS KIND ENOUGH TO ALLOW ANGELICA TO SIT IN HER office while waiting for Benjamin. She explained that he could be a bit obsessive at times and sometimes spent the greater part of his day locked in his own office across the hall. Normally this would be a welcome rest for Angelica, but with every passing moment she more firmly regretted her decision to leave the restaurant in the manner she did, and her mind wandered back to Alexander. "What conclusion would he come to?" she wondered. *"Why did she leave me?"* flashed across her mind. She began trembling at the thought that she may have injured him, even in the slightest, and decided that she would beg for forgiveness if she felt it was warranted. She calmed herself and remembered the look in his eyes. He understood her. He would understand the folly she made and would welcome her embrace warmly. Her thoughts drifted to the future. She wondered what their house would look like. She had always been fond of cottages. She imagined a modest dwelling painted white, with brown trimming. Large shrubbery contrasted well with the browns and surrounded the home entirely. Cyprus vines claimed the fences that lined the walkway. A slight walk from their home was a pond that sparkled in the sun, and moon light. It was also surrounded entirely by trees, as if hidden from the world. A few paces from the shore had been built, by ancient lovers, a bench that through the years had become a part of the earth itself. She and Alexander would sit on that bench for lifetimes. She would look into his eyes and he into hers. Time would be lost in such a place. It is the power of love after all that can slow time, she had learned that earlier. All Angelica wanted now though, was for time to speed up so she could be with him once again.

Finally, Benjamin emerged from his office after what felt, to Angelica, like hours. He looked as tired as ever but had an added countenance of determined resolution. He peered into Macey's office and looked distraught at the sight of Angelica, as if he forgot where he was or the events of the day.

"Ah.. Yes. Angelica.. I'm sorry to keep you waiting, how long have I been?" he said, regaining his confident nature.

"No problem sir, I'm.. I'm really not sure." she stopped abruptly deciding not to attempt to explain their apparently equal lapses in time.

"I see.. again, I'm terribly sorry. Here is your prize, the letter for my old friend Wilbur." He handed her a thick white envelope sealed with the wax stamp of what looked like the profile silhouette of some great statesman. "The details are covered in the letter, all the ones I know at least."

"Thank you, sir." she said with a curtsey after taking the envelope.

She wondered where Alexander might be and although it was getting late, she hoped that she could somehow see him before the day was completely over. She hurried toward the door.

"Oh Angelica! One more thing." Benjamin rushed after her and she turned quickly. "So that you may avoid being turned into a spider... Or any other hardships you may face." He reached into his pocket and revealed the crucifix that she had given him earlier, and handed it to her.

"I love it sir, but I can't take it.. I was only kidding about being a great spider, I'm not afraid." she said, struggling for what words to use, and preoccupied with other thoughts.

"Please, I insist. Consider it a thank you for running this errand for me." He took hold of her hands and closed them upon the crucifix that she was offering back to him.

"Thank you.. I will cherish it sir." she said with earnestness.

"I would accept nothing less, my dear." he said with a smile, "now go on, I won't make you suffer any longer." He bowed and turned back toward his office. Angelica hurried again towards the doors and back into the walkway outside.

As she began her return she noticed a modest but ornate carriage waiting outside the shop. As she admired it Benjamin rushed out donning his hat and suit jacket, passing her he nodded and entered the carriage which then sped off. His urgency reminded Angelica of her own and she vaulted steadily in the direction of her Uncle's restaurant. She was resigned to the obviousness that Alexander was not waiting for her there, but she wondered where exactly he might be. She could not decide. She knew so little about him and her infatuation with the thought of learning more but being currently unable to do so, pained her. She entered "The Dancing Sheep" slumped over and downtrodden. She had hoped to have some revelation of where Alexander might be or even better, have seen him during her walk back, but as she entered the restaurant and her final hope of seeing him before the day's end vanished she nearly broke out in hysterics.

Wilbur was talking with a customer when she entered and quickly excused himself from the conversation after seeing her distraught countenance. He rushed over and hugged her, squeezing her tight. She began sobbing.

"Oh darling! What happened? My God! The nerve of that Benjamin.. What did he say? I should have never sent you. I'm sorry! So very sorry. It will be all right I promise." Wilbur said disdainfully, and without relinquishing his embrace.

"Uncle... If I hurt him.. I won't be able to forgive myself!" Her sobs were heavy and she clenched Wilbur tight. "Where is he...?! Where has he gone?! Oh Uncle my heart cannot take it. I don't know the boy, yet I miss him! I miss him so dearly. Why! Why did I leave him? And without saying anything,, what.. What was I thinking!?"

"Who Angelica.. Who!?" Wilbur said, perplexed but refusing to denounce the importance of the situation in any way.

"Alexander! He sat there Uncle, right there!" Angelica pointed to the spot where he had been sitting. Wilbur released his grip and held her by her shoulders in front of him so he could look her in the eyes.

"I'm sorry darling! I did not see him leave. I was in my office, I know though, that he did not stay long enough to receive his meal." he said sympathetically, trying to understand exactly what he had missed. Angelica had regained her composure periodically but couldn't help an occasional sob.

"He said nothing Uncle! But that was enough! He said everything there was to say without uttering a word about it! Do you understand?" she said, answering a question that Wilbur was too tactful to ask.

"I do darling." He forced a smile.

Angelica noticed immediately the immense effort that Wilbur went through to produce the effect and recoiled.

"What is it Uncle? You frighten me!" she exclaimed more scornfully than she intended.

"I'm sorry darling. I've just had a long day.. I understand.. I do, I promise. Love is a powerful force Angelica.. You've had a long day too, go home and rest. Tomorrow if Alexander does not come by the time he did today, precisely one o'clock, we will go to his estate. We will wait all day if we must. You have my word you will see him tomorrow."

Angelica had completely regained her composure.

"Thank you Uncle!.. I'm sorry I was so emotional.. I just.. I couldn't help it." Angelica said, red with embarrassment.

"Never be ashamed of your passion Angelica." Wilbur said while pulling her back into his arms and embracing her tightly. "And darling.. how did it go with Benjamin?" he said, quickly changing the subject.

"Well Uncle. He was pleasant enough, in fact I really took a liking to him. He gave me this for you." She produced the envelope Benjamin had given her and handed it to Wilbur. "He said all the details he knew were accounted for in that letter... A good thing you sent it today, he left immediately after giving it to me."

Wilbur appeared to be masking concern with another laborious smile. This time, Angelica did not question out loud why.

"Thank you darling. Now please, go get some rest! Tomorrow comes soon enough."

"But what about you..? Don't you want help closing up?" Angelica said concerned.

"No.. no, I'll be fine. Thank you though. I'll be home late.. This letter.." he cut himself off, "Don't worry about me, I'll be okay, it hasn't been busy." he said with another forced smile.

Angelica politely curtseyed and exited the restaurant. The few lingering questions that remained vanished at the thought of Alexander. A shiver ran up her spine and she yearned to be embraced by something. For tonight, she reconciled that her bed would have to do. It was a small bed, just large enough for herself, and the act of entering it required her to move several pillows to the adjacent ornamental bench. The covers were thick and smothering, she was determined to never feel the coldness she felt when living with her parents again. She had decided that after her parents split she would start anew. After acquiring a new family and a welcoming environment her next objective was to build a happy life, starting with her bed. She took great care in selecting the perfect ingredients. Choosing soft but mature colors Angelica crafted a relaxing tone, a single light green pillow acted as her primary with the following pillows growing in natural distinction until reaching an almost teal color, five pillows in total and then an Egyptian blue, heavy blanket. She typically removed all but two of them before sleeping, one supported her head and the other, in her own half joking words, "supported her heart". She kept it next to her for comforts sake, knowing that a stuffed animal would be too childish.

As she reached her bed, and after removing all but one pillow, she couldn't help but smile. She slipped under the heavy cover and placed her head on the light green pillow. The moon shined brightly into her bedroom and she felt glad to be exactly where she was. Her final thought before falling asleep was, for the first time in her life, "tomorrow."

SIX

———

THE COURTROOM WAS FOREIGN BUT FAMILIAR. THE OBSERVER RE-
mained as far back as manageable without detracting from the
spectacle that he felt inevitable. Large stone pillars bore the weight
of the thick marble roof which hung high overhead. The seating
accommodations, all of stone as well, formed a semi-circle around
a speaking stage and each row back was situated higher than the
previous to allow everyone in attendance to witness any oration
or scene that might unfold. The public seating eventually gave
way to a row of distinguished, raised chairs partitioned by carved
stone. The ornate chairs then gave way to a view of what looked
like a courtyard. The observer noticed ancient trees draping over
the stone walkway in the distance. Two guards stood just outside,
ordained with golden armor over white linen. Their helmets covered most of their faces leaving just enough exposed to prevent in-
hibiting vision, with a round polished top. The armor and helmet
gleamed in the sunlight and while admiring them, the observer
noticed the shine of metal. Each of the guards wielded a long spear
of wood, with a sharpened steel blade at the end.

There had only been a few others sitting in the hall with him
when he began his observations, but he paid them no mind. Soon
enough though, the chamber began filling. Men, most of whom
were well groomed, filled the available seats around him. Most
wore clean white togas with an onlooker's attention drawn primar-

ily to the individual's eyes, or, if the eyes were unsatisfactory, a fanciful pin on the shoulder which also helped hold the garb in place. Occasionally more distinct figures entered, typically with crimson togas or shawls and accompanied by lesser companions flanking them. Some figures looked especially forlorn and at the same time bizarrely familiar. The observer viewed with great curiosity.

Additional guards eventually escorted a group of men to the distinguished chairs which they gladly occupied. After the men were situated a single guard entered, followed by an elderly civilian, wrists clasped with chains and pulled along by the guard. The old man looked weathered, he was partially bald with a long grey beard and a poverty stricken face. He somehow maintained an energetic countenance despite his poor circumstances. He was brought before the men in the raised chairs, which the observer now identified as judges. After a short time, and once the audience was situated and silent one of the centermost judges spoke, addressing the old man,

"You have been found guilty sir. Your sentence has been explained and accepted. The state hereby formally sentences you to death."

A small but well-crafted circular table was brought in. Upon it was a cup filled with a dark liquid. The old man looked at it with indifference and his demeanor indicated that he was prepared to drink it. As he began motioning towards it footsteps began echoing through the room. No one except the old man, along with the observer himself, seemed to hear the noise through the deafening silence of anticipation. A woman entered. Again, no one but the observer and the old man acknowledged her.

Her steps were short but determined, her lean figure was accentuated by the pristine, flowing white of her toga, which also, the observer noticed, made everyone else look dirty in comparison. Middling blonde hair hung beautifully behind her, exposing a tan and radiant face. Her thin, delicate lips hid pearl white teeth that one could only see in quick instances as she entered. The observer immediately recognized the woman. She was a resident of a far-off town called Wilheimer Falls, named after the drunk Alfred Wilheimer. The observer sat mesmerized by her appearance and his heart throbbed. She stood before the old man who had, before she entered, picked up the cup that rested on the small well-crafted table, no one else took notice of her.

The old man looked around the room like a prophet might, surrounded by silence the inhabitants of the chamber waited for the man, who had apparently accepted his fate beforehand, to drink. After surveying the chamber, the man looked directly to the woman who he appeared sufficiently convinced that no one else could see. A pristine smile formed on her lips and the genuine nature of it was echoed by her forgiving eyes. Tears began streaming down the old man's face and he began to smile with her. She extended a gentle hand and placed it over the top of the cup that he was holding, motioning and aiding him in placing it back on the table. She embraced him lovingly, he was sobbing. She looked then to the observer whose heart was still pounding. Her eyes met with his.

Alexander woke up, the dawn illuminating his room in a manner only possible by flawless architecture. His heart was beating rapidly. Looking around he began to calm down upon the realization that it was, indeed, just a dream. Remaining under his heavy white cover he struggled to make sense of the ordeal. Alexander was of the rare variety of individuals who placed a high significance on dreams. The mode of understanding which he employed was natural for certain writers or orators who found that while writing or speaking they often embarked on certain sentences or topics which they had no intention of initially undertaking and tended to describe the topics in a manner that was not formally considered beforehand. Ensconced by such happenings, Alexander found through study that religious thinkers had deemed it divine instruction, divine implementation, etc. Experiencing the poetical phenomenon himself, but not willing to accept a religious stance, Alexander nevertheless placed a sizeable weight on the things he knew without knowing, the things that he knew *unconsciously*, the things he tried to tell *himself.*

Again his heart rate picked up. Turning pale, he frantically threw the covers off and rushed to get dressed. Alexander flung open the closet door of his bedroom and removed a black leather suitcase. With one of the few remnants from his father's time abroad in hand, he began haphazardly packing it with all the clothes in arms reach. When it was full, he closed it quick and ran from the room. The room adjacent to his own belonged to a servant of the family who was entrusted with handling the logistics and finances of the house. Alexander began pounding ferociously on the door.

"Luther! Luther! Open the door!" Alexander shouted, while still pounding.

Covers could be heard being upturned and footsteps rushing toward the door, Alexander remained knocking vigorously.

"What's all this fuss!?" the man said in confusion, he was still wearing his pajamas and it was clear he was sleeping prior to the intrusion.

"I must be off to Breckenshire! Have the driver ready immediately, I'll leave this very second!" He said with confidence, leaving no room for dispute.

"I'll be in the front way." Alexander said, turning and walking with his suitcase towards the stairwell, which led to the front door.

Breckenshire was a smaller and less extravagant estate, but it was redeemed by its overview of the river. Alexander's father had purchased the land at a steal and erected upon it a lively summer home for the family. A large porch overlooked the river and fed into an almost entirely glass dining room that spectated both the river and the porch. It was painted a docile white and had inviting steps leading to the front door. Alexander had not visited it in years but the financial and logistical caretaker, Luther, had funds allocated to ensure its upkeep indefinitely.

Not wanting to think, and completely sure of the meaning of his dream, he paced furiously until finally the carriage was ready. The driver opened the door and Alexander hurriedly entered, instructing the driver to leave immediately. Alexander sat anxiously, Breckenshire was a full day's trip away.

SEVEN

ANGELICA WOKE UP EARLIER THAN NORMAL, BUT FELT REFRESHED. She noticed that her excitement made the night fly by, it was only a moment ago that she had closed her eyes. Looking at the dimly lit clock and reading the time of five thirty-six a.m. produced a wild impatience in her bones. She managed to smile and closed her eyes, deciding to remain in bed. Although the time had elapsed quickly, the warmth of Angelica's bed was proof of the depth of her dreams. She felt deeply sunken, as if she had not moved a muscle in hours, and decided to remain occupied by nothing at all for the next hour, until the time came when she would get ready for work, at seven a.m., The Dancing Sheep opened at nine.

A man of habit, Wilbur knocked gently on her door at the exact moment when the small hand of the clock struck the much anticipated seven o'clock. He opened Angelica's door carefully and although always prepared to rouse her if necessary began calmly.

"Darling.. Angelica, time to get up dear.. It's seven o'clock." Wilbur said, the sun barely breaking the horizon outside the window, which was situated on the wall directly opposite the bed.

"Okay, Uncle, thank you." she said, attempting to emulate her usual tired tone, and thus hide her excitement.

Upon the exit of Wilbur, Angelica threw off her covers and began to laboriously sift through her closet searching for a perfect outfit. The first article she grabbed was a flowing white dress that she had worn as a bridesmaid for her cousins wedding. It was an immaculate white and appeared to be its own source of light in the dim early morning. Naked, she stood staring at the garment that she had spread in full length on the bed in front of her, it was beautiful. It had a divine quality that Angelica cherished, it seemed ancient. Gazing, she recalled Genesis 29. Jacob traveling across the world to find his uncle Laban, and is captivated by a woman working for her family. Instantly he agrees to surrender seven years of his labor to acquire her hand in marriage. 'I wonder what Alexander would give for mine..' she thought, blushing. Finally putting the dress on she admitted how bible-like she did feel, but laughed aloud at how inappropriate it was for anything other than a wedding. She placed it back in her closet and reminded herself to be more realistic.

After a few more unsatisfactory attempts, Angelica managed to calm herself down. 'I've never worried this much about my appearance before,' she thought triumphantly, grabbing the nearest things in her closet and putting them on quickly. 'He will love me no matter what I wear.' The outfit that had materialized, similar to most things Angelica haphazardly donned, went so wonderfully with her figure that it appeared planned in advance. A black skirt extending from her midsection to just below the knee, and a long sleeve gray knit that was elegantly hidden by the skirt from the abdomen down. She looked in the mirror and smiled, she could almost feel Alexander next to her, caressing the top of her hand and pleading to hold it. Opening the top drawer of her desk she took a hairband and banded her hair tightly up and slightly off to the side. Letting oxygen completely fill her lungs and expelling it slowly she opened her door and walked into the dining room where Wilbur was waiting as normal.

"Are you ready darling? You look beautiful as always. I haven't forgotten what I've said. Nothing has changed I presume?"

"Everything has changed Uncle. For the better. I have seen his eyes. I know I am loved. A different kind of love, it is a love in the eyes. Why did I spend so much time worrying whether or not the boys spoke to me, what their reasons were, why they were silent or didn't understand my humor. None of that matters! I have met a boy with a passionate soul, he has shown it to me! He needn't say a word if he wishes it so, I have been told everything. He will come today, and we will be together, I'm sure of it Uncle. How silly you are to think we may have to track him down. First thing, you'll see, he will come."

The Dancing Sheep was a moderate walk and Wilbur insisted on the benefits of the fresh morning air, he placed it just below fresh night time air but above cool midday air. "Good for the lungs," he would say, confining most expeditions to be traveled by foot. Angelica found herself struggling to walk. She wanted so badly to run, imagining Alexander would be waiting for her at the restaurant. Angelica thought back to the story of Rachel and Laban.

"What would you give for love Uncle?" she implored, finally slowing to his pace. He fixed his arm outwards allowing Angelica to grab hold. He let out a deep sigh.

"Anything Angelica.. Did I ever tell you how I met your Aunt?"

"No Uncle! Please do tell!" Angelica said squeezing his arm tighter.

"When I was a boy, Wilheimer Falls was not like it is today. It was busy, yes, but most of the people were just passing through, traveling west. My father owned The Dancing Sheep back then, and Benjamin and I would spend our days talking to all the different kind of folks. We loved the stories they told, all the adventures, glory, fortunes, kings, revolutions we just couldn't get enough. We were captivated to say the least, anyone could tell us anything and we would believe it, we were convinced that there was a big wide world of adventure out there. One day when we entered my father's restaurant there was a girl about our age sitting at the bar next to her father, he was a lean man that looked like a lot of the men we had seen, worn with travel, an odor of adventure, the cowboy qualities we so wished to possess. His daughter was an enigma to us, we had grown up without a proper compass of women much less free-spirited women. They were either overprotective and worry full like Benjamin's mother or too magnificent to be bothered by us, or nuns of course, which we avoided at all costs. Katherine was her name, your aunt Katherine. I remember that day well, she wore a white flower dress, confidently, but managed to impress upon us her tomboy qualities. Her black hair in pigtails lazily banded and hanging behind her back, she wore a mean grimace that I only noticed when we entered and she turned curiously before deciding that our entry wasn't worth her attention. It was not love at first sight Angelica... I was absolutely intimidated, I wanted nothing to do with her, I begged Benjamin to let us go talk to someone else, I prayed my pap would call for us. Benjamin approached her and said hello, which she ignored. If you knew Ben, you would know how much he demands attention and refuses to be anything but the center of it. He pulled one of her pigtails with a stern jerk, she spun her chair and slapped him square in the face without missing a beat. There was a grave silence and I, of course, was terrified. Benjamin, the damned fool, burst out laughing and offered his hand.

"I'm Ben and this is Wil, nice to meet you." he said with a grin that only being the center of attention could afford him.

"Katie." She took his hand and kissed it as if he was a woman and she a well-groomed gentleman. Ben curtseyed accordingly.

She told us stories of her adventures with her father, how he was traveling west to California in search of gold. Her Uncle had gone a few years earlier and so they had a place to stay eventually. The wonderful thing about Katie was that she left in all the gruesome bits… All the inappropriate parts that some of the men would find not worth mentioning let alone remembering. We spent our days laughing gaily over anything and everything. They were in no rush to move on she said to Ben and my relief so her father and her decided to stay the winter and begin traveling again in the summer. We became close that winter, the three of us. It wasn't until she was gone that I realized I loved her.

That day passed like a dream. I remember her coming to the Dancing Sheep with her pap while me and Ben waited. All three of us were crying.

"Say your goodbyes." her father said; he looked pained.

Ben stuck out his hand which she promptly kissed and he curtseyed. When she came to me I remember feeling happy, happy that she was here right now. The thought of her leaving hadn't even hit me yet. I was crying because I was so happy that she was there, in front of me, that very second. She hugged me tight and I hugged her. Neither of us wanted to let go. It wasn't until her pap placed a hand on her shoulder that she realized and let go after a few more precious seconds. She was gone.

The next day Ben and I sulked. The reality started to sink in that she actually had left. Ben said "If only we could go to California with her." And we both cried. The more I thought about it the more I missed her. The more I realized that I would do anything to be with her. I realized I loved her. One morning four days after she had left I was dead set on my goal. I let myself into Ben's room and woke him up whispering a question I already knew the answer to.

"You ready for an adventure?"

Ben threw his covers off and reached under his bed, where a pack was already made. He knew me too well, he told me he had just been waiting for me to say the word. We left that morning without telling anyone.

With the exception of the first few towns that her and her father would be required to pass through, we only knew the general direction that she was heading. It didn't matter. One thing we learned from all the stories we heard was that fate was unquestionable. Things would always work themselves out. Those who were meant to be together, whether it be friends, family, love, it didn't matter, they would find each other. We were off quick and after just one day we arrived at the next town. A small little town it was. Just a few shops, two inns and of course a bar. Just one street, that was all. We decided to investigate at the bar and find out what we could. When we entered… My god Angelica, Katherine was sitting right there! Next to her father just as she had been at the Dancing Sheep! This time she turned without hesitation and jumped from her seat. Running to us we all hugged and cried and danced and bowed and curtseyed, we were so damned happy.

Her father was a gambling man you see… And Angelica, after one day of travel had refused to go any farther. She would not take another step away from Wilhiemer Falls. So she made a bet with her Father. She knew me like Ben knew me. "They will come." she said, "If they do, we go back. If they don't, we go on to California and I won't complain, not for anything." They had agreed to wait one week in that town for us. And she was right, I could not go a week without her. She won the bet and they moved to Wilhiemer Falls and we would never be apart for that long ever again.

It was a much slower burn, much more manageable, I didn't even realize I loved her until she had left. I love you and therefore I love Alexander. I see your eyes and the fire in them. He will come."

The story had made Angelica smile; her face was red from laughing.

"You guys sound so cute Uncle! I had no idea Auntie was such a cowgirl. Thank you! Thank you for sharing." The story had warmed Angelica's heart but hearing Wilbur mention Alexander's name had made it resonate much more intensely. She desperately wanted Wilbur to keep talking, to say anything more about Alexander. She wanted to know everything.

She hoped that he would be waiting at the Dancing Sheep, there was a bench outside, a quite comfortable one, completely red and repainted every summer to retain its shine. If he had woken up particularly early, for some reason or another, maybe as she had, maybe just maybe he would have decided to wait on that bench. As Wilbur and her drew closer to town she released the grip she had on his arm and slowed her pace. The sun had been out for a while now, but the air was still brisk, dew glimmered on the grass lining the sidewalk just before entering town. Her heart began to beat quicker. She recalled a conversation she heard between two of the bar patrons. It was about gambling, "that moment!" the man had said to his companion, or maybe not companion, the other gentleman didn't seem especially fond of him, she could tell by the way they exchanged looks, "Is the realist high I've ever felt, that moment right before the cards are flipped and you don't know if you've won or not, you don't know if you've played the stage right." Angelica wondered if that man had ever been in love.

EIGHT

BENJAMIN HAD BEEN TRAVELING WELL INTO THE NIGHT BEFORE reaching his destination and was hurrying back to Wilheimer Falls. His eyes were dark and he could feel a fatigue in his bones that only sleep could remedy, still he feared the worst and could not close his eyes until all was right. He held in his hands the letter that Angelica had brought to him, which was already worn from his own handling of it. He reread it again:

> *It is with gravity that I send my dear niece to you. Her cough has returned in a preliminary sense, that is to say it is still mild, but my knowledge is not sufficient to determine the nature of it. I, of course, fear the worst. After her initial fever some months ago her strength returned in its entirety, I maintained diligent watch and per your recommendations ensured proper nutrition, exercise, and fresh air. It was not until a week ago that I noticed a paleness, imperceptible to probably anyone not actively looking for it. I fear it to be that brutal paleness of consumption, of tuberculosis. This color to me signifies the validity of the first sickness which may have never passed, but was only pacified for a time. My fondness for Angelica is unequalled and I am racked at the thought of losing her. It is with great fortune that you have returned at the probable climax of difficulty, for you are the only one with the connections necessary for*

the required care. My position is not substantial enough to offer anything in return but thanks and so I ask as old friends for this immense favor knowing that you will not refuse. I know you too well Ben and so I thank you in advance.

Reflect for yourself Angelica's countenance and determine the quality of her condition free from my presumption. You, being removed from the affection that towers over me, can provide a more accurate diagnosis. Time terrifies me to no ends now and I think we may be short of it, if anything points you to the conclusion that I am pointed, please begin measures with haste and avoid with me the rigmarole of deciding a course.

Sincerely, Wilbur

Benjamin folded the letter as he had countless times before and placed it back in the envelope which had now lost any coherent shape. He had by his own will accepted Wilbur's demands. He noted the most likely situation, although for Wilbur's sake retained as much optimism as possible. His meeting with Dr. March, who was one of the most respected physicians in the country, went well but not exactly how Benjamin had hoped. In his franticness Benjamin imagined retrieving the doctor from his home in Chicago and returning promptly, treating Angelica immediately upon arrival. Unfortunately, as accommodating as the doctor was, he was treating several patients a day and was not in a position to travel. He promised to treat Angelica the moment he brought her, but warned that anxiety and travel could potentially make the condition worse. He said all this in a somber manner of course. Benjamin decided begrudgingly that arguing would only waste time and it was too precious a commodity to be wasted. He concluded that Chicago was his starting point and that his objective was now to retrieve Angelica as quickly as possible and present her to the doctor, instead of vice versa. The trek back began instantly.

The meeting with the doctor occurred during the cold moments before the sun rose, when the darkness intensified as if bracing itself, hoping to perhaps fend off the light for good. A heavy fog lined the Chicagoan streets and the urgency of Benjamin's carriage instigated a preemptive and energetic start of the day for the city goers. And although the plea with Dr. March was brief the roadway was congested as the sun rose and the white mist was vanquished. Benjamin wondered if he had made a mistake in insisting the doctor grant him use of his own fresh horses for the journey back. Looking at the road and lack of movement, maybe the steeds would have procured enough rest from the idleness. Or better yet, the time saved from retaining his own horses would perhaps have allowed him to beat the traffic, they would have just had to push themselves a bit harder, that's all.

NINE

WILBUR WALKED NEXT TO ANGELICA, HIS HAND EMBRACING HERS. He noticed a subtle clamminess to it, a perspiration not of sweat but of some other liquid, of a heartier consistency. He had not slept the previous night and felt that this actually heightened his senses, he had been hyper sensitive recently out of fear. The previous months Wilbur had been in a state of hidden panic which he managed to hide almost entirely if not for the dark circles that formed under his eyes. Angelica had been struck down with a violent cough and was detained to her bed for several weeks early on upon her move some months ago. The blood which accompanied the racking fits especially traumatized him. He, like most others, couldn't help but love Angelica. Wilbur ascribed to her rapidity of sickness a certain divine quality. He was being punished. Ever since the initial sickness he had spent his nights, and any free moment he could spare, engaged in worship and study. He consulted constantly with local doctors to ensure every possible medical avenue was exhausted toward Angelica but was always sure to ask them, *"and how does God fit into this?"* with his tired eyes. The reality was, that no doctor could tell him that his obsession with compensating for a godless youth was directly damaging, at least not to Angelica. Even his correspondence with Benjamin, although ripe with practical medical information, yielded reluctantly uncertain answers in respect to the religious aspects of his inquiries. His life was too good for how little God it contained. Angelica was the message and the salvation. A God-filled youth that brought light into his eyes and then he was shown the darkness by her illness. A clear message to Wilbur: the salvation that is Angelica cannot be held captive in a godless home. Upon reflection Wilbur noticed that all too often individuals accept good fortune without question. Something pleasant is taken with glee and self-admiration, pride fills those who maintain good fortune. It's only when something is removed, when something is ripped from ones grip that answers are required. A man who finds a ten-dollar note asks no questions, a man who loses one is distraught. No one praises someone for generations, they only curse them.

The introduction of the young man Alexander onto the scene had complicated things slightly. It made the thought of Angelica's sickness more painful but Wilbur couldn't help but see it as a good sign. It was an omen, a sign that Angelica would last, God would not be so cruel to start such a powerful motion only for it to end abruptly. Wilbur could feel Angelica's anticipation. In his sleepless night he had heard her awaken around five in the morning and his initial panic that it was fever related subsided when he saw her eyes. As pale as she had subtlety turned she seemed invigorated. The bounce in her step which never fully left, regained a quality that he forgot existed; even questioned if it had ever been there to begin with. He hoped, he suspected, as much as her that he would be there at The Dancing Sheep when they arrived, or come shortly after. He knew though that such an outcome was unlikely. Wilbur not only knew the boy's past, he had been close to it. A tragedy that could possibly leave one with an inability to access the heart. An inability to accept love.

As Wilbur and Angelica approached the Dancing Sheep, they both slowed down without realizing. The wind accompanied them in decelerating and they both stood looking at the unoccupied red bench, it shined with a pessimistic gleam. The breeze picked up and jostled them both out of thought and back to the present. Wilbur sighed, almost accidentally.

"I'm sure he will come darling… One O'clock…" he said, wrestling the keys out of his pocket and opening the door.

"Yes, Uncle." she said, unsure of what to think or even if to think.

Angelica could not decide what she thought of the advice "don't overthink," which she had heard often; not necessarily directed at herself but as a general phrase of wisdom. If one could overthink, could they under think? How does one decide the perfect amount to think? It all made her head hurt and so she opted to feel instead. To 'think' with her heart and body. She had learned such a talent in ballet. Thinking with the mind is a slow, cumbersome act that inhibits motion. Dancing could only be done without the mind and therefore one had to learn how to think with the body. As all dancers know this is achieved by countless repetition. Incorporating a movement into one's soul so that they could then dance with their soul.

Wilbur was holding the door open, Angelica forced a smile, nodded and entered.

Angelica noticed that time had slowed to a near stop. She could hear the low sounds that she had never noticed before, the fan blowing gently behind the front counter, the grill sizzling consistently in the kitchen with an occasional jolt of energy. The thick lacquered oak door had a small bell that signaled each customers entrance. With every jingle Angelica's heart raced and then dropped when the customer identified themselves as not Alexander. Angelica thought back to her dancing days.

"Uncle… How can one love with their soul?" she said slowly and carefully, furrowing her brow in a generally inquisitive matter, like she had not fully known how to word the question.

"Hmmm…" Wilbur paused for a moment and put his hand on his chin, "well what exactly do you mean?"

"I learned to dance with my soul... when I was younger. We did it by practicing. Lady Bereda always told us that only when we practiced enough could we stop our thoughts, and only then could we dance with our souls."

"Darling. Your Lady Bereda is a smart woman, it's true, she's right. In the case of love, it's the same. Thankfully we are creatures of love. God has created us in his image and he is love itself. We practice love all our lives, we feel loved and we love. Our soul is a magnificent portrait of passion. You love dance and that's why you can dance with your soul. The repetition only acts as a mechanism for you to develop your love deeper, but the love is there already, waiting to be directed. There are geniuses who find that they wholeheartedly love something without such repetition. But there is another kind of genius, the one who finds the person that they love wholeheartedly without such repetition. It's a love that other individuals can spend their whole lives cultivating." Wilbur's voice escalated as he spoke as if the thought had just come to him and he was saying it all at the precise moment it arrived.

Angelica's smile had grown and her eyes were watering. Her pleasant teeth escaped the slight break of her lips. Wilbur smiled and sighed.

"Let's go Angelica... Forget the one o'clock. We will find him. His estate is just outside town. Alexander will be there. He will be there working up the courage to come and see you and we will surprise him. His fear will vanish when he sees you, I'm sure of it."

Angelica leapt into Wilbur's arms, as they turned he grabbed her sweater from the back of a chair she had placed it on and put it over her shoulders. As they exited Angelica heard the bell ring for a final time, she looked at it and smiled.

TEN

——————

Alexander sat in an idle carriage, his face buried sternly in his hands, the carriage had been stopped for several minutes now. His knee bounced capriciously up and down and as he relieved his head from the pressure of his palms, he felt his hands begin to shake with the same rapidity of his knee. He clasped them together not knowing what else to do and looked outside. They had been traveling for hours, the driver and himself, and by now were deep in the wilderness. The sun shined directly overhead and illuminated the dirt road in front of them; it looked like it went on forever. The view to the side was darker due to the thick canopy that the trees provided, the forest floor was covered in leaves and sticks. Alexander let his mind wander back to all his expeditions into the woods. He thought back to the ants. He was a dreamer ant... But the forest... The forest looked so cold and so lonely.

"Back to Wilheimer Falls!" Alexander shouted. "To The Dancing Sheep." He replanted his head firmly into his hands, clutching his hair.

The carriage instantly took off and turned around. He would go to Brekenshire, he thought, but first he must get Angelica.

LUTHER, LIKE MOST DAYS, SAT AT A DESK IN THE STUDY WITH A book open. He had taken care of Alexander ever since the tragic event and noticed that Alexander took after him in many respects including temperament. Luther wondered constantly how much of an influence he actually had in the young boy's thoughts but never reached a satisfying conclusion. This was a good thing he decided because despite his position on the matter, he did want Alexander to be happy. Raising the boy challenged him daily, even when Alexander was physically much younger, and before he went off to study. It was as if his mind resided on some higher vantage point and would only come down briefly, when forced, and then return to its peak. Luther wished to explore the child but realized that their spirits were too different. He wasn't even completely sure what he meant by "spirit", that was one way he did manage to rub off on Alexander, his absolute refusal to acknowledge any intrinsic meaning or supernatural entities. People tended to call a lack of religiosity or spirituality as a kind of void but Luther saw it more as an additional quality. Not a lack of spirituality but a positive dimension of a negative entity, leaving one *with* no god.

Luther had been best friends with Alexander's father Thomas and was devastated by the accident, which followed crushingly close to his own wife's death by flu. He had been well read and casually religious, like most people, but the successive disasters had ripped any notion of divinity that he might have attributed to the world prior to the tragic events. If forced to label himself, he would reluctantly refer to himself as a nihilist. Reluctantly, because he still moved and operated and concerned himself with everyday activities. He cleaned, took care of bills, tried wholeheartedly to raise Alexander as a proper gentleman sending him to wherever he saw as prestigious and even expanding his fortune by investing and acquiring land. He saw this as the great nihilistic dilemma. The world has no meaning yet he cares, he so terribly cares.

A loud knock startled Luther out of contemplation and he closed his book, carefully putting his bookmark where he left off. He walked through the halls and past Alexander's room. The door was ajar and he noticed, looking in, that clothes were thrown all across the room. He recalled the event that occurred earlier and that he had forgotten due to the fact that it occurred so early and was not especially abnormal (for Alexander to make concise requests.) Luther had stopped questioning long ago and they had a lively relationship that involved only serious discussion or simple demands. He continued on down the flight of white marble stairs that led to the front door. When he made his way and opened it he was greeted by a drowsy looking man and a sickly looking woman. Luther had also stopped long ago attributing beauty to anything or even recognizing redeeming features in anything. He found it refreshing.

"Hello, how can I help you?" Luther said formally.

"Hello.." the tired man began but the pale female enthusiastically interrupted.

"Hi.. I was.. I was uh. Wondering if Alexander would come out?.. To see me.." Her breath was short and she had to struggle to get the words out in the correct order. She looked startled at how quickly her voice flattened.

"He is the master of this residence but I'm afraid he is not present at the moment. My name is Luther, I'm his caretaker, is there anything I could help you with by chance?" Luther said curiously. He was beginning to understand but had trouble taking it all in clearly. He had noticed in Alexander, as well as an immense curiosity, many nihilistic qualities. He had not pried into Alexander's life but had attributed a thirst for nothing but concrete knowledge to the boy. This made the earlier event in the morning much more interesting and Luther felt himself becoming more and more curious, but let his face remain neutral, the woman looked disoriented at his words.

"Not here…?" she said, confused.

The man with heavy black bags under his eyes sighed. "Sir. Have you any idea where he has gone? It's terribly important that we see him at least to have a word."

"I'm afraid I don't. The boy goes off so much I have stopped attempting to keep track of him. He is fond of flowers though, he picks them frequently, sometimes all day. I wonder if he is maybe off doing something silly like that." Luther looked at the woman and smiled. He understood.

"You're Wilbur yes? I recognize you from the paper, you own the Dancing Sheep? A wonderful establishment. I wonder if maybe I could have a word with you in private?" Luther said enthusiastically. His feigned confidence that Alexander would return and his willingness to change subjects had alleviated the distress that materialized previously in the woman's face.

"Right this way." Luther gestured inward. Wilbur looked at the woman and nodded.

"Make yourself at home my dear." Luther turned sharply and heard the gentleman scramble to follow.

They entered a lounge. Two large velvet couches sat parallel, with a table in between. The velvet was a crimson red and the frame was made of a generous wood. The table was simple and hefty, the surface shone like glass, and nothing obstructed it. Luther did not sit nor offer a seat. He turned towards Wilbur, leaning one arm on the couch and placing a substantial amount of weight onto it. He looked Wilbur solemnly in the eyes. He noticed Wilbur's eyes didn't have black bags under them as he had originally thought, but more so deep black indentations. It was as if the dark pouches that antagonize those individuals who have more important things to do than sleep had abandoned him, leaving only their corpse behind. He could see the tiredness.

"I'm sorry. I wasn't exactly honest back there. Alexander left in quite a hurry this morning. He left to his cabin in Brekenshire, almost a day's ride away. I think I can guess the circumstance." Luther said. His weight remaining almost entirely on the backrest of the couch.

"I see… Yes. The circumstance is quite obvious. She loves him… And I love her." Wilbur said releasing a deep sigh as he finished. He turned and walked a few paces to a window that sat in alignment with the heavy wood table. Luther followed him with his eyes. The view outside was wilderness. The concentration of trees darkened the otherwise gray air and Wilbur could see a small stream in the distance. He could not hear it but imagined the melody it was playing.

"And she's dying…?" Luther said lowly.

"I'm not a doctor." Wilbur said without turning. "Is there a possibility that he returns?"

"The boy is indecisive, you know his history as well as anyone."

"Indeed, well then…" Wilbur began but was interrupted. A vicious coughing fit could be heard from a distant room. Both Luther and Wilbur began running to the commotion.

They found Angelica on all fours, the coughing had not stopped. Wilbur knelt down next to her and placed a hand on her shoulder, his eyes wide and panicked. The frequency of each cough left her struggling to breathe and each breath attempted was deeper than the last and made a deep wheezing sound. Luther frantically ran to another room and returned with a cup. He knelt beside Wilbur and forced the cup to her lips. Tilting the cup and allowing the liquid to enter her mouth. The first attempt was thwarted by another deep cough, sending fluid flying in every direction. The second attempt had more success and Angelica managed to subdue the fit long enough for the substance to lavish her throat. It soothed her for now and the fit ceased. Wilbur looked with dread to Luther who returned the glance.

"Darling we must be going." Wilbur said holding her tight. She had moved to a sitting position.

"But Uncle... What about Alexander?" Angelica said, her composure somewhat regained but the streak of tears still remained from the trauma of being unable to breathe.

"Luther has informed me... The greater possibility is that he would go directly to The Dancing Sheep opposed to returning here. Our time is much better spent waiting there." Wilbur said, his hand was moving up and down her back in a circular motion.

"I'll have a carriage prepared for you. I would rather you not walk; seems a mild bug has seized you. Rest is very important now so that you may procure your health as quickly as possible."

Luther stood up and left to retrieve one of the few servants who was capable of handling the duty, the primary driver was still off with Alexander. The carriage was prepared swiftly and Wilbur and Angelica were off. Luther watched as it picked up speed and headed towards town. Alexander was wealthy and debatably good looking, leading many women over the years to seek some form of acknowledgement from him. Alexander had always operated in a way that unknowingly shunned them, he had always proceeded as normal as one could say Alexander acted but the very nature of those actions disinterested them. It was as if he did not know they existed, they did not have the substance to demand his attention, to bring him down from his residency in the clouds. This woman though. This Angelica. The boy had never left in such a hurry. His motions had never been so drastically altered as they were this very morning. Luther watched the carriage escape his vision, his lips parted, "He loves her." He said to himself.

THE CARRIAGE WAS OUT OF DATE. THE BROWN CUSHIONS HAD BEEN worn from use and provided little comfort, everything else was bare. The windows lacked the usual curtain that could hide the world from the occupant, or more importantly hide the occupant from the world. Angelica felt weak. Every few seconds the carriage would thump in the back-right corner, clearly the wheel had been worn. Although rather insignificant, and barely noticeable to Wilbur, each bump made Angelica shudder in pain. 'What is going on..' she thought. Wilbur remained silent and she noticed that he was avoiding her gaze. She opted to look out the window. She was sweating.

Entering town, it was as busy as ever. The sidewalks were full of purpose driven citizens and they didn't pay any attention to the carriage. The gray weather and gleam of light from the storefronts comforted her. They made her imagine being caught in a rainstorm; soaking wet and desperate for shelter and coming across a campfire. Maybe there was a boy sitting at the campfire. Perhaps he would look up at her and the flame would be reflected in his emerald eyes. The glass of the shops emanated in a way that she was certain produced warmth in the brisk afternoon breeze. She wondered if that man Luther was telling the truth. It really didn't matter much to her at the moment. Whether anything that she knew was true or false was irrelevant, she just wanted to see Alexander again. To look him in the eyes. She wondered if maybe it was all a dream. Had she even met such a man? She was having trouble recognizing what was happening at the moment. She did not recognize the vehicle they were traveling in. Was that her Uncle Wilbur? He looked so tired, his eyes were dark, he was just staring perilously out the window. Things were becoming blurry… It was a dream, she decided.

They began to approach The Dancing Sheep and Angelica peered attentively out the curtain-less window. A figure was on the bench. That crimson bench stood out like a sore thumb in the gloomy weather of Wilheimer Falls, and there was a figure on it! The figure looked grieved, his knee was shaking, his head was in his hands. Angelica's heart raced. They were still far but it was surely Alexander! 'I must apologize to him!' she thought, 'I should never have left, but that man Luther was right, he would be waiting!' Angelica put her hand on Wilbur's hand and squeezed. He looked at her with a frightened expression, he noticed the figure also.

ELEVEN

BENJAMIN SAT. HIS TIREDNESS REMOVED FROM HIM ANY RESTRAINT he had previously held, and his grand posture had evaporated. His legs trembled and his head was heavy, leaving his hands to support it rather than his neck. He had arrived at The Dancing Sheep not long ago but knew how important time was at what he predicted was Angelica's current stage. The red bench was comfortable despite the circumstance. It was a landmark in town, the vibrancy and stellar upkeep of it emanated the season of summer. Even in the dead of winter the bench seemed to retain its heat and spectacular glow. The desolate air and shivering sky tended to obscure any reference to that warm contentedness of summer, yet the bench managed to remind them.

Gaining the courage, Benjamin allowed his head to rise and relied concernedly on his neck for complete support. Looking up he observed the distant approach of an antique carriage. Without knowing how, he could feel that it was her. As it grew closer, he used what mental energy he had left to concoct a satisfying and articulate explanation. He found it too difficult. It was clear to him that although she had been sick before, and quite seriously, that there had not been the slightest acknowledgement from her of any possibility but life. As the vehicle stopped, still a short walk from the Dancing Sheep, Benjamin kept his head embedded in his hands. Through his peripherals he recognized her. It was from her gait, he looked up with a stern curiosity that most men can do nothing but obey. She moved with a delicate voracity, each step allowed one to imagine her springing high into the air, and each step seemed consciously stifled in order to muffle such enthusiastic living. Even with such an energetic stride and a sizeable distance still between them, Ben noticed the paleness. All color had left Angelica. His knee remained shaking and his head returned to the comfort of his hands. He had, as he perceived it, entered an informal agreement with Wilbur, her life was completely in his hands and he knew what that meant.

Benjamin's carriage was halted just a few feet down the road as to not obstruct the restaurant. As Angelica approached, he noticed a perplexed expression grow on her face. He noticed for the first time Wilbur walking beside her. He noted the fatigue in Wilbur's decorum and his lugubrious movement; Benjamin wondered if he himself could even stand. If he could, he would surely move similar to Wilbur. Placing his hands on his knees he forced himself to his feet, a sigh escaped his lips and he made no attempt to correct his posture, his shoulders remained hunched with his hands resting in front of him. Any energy Angelica had displayed vanished as he rose, as if it was his fault. She stopped and turned, hugging Wilbur tightly. Benjamin strenuously approached and placing one hand on Angelica's shoulder and one on Wilbur's, he spoke,

"I'm so… Sorry." He paused, searching for words. "I… Doctor March… He couldn't come.. we must leave.. Immediately." The urgency of the situation pushed him forward and as he went he regained his fluidity.

"What? Go where… What are you talking about?" Angelica had relieved her embrace of Wilbur and was shaking her head vehemently.

"Darling… My love… The coughing fit back at Alexander's… It must be treated." Finishing the sentence Wilbur leaned back slightly and gazed at Benjamin. Ben noticed an imploring quality to the stare.

"Chicago, Angelica, I'm afraid we must be quick. It looks like… It looks to be tuberculosis."

"What? Tuberculosis… Me? No… It's just a cough is all. Before.. The blood, I have a weak throat is all… The doctor said I would be fine." Angelica raised and shook her hands in a dismissing manner, her attempt at a smile was too forced to be a product of anything but shock.

"Come… Look…"

Benjamin motioned to his carriage and upon reaching it he removed a mirror from inside. The mirror was a fine silver almost as reflective as the mirror itself with silver roses every few inches. Benjamin held it up in front of Angelica's face.

'THIS CARRIAGE IS MUCH MORE COMFORTABLE,' ANGELICA THOUGHT. She was burdened with none of her own weight. The seating fully accommodated her body and her head leaned back lazily, sweat had accumulated on her forehead. Out the window the scene moved quickly. She looked across to Wilbur who sat opposite her, he had fallen asleep. The dark leather accentuated the blackness that had formed under his eyes. The wooden structure of the seats, which were all individually crafted, held his limp frame completely upright. His mouth hung open slightly and his lips had a distinctive downward slant, as if he had been frozen in a shriek. 'He looks dead…' Angelica thought, intensifying her gaze and remembering back to her own image in Benjamin's mirror, 'I look dead…'

She sighed and returned her focus back to the window. Not to enjoy the view per se but to distract her from the current train of her thoughts. Movement is a good distraction. There is meaning in movement. The longer motion is halted the more apparent death becomes. In the stillness of life one is confronted with the stillness of death. Non-movement translates seamlessly into death. There is no meaning in life without movement. Ask the philosopher general who's seen a thousand battles if the outcome of the next engagement will change the universe and he will laugh. And then watch him fight with his entire soul: he will bark orders, make adjustments, and if needed he will sacrifice himself. All due to motion. Wherever there is motion, no matter how subtle, meaning presents itself. Many individuals live in the sad pendulum of existence where motion is present but stationary. An ebb and flow without any distinctive course. Their eyes are closed for the brief instances where the pendulum changes its momentum. The meaning is arguable, for the individual constantly returns to where he has already been, he would almost be better off in a conscious idleness. The potency and explosiveness of motion takes its most graceful form, as some individuals learn, in love. An individual who looks into the eyes of the one they love sees everything, for love is not only motion, it is a mirror, and it reflects not only the purest form of the individual, but the meaninglessness that resides behind them. It illuminates all paths, but especially the one which must be avoided at all costs, the path already trodden. How dark the path that precedes love is.

TWELVE

───────

IT WAS MIDAFTERNOON WHEN ALEXANDER'S CARRIAGE ENTERED town. He could have arrived earlier but had elected to first pick an assortment of flowers from a bed he had discovered during one of his hikes. The decision to change course from Brekenshire had sent his heart into a momentous fit of rapidity that had not ceased but for short intervals where although his heart seemed to beat slower, it beat harder and more profoundly. As he drew closer to The Dancing Sheep his breathing grew more consistent and he sat back relaxing, the bouquet laying across his lap. Typically, calmness comes from preparation, Alexander had not the slightest idea what he would say or even what he would do. He proceeded with a lack of appreciation for the luxury of his current comfort, he made no notice of his nonexistent plan or any outcome, he was simply in motion.

As he approached The Dancing Sheep he noticed first, as he always did, the vibrant red bench that drew every eye in the dreary winter weather. There was a man sleeping on it, he looked uncomfortable, only a small portion of him was actually supported by the bench. One arm was distorted under him while the other hung lazily off the bench, along with both legs. It was clear that the man had not intended to sleep but only after an extended length of sitting, could take no more. Alexander only acknowledged the man's existence for a brief second before his carriage stopped and he leapt energetically from it, being careful not to disorient his floral arrangement. A confident smile had formed on his lips and again he made no attempt to assess the situation but began walking decisively toward the door. The man had begun stirring at the noise created by the arrival of Alexander's carriage in such close proximity. After moments of maneuvering the man sprang up.

"Wait!" he shouted. Any evidence that he had been sleeping deeply seconds ago had evaporated.

Alexander stopped abruptly but did not turn. His gaze did not shift, but remained firmly on the handle of the front door.

"Alexander!..." The man sighed. "Come... Sit..." He moved consciously to one side of the bench leaving plenty of room for another occupant.

Alexander chose to ignore the man. He returned to his task at hand and grabbing the door handle, he had completely forgotten the insignificant event that had just occurred. He pulled with a quick confidence and entered. His hand tightened around the flowers which were held down near his side. Scanning the room, he saw no sign of Angelica. He scanned again. No sign. His heart quickened. He felt hot. He scanned again, this time walking slightly further to ensure he missed nothing. Angelica was not here. The only face he recognized was Wilbur's wife Katherine, who like Wilbur was an acquaintance whom he had never spoken to, save once. She was attractive for her age and managed to stand resolutely upright without the snobby appearance of a proper lady. Her brunette hair hung loosely down to her shoulders and she wore a modest plain dress. Her wrists were clad with a subtle assortment of jewelry. Alexander approached.

"Hello..." Alexander said after several awkward moments of standing in front of her. He realized how little he had prepared for. The possibility of Angelica not being there had not even occurred to him.

"Is Wilbur? I'm looking for Angelica.." he said.

The woman's expression remained neutral but her eyes revealed the strenuous effort required to not react. "She's not here."

"Well, where is she?"

"Chicago."

"When will she return?" Alexander asked. His eyes had moved to the floor.

Katherine sighed and sat down on a nearby stool. "Not sure." She poured herself a drink.

Alexander's eyes remained firmly on the ground. He searched for a reason for her departure but could find none sufficient. The singular reasonable answer was that he had been mistaken in his assessment of their mutual feelings. Looking into Angelica's eyes he had never felt such a connection. He felt as if he could tell her anything and she would understand, or even tell her nothing and she would still understand. 'How could I be so wrong?' He thought back to their first and only encounter. One sentence maybe two, nothing specifically intimate. 'I was right to go to Brekenshire... Christ, what was I thinking?' Alexander looked up and Katherine was gone. There was an empty glass where she had been sitting. He placed the flowers on the bar and walked through the door, it seemed heavier now.

Once outside he noticed the man still sitting there, on that red bench. Alexander sighed and sat next to him, the man said nothing. Both men waited for some time, it was clear to both that neither was comfortable in the situation. Each man had thoughts that required immediate attention and so they sat. Finally, the man erected himself and spoke.

"Benjamin. I'm a friend of Wilbur's, but more importantly a friend of Angelica's. You were right to come here."

"Angelica?" Alexander sighed. "I was right to come? are those your words or hers?"

"Well… Mine of course, hers were a bit more sentimental, she said a great deal about love and all that."

"And all that…? Benjamin speak plainly… What did she say?!"

"Sorry, my manners are a bit lacking and I'm tired obviously… She loves you. That's what she said, 'I love Alexander,' to be honest I probably shouldn't have told you that, in fact I had resigned not to. I just saw that look in your eyes, why do you curse me so? I shouldn't have said anything, I'm sorry."

"Why… What is going on. Where is Angelica?"

"She is on her way to Chicago, I'm afraid she's quite sick. Tuberculosis most likely, it came on quick but it was not her first fit."

Alexander stood and rushed back into the restaurant. Benjamin remained on the bench. When Alexander emerged he had flowers in his hand. With long strides he hurried in the direction of his carriage. Benjamin stood and raced to put a hand on the boy's shoulder. Alexander turned.

"Where are you going?" Benjamin asked, a concerned look materializing on his face

"Isn't it obvious? Chicago of course" Alexander's eyes looked tired, tightening the grip he had on the flowers in his hand he nodded to Benjamin.

"I'll join you, I know exactly where she is. But I must know in advance, there is a possibility that the travel will have hastened her condition, that she may have died… or die. I only say this because I care for her and therefore I care for you. Is that something you can accept? Can you handle that?" Benjamin asked placing his other hand firmly on Alexander's shoulder, his face had become neutral.

"I'm not sure that I can…" Alexander's labored smile gleamed under his otherwise expressionless face.

"Alright then…" Benjamin sighed, starting towards Alexander's carriage and opening the door. "After you."

Alexander entered, followed by Benjamin. Benjamin instructed the driver on the location and the carriage began instantly. The men sat opposite each other. The moments on the bench had acclimated each to the other's presence. Alexander recognized that other than Angelica he had not been this close to an individual in a long time. He wondered what caused the sudden influx of actual individuals.

"She went to your home you know." Benjamin said, looking out the window. "Obviously you weren't there. Why come now?"

Alexander spent a few moments in preparation. He was surprised to feel no pressure from Benjamin to respond with any haste.

"I was frightened... Well frightened may be the wrong word, or it may be the right word, I'll let you decide... I haven't decided my fondness for words they can be so cumbersome in certain circumstances. It was a dream. I was in Athens. I recognized it from the architecture. From the courtroom. From the people. 399 BC to be exact. The trial of Socrates. It was all so vivid... The champion of reason, who died to uphold his ideals. An event of particular inspiration in my life. You see, I often wonder why I do the things I do, why I do anything. Luther calls me a nihilist but I just think he wants to imagine I'm like him. I'm not entirely convinced by his position and anyway, I already told you I'm not sure how I feel about words, I think someone like him must be wrong. Why do I do what I do? My ideals. Like Socrates. I've spent many years in what people would call loneliness but it's a small price to pay for my ideals."

"They say it's the saint who sacrifices the temporal for the eternal, who chooses to live for something infinitely greater than himself. If only Socrates had been born later maybe they would call him a Saint."

"Or perhaps he would prevent the whole charade that you're alluding to. I like to think he would. Ideals like his, like mine, cannot allow for such superstition. The faculties of reason, the faculties of Socrates, are un-reconcilable to those presented by people like Jesus. They lay on opposites sides of a spectrum, or better yet two separate caverns. Each individual must choose only one if he hopes to reach any depth. Socrates in his death descended to the bottom of the cavern of reason and he waits for me there... Or waited for me. Oh sir. The angel that is Angelica has illuminated my surroundings! The cavern is bleak; I wish to descend no more. In my dream she stopped the man! She stopped the fool Socrates! The death of reason some would say but it is not so. That was my initial thought and that is what frightened me, that is why I left. I had no intention of returning. But the more I dwelled and pondered, the more I understood. What kills a man? Is man's death when his heart stops or when his ideals vanish? But what are ideals? Aha! Maybe I am a nihilist. But my heart had not beat a day in ages... Was I not dead? I was. Angelica has brought me to life. My ideals are vanished but my heart is beating. I am alive!"

"But is there not reason in unreason? Surely in certain cases it is reasonable to be unreasonable. You were right to come back I think, Alexander. Socrates was reasonable, in your dream, to be stopped, to want to live, to want to love. His ideals were true. And you see it now, the only way which I have, Angelica saved Socrates, as she has saved you."

"I love her... And I don't even love myself. My indecision has cost me precious moments with her. A lifetime is too short Benjamin. I could have an eternity more with her and I would still be tormented by those moments I squandered."

"You're right to curse time. The clock, I think, is too bold and we men give it too much authority. The best one can do is to do all he can. Time has no bearing on that. It's funny really... We waste time worrying about time. You said you are alive... So live. Don't let time stop you from living."

The men sat in silence. Alexander, after some time, buried his head in his hands and tried hard to stifle the expression of his accumulating sorrow. Tears escaped.

"Tuberculosis... Benjamin... What if I don't get to see her again, how will I live with that?"

Benjamin switched to Alexander's side of the carriage and placed a hand on his shoulder, unwilling to answer his question.

Alexander sat upwards and wiped his eyes clear.

"I've never felt this way before... For the first time in my life, I am willing to be optimistic. And what a time for it, at the almost certain apex of hopelessness. Still, I cannot shake this feeling... For Angelica."

THIRTEEN

THE VOICE WAS FAINT, "WE'RE ALMOST THERE," IT SAID, ALMOST inaudibly. She had lurched forward attempting to ease the contortions that her body demanded in order to produce the depth of cough necessary to expel the blood that had congealed in her lungs. Her bones felt frail and she failed to catch herself, landing squarely on her face in the quickening carriage. Already in intense pain the fall produced an instant numbness in her face, every faculty possessed was engaged in accelerating the intensity of her cough, hoping that it would pass. Her focus was almost entirely on the floorboards in front of her, which occasionally rattled as the vessel traveled over the turbulent city street. She felt a light hand on her back caressing energetically up and down. All sound with the exception of an occasional muffled yell and her own intense coughing, went unnoticed. The fits had become so consistent, although progressively worse each time, that she had ceased to recognize them as her own. The sound seemed to emanate from somewhere outside of her vantage point, and the actual hacking was something impossible to imagine herself producing, not to mention the blood that had accumulated in front of her. Thick red droplets painted the floor as well as her hands, every time she looked, she noticed that more had accrued and she wasn't entirely sure where it came from. She coughed deep. By now she had become accustomed to sizeable deprivations of oxygen and so her coughing remained as clean and proficient as one could say coughing could be. She could feel with each hack the blood accumulating in her throat and nearly suffocating her. Thankfully she expelled it as she had the previous times and it amassed where the rest had, in front of her and in the middle of the carriage. Angelica took a deep breath and fell from her knees onto her side, on the floor of the carriage. She laid, feeling the tears on her face, each breath was excruciating. Wilbur had a firm hand on her shoulder. She noticed tears on his face too. She looked outside, all motion had stopped.

THE MEN HADN'T SPOKEN FOR HOURS. BENJAMIN SAT WITH HIS head resting entirely on his hand, he drifted in and out of sleep, each time the fatigue on his face drifted and his posture heightened. Alexander stared across to the empty seat next to Benjamin, although he had closed the shade of the window, small flickers of movement were still produced by the motion outside. Motion, Alexander thought, was an immense distraction. Motion instructs an individual on how to think. It inevitably produces something that must be acknowledged and the recipient is jolted into a deterministic spiral. External inputs like motion cannot be ignored and so must be avoided. Alexander stared intently, not to investigate any focal object but to subjugate all motion to that object. He needed to think.

"To curse time…" Alexander said out loud, repeating what Benjamin had said a few hours earlier and with clear anxiety in his voice. "If I could speak with Father Time I would tell him to stop. I would have him bring me back to Angelica. 'Right now is fine,' I would say, and then 'be gone.'-"

Ben jostled upright, he had not been asleep but in deep thought, his expression suggested that he had forgotten Alexander was in the carriage with him. He took a second to compose himself, inhaling slowly and exhaling completely.

"He would, of course, refuse but I would refute him! 'Too many moments you've taken from me!' I would say, 'And I have not batted an eye or cursed you. I have allowed you to satiate yourself however you like. To do with my time what you wish. But this minute sir, I refuse to give you.'-"

Alexander sat backwards, resting his entire weight on the seat. He closed his eyes, not to sleep but to regain his composure. He opened his eyes and sighed, leaning forward and placing his head into his hands. Benjamin started, in a low voice,

"A beautiful sentiment. Poetry... But I think you have the wrong idea Alexander. To beg Father Time for a favor would be to become his slave. Most men are already subordinate to him, to sacrifice even more... I think it's best... to not worry about him."

Alexander sighed, "Poetry? I am only a poet Benjamin, in the sense that I am mad. I don't know what I think and you disorient me further."

Alexander opened the curtain, illuminating the space, and livening it with a flurry of motion. The two men returned to silence.

THE DESTINATION WAS DRAWING CLOSER. BENJAMIN HAD OCCA-sionally protruded his head from the vehicle to instruct the driver of certain directions and shortcuts to expedite the trip. Attempting to seem relaxed Benjamin sat back fully and crossed his legs, although he couldn't help but bounce his knee. "A few more minutes," he said quietly, almost as if to himself. He took a deep breath and looked at his watch, the once open curtain had been closed without protest a few hours ago and so he looked cautiously at Alexander, and then back to the floor. Alexander sat motionless.

It would be soon now. He tried his best to remain still but would occasionally be overwhelmed with emotion and would show it by leaning forward and burying his face in his hands, only briefly, before returning to his idle state. He appreciated that Benjamin made no acknowledgement of it. Alexander had much time to think, and due to thought, his optimism strengthened. He recognized and welcomed it, 'not literally...' he thought, 'the emotion has simply shifted, this life is cruel and Angelica Hamilton will die. But she will look into my eyes once more, and I will look into hers. This is my optimism, a final glance. God will grant me this.'

The carriage stopped; little was visible due to the curtain. Alexander could make out the vague images that resided outside, but not much. The house was large and white, the yard had many trees, that was all he could see. He looked to Benjamin, his lips were dry and cracked and although the blackness had vanished from under his eyes, a different shade had replaced it, not quite a natural shade but a blueish hue that originates from the deepest level of concern. With the back of his hand Alexander lifted the curtain to make out what he could. The house was immense. Large white pillars emerged from a patio that extended the entire length of the place, including behind. Two spacious floors, he could tell from the quantity of windows, eventually gave way to a third more economic level with a single window. Alexanders attention was drawn, though, to the stairs leading to the front door. They were wide and immaculate, white like the house with ornate and spectacular handrails leading upwards. About ten steps in total. Sitting towards the middle step was Wilbur. He was contorted as much as the steps would allow, leaning heavily against one of the hand rails. His face completely hidden by his arms which were secured firmly to his head and neck. He looked as if he had just been stabbed.

Benjamin must have seen something in Alexander's eyes. He looked deeply, putting one hand lightly on Alexander's knee, but said nothing. He opened the door and stepped out. Alexander sat motionless. Benjamin closed the door behind him and a few seconds later the carriage returned to motion. The direction, Alexander knew not.

I've seen it before. The vibrant dread that distinguishes the faces of those who have just lost something dear to them. Their eyes still have something of the former self, as if a fire has been just extinguished but remains hot. It fades eventually, and quickly too, depending on the intensity of the flame. I see the eyes in my dreams. Some would dare call them nightmares but I have been visited so consistently by such dreadful eyes that I am entirely acclimated and the horror is wholly normal. I have grown so accustomed to the feeling that I find a sort of bizarre comfort in it. Such an ocular quality to my ethereal travels is welcome, much preferred in fact, to those characterized by the spirit of the vanished Angelica. On such a thankfully rare occasion we walk. Sometimes just stand. To walk would be to concede an elapsation of time and an eventual end to our embrace, yet despite all our efforts we are robbed again and again. Waking is then the disorienting culmination of all prior memories, and memories are the decaying collection of dead moments. She is absent when I stir in such a realm yet I fear my fondness has not yet climaxed. Every moment I feel more and more bereaved and astonished at her banishment. I attended nothing that would solidify her vacuity in my mind, yet I know she is gone. She has left me as my parents have.

PART TWO

———

Prologue

*In times of distress one turns to family, the humblest and most imme-
diate of sanctuaries. When one's family has abandoned them, where
does he turn? He does not turn; he waits, he endures, and sure enough
a rescuer will appear, from where? A repressed branch of my expansive
tree. A forgotten oasis never even acknowledged as reachable. She is my
cousin, Eliza. Appearing in an hour not so much desperate but void of
all feeling. An hour consisting of all the forgotten seconds throughout
the day in which life's true purpose is laid bare. She came to enliven
such a moment. To entice within me the most truculent and vivid
ambitions. For a time, I thought she pitied me, but it was her nature
to eradicate such notions; she embraced me. She is the central pillar for
which my abode in this firey land is constructed.*

FOURTEEN

———

ALEXANDER OCCUPIED A LARGE WOODEN ROCKING CHAIR, ROCKing it back and forth in a slow rhythmic motion. His eyes open but unconscious, staring at a blank wall in front of him. Luther was worried at first but his angst slowly faded as Alexander engaged his conversation. The worry with any nihilist like Luther is the possibility of being correct, but more so of convincing another party of the un-deniability of the proposition. Such was not the case with Alexander, though, and despite the death of an acquaintance (you must understand for Alexander this is the farthest a relationship can go) he remained responsive and although his usual routine had changed he was considerably aloof and vigorous in his studies. Luther would engage from time to time in nihilistic arguments to gauge the mental sharpness of his companion.

"We can skip the part about life being meaningless Luther, I've heard you say it a thousand times 'We are merely animals,' so it begins."

"Of course... Well after that, the nihilists first intellectual movement is one of devaluing, as man has been very busy to throw such valuations around haphazardly. His first action is the return to nature in which nothing has a true value, or rather, everything's value is precisely 0. The result of the world and anything superficially gained will revert to 0 after a given duration due to the inevitable death of all humans and so on. The nihilist though, as most philosophies do, must acknowledge the possibility of being incorrect, he must take a stance of uncertainty for he is just man and no man can know the truth by anything but coincidence. This stance of uncertainty is the nihilists driving force. The uncertainty that cannot be disregarded combined with the hearty stance of meaninglessness force upon the nihilist no other objective but personal development, for the nihilist can by no other means justify living, initially, without meaning and so uncertainty is the driver and protector. Embracing the personal development dictated by a search for some value or meaning he finds only more proof. Although he must admit uncertainty in all cases. Nothing is possible but the receding uncertainty, or perhaps the concession of ideals. Such a concession is difficult because the nihilists entire foundation is the positive force of no meaning. The only reasonable choice for the nihilist to retain his freedom is to emerge from the despair of meaninglessness with all but the most minute certainty eradicated. The prior state of development has freed him of the handy force of uncertainty and placed him with a firmer state of nihilism. This state of nihilism has risen from a valueless state into the euphoria of an equally valueless state. The nihilist has made progress which can be totaled at 0, but progress was yet made. The value of 0 has been calculated innumerable times and remains 0. Here the nihilist can make the intellectual movement of constructing something, inside the 0. The nihilist makes the move. All values are equal. This value upon inspection redacts with the good, as some are saddened, the bad. History's previously misguided valuations are redacted, the unnecessary is trimmed. This is the starting for the nihilist. "

"You've already betrayed your ideals Luther... You've admitted that your precious nihilism cannot do anything but consume itself."

"How so?"

"This stance of uncertainty you've taken. The way you present it, and I must admit a very persuasive way of seeing it is as follows:

everything is derived of two parts, that is, the core of the proposition, or belief or what have you, and the uncertainty. Most people live primarily without acknowledging the uncertain aspect of their proposition. Why would they? There is no advantage to it. But the nihilist you present acknowledges nothing *but* the uncertainty. He has nothing else too acknowledge because life to him is obviously meaningless, although he is unsure. But it is in this uncertainty that his meaning is unescapable. As you say he is uncertain, and what is he uncertain about Luther? His uncertainty. So his 'driving force,' as you say, is his inability to dismiss meaning, because in uncertainty is the meaning of all other beliefs. Contained in this driving force is the potentiality of all other systems of thought. The nihilist according to you has more meaning than anyone else… I dismiss this optimistic nihilism. I think your younger self would be ashamed. He would say 'Yes you've moved but in the wrong direction,' for the nihilist would never presume to know what direction to go. He would remain in non-movement as he should."

"I wonder… Yes, I suppose it's true, maybe the true nihilist is the one who ends it?"

"Perhaps. Let's think on it, digest it. I imagine every idea is purest at the point of conception. The laborious task of translating it into something coherent to others is where everything is mucked up. That's my initial thought anyway."

"Indeed… digest it. Let's assume I will survive the night," said Luther, both laughing afterward.

Alexander and Luther then sat in silence. They recognized early that they were both slow thinkers. Slow being, obviously, a lazy word, a more accurate description would be *deliberate*. Both recognized that among their peers they spent more time in a state of raw contemplation, in fact Luther was sure that Alexander would collapse into a state of perpetual pontification if not for the constant elaborate prodding constructed by Luther. As nihilistic as he is, Luther has an unconscious admiration of the concept of balance. Not conceding to a laughable ying and yang but some element of his human nature disallowed him of standing action-less as Alexander succumbed to the debilitating beast called philosophy. Whatever academic strides possible always felt inadequate compared to the physical welfare of the boy.

FIFTEEN

———

"It was a terrible tragedy," Macey said, "such a lovely woman. I am truly heartbroken, not just for myself but for my friend Wilbur as well."

"It's so hard to find consolation among such events," said Sherry, a regular customer of Macey and Mills, "but one must look to God for answers."

"Of course," said Macey, "I know his plans must be grand to deprive us here of such a radiant light. She was such a pleasure, and of course her Uncle had become so fond of her... Even Ben seemed stricken by her departure."

"It's not our place to know Macey. We can only attempt to understand, as is our nature, but after that it is beyond our grasp."

"Yes of course Sherry, but I imagine this grief will last for some time." Macey looked down towards the floor. The carpet was freshly swept and the fabric retained a uniform indentation from where each deep broom arc was initiated.

The town of Wilheimer Falls, after the death of Angelica, operated as before with the exception of almost every acquaintance of hers becoming devastated. Even then the number was negligible despite an admirable impact considering the duration of her visit. Wilbur had retreated completely into isolation, his biblical studies and proclivity for the drink surpassing his duty towards his father's restaurant. Macey excelled at being unaffected by things and so other than an absent glimmer in her eye she operated as normal. Alexander managed to continue as normal. Normal meaning a drastic flip in his orientation towards the world, but normal none the less in his systematic method of analyzing and coming to conclusions.

SIXTEEN

BENJAMIN APPROACHED THE TABLE, IN ONE HAND WAS AN OLD bottle of bourbon and in the other was two short but formidable glasses. Sitting, he placed the bottle in the center of the table over a silhouette of a sheep's head and laid a glass in front of each chair. Benjamin had taken over The Dancing Sheep while the previous owner Wilbur shut himself inside, with his wife Katherine, to properly grieve. Word had spread quick and the thought of the great Benjamin Mills in a bar setting had seduced the bulk of the American intellectual scene and those more social fellows began immediately the trek to what they had poetically called "Gray Town." It was a perfectly romantic setting for what the romantics would call something like a rescue operation for their old friend Benjamin. He sat back comfortably.

"That was fast…" he said with a sigh. A figure stood in the doorway. "Don't you have a damn home?" he added jeeringly.

"A damned home if anything, yes a damned home that's much more appropriate. Clever too. But you know… fake ascetics like me gave up homes a long time ago, it's something in all honesty not too hard to part with." The figure took his coat off and hung it on a rack near the entryway. He was short but lean, the ends of his mouth curling upwards in a grin, his coat was clean but showed clear signs of strenuous travel. He sat across from Benjamin, taking the bourbon he poured in silence until his cup was about half full. "Your last publication did not sit well with me you know…?"

"As a man or as a psychologist? Yes, either way I imagined it would stir things a bit. Seeing the circumstances, I can't say I haven't been expecting you."

"Yes, the circumstances... we cannot rush ahead..." The man sat in silence for several seconds, gathering his thoughts. "It is these precise circumstances that have currently thrust you back into the public sphere; back into a position of accessibility, and the young boys of the academy who are so fond of you weep for the lost Angelica, and they write poems of her beauty. It is to this gray town that they now make their pilgrimage."

Ben closed his eyes slowly. Despite gathering tears, a slow smile crept onto his face.

"And what did they write Phillip?"

Phillip sprawled a stack of newspapers across the table, "How far do you make them travel? To get newspapers."

"That's the thing about getting older, you accumulate resources. I have them sent to me, from everywhere."

"Indeed." Phillip said, "This is from one town over, which means they are getting close, but in time you will be able to open any one of these and read about it. You've only missed it due to the delay in receiving from that side of the country."

Those blessed to know the maid will say
This little town was never gray
For beauty often forgets the cost
Of all prior memories which are lost
When amidst the clouds, a garden
Time will stop and terror pardon
Grace allows us walking lighter
To view the flower as the writer

"THEY ARE QUITE FOND OF THE THOUGHT OF HER, AND GENUINELY fond too. It's as if they've uncovered some rare inspirational artifact. The fact that this town is so seemingly dull makes the thought of such a radiant light all the more intriguing. For what other reason, in their minds, would you return here, if not but entirely for *her*? Yes, as ridiculous as that sounds, it is the way the story will surely be written. And I think I know your character well enough to predict that you won't object. Indeed, because it is a sin to interfere with that which is poetic, no matter how untruthful it is. Yes, they will arrive at this gray town and deduce that it is because she, Angelica, is no more and without her the clouds have returned and there remains no source of sustenance for that which is beautiful."

"No…" Benjamin's face was composed. Something deep inside him was satisfied that somewhere out there, art had taken the shape of Angelica. It had been a subject that he, himself could not muster the courage to annunciate. Her death had hit him particularly hard, and he often contemplated why. The way he saw it there were three main reasons: the first being that it had utterly devastated his childhood friend Wilbur, who wordless left town almost immediately with his disheveled wife, who was also another childhood friend, Katherine. Benjamin had experienced death often, being rather popular among whatever population he chose to mingle with, yet never was he affected to this degree. He felt as if somehow this particular death represented the death of all those before her. Every unfair expiration he had ever heard of, that deprived the world of something great, came flooding back to him those few days after. It was the first death that truly made him contemplate the concept. Yes, men often pretend to contemplate it, in classrooms and peering into the sunset, but in reality such contemplation can only be done staring at something like a weep-ing soul. And so the soul of his acquaintance Alexander had wept. Maybe it was that the boy had a lofty soul? Either way Benjamin was intrigued by his eyes for the entire duration of their trip. He had appeared unaffected in all manner except those eyes, which Benjamin saw something shift.

The science of the soul is not yet adequately formed but it is obvious to most that it is through the eyes that one can study the soul. A man who accomplishes a great task gains some unexplainable aspect to his eyes. A genius will have a gaze like no one else and so it falls to those who spend their lives meeting people and studying each set of eyes to shepherd men with great eyes, towards great things.

"There remains a light regardless of the gloom currently occupying the town." Benjamin added after a few seconds of thought, his expression remaining unchanged.

"Oh...? Someone notable?"

"Yes. And intellectually so."

"Coming from you, Benjamin, that means a lot." The man's face flushed, as he took a sip of the bourbon, with a tinge of interest.

"You were right in some respects Thomas, I am here in Wilheimer Falls, and I will remain here and at the service of such *public*."

SEVENTEEN

Dear Luther,

It pains me so, of my beloved cousin Alexander. His hardships even prior to your invitation have steadied my gaze towards a simpler society. Although I have not seen him since childhood his eyes remain in my heart, he is a survivor. Although I am contained here at the moment, it would be my greatest pleasure to reunite with the forever young Alexander and live in Wilheimer Falls as long as I am welcome. I will leave following the formal end to the school year and arrive sometime after. I am a natural traveler and am thus reluctant to give an exact date as I may drift to certain destinations along the way. Because of this it would be better to not acknowledge any specific date of arrival but instead admire my pending presence. I look forward so greatly to seeing you again and being reunited with Alexander.

Yours,

Eliza.

Dearest Alexander,

It is with girlish enthusiasm that I can inform you of my departure from New York en route to Wilheimer Falls. My studies have ceased for the year and I intend to reinvigorate that friendship which so characterized my childhood as to leave me a perpetual romantic. My admiration for you not just as my older cousin but as a sort of rival perhaps went unnoticed to you but it has been a sincere motivator to my distinguished path of learning. If only I could travel back and engage with that young boy who occupies so vivid a space in my memory perhaps I would have a chance at enlightening him. Alas my excitement blooms in wait for this trip and it is with a smile I sign this letter

Love,
Eliza

SHE PLACED THE FLASK AGAINST HER LIPS. THE SUN SHINING through her carriage window and reflected against the brilliant metal, illuminating the entirety of the vessel. Finding the flask empty she tossed it down to her side with frustration. Sliding the window open she was kicked by the swiftness of the wind, causing her black hair to flow rapturously. Embracing the cool chill and knowing that it was potentially the last that the winter could offer she opened her window a smidgen more, sticking her head out completely.

"Simon! My flask is empty! As is yours! And we're all out of wine!" she shouted with intermingling laughter, no doubt from the frankness of the wind.

"Aye Eliza!" the man shouted back. He flogged the horses with a renewed vigor. Satisfied she returned into the vehicle. As she closed the window the silence managed to engulf her. Whether it was because she had just closed the window or because she was out of wine, she could not tell. She sat back and smiled in the solitude. Long trips were not foreign to her and she relished in time alone to reflect on previous adventures. Such solitude was generally only acquired in such adventures due to the necessity of travel and so it goes and goes in a circular fashion; one trip demands a second to reflect and that demands a third and so on.

The carriage dashed along through the thick woods on a thin hardly visible road until finally a clearing appeared and with it came a small town in the distance. The buildings clustered in the familiar fashion of a town subjected to no planning whatsoever and from a distance looked almost like debris left behind by a disaster. The approaching town stirred an excitement in Eliza, not because of the wine but because of the people. Eliza loved people and had decided that people are the truest medium to learn from. She thought often about great conversations she's had and how she learned more from them than any book she ever read. Even bad conversations taught her something. Yes, it's said that learning is not an action but a state of being and so Eliza yearned to remain perpetually in that state, and even when in the act of teaching was very careful to extract something about herself from it. The carriage approached the tavern that doubled as an inn. A two story building situated almost immediately to the right when entering the town. It was shabby but appeared to be maintained well, as if a battle against time was perpetually ensuing (is it not?), but did manage to invoke a welcoming atmosphere. "One Frog," read the sign, with a poor outline of a frog just underneath. As the carriage stopped Eliza leapt out.

Her tight azure dress hugging her hips and chest allowing only the looser lower portion to flow with the wind. Her dark hair, despite the frequent barrages from wind, had regained its usual posture, falling just down to her shoulders with the slightest waves toward her delicate neck. Her pale skin and wide eyes made her appear older than most would guess and her gaze lavished with warmth those lucky enough to endure it. She entered the tavern, pushing the doors as gently as they would allow, although they still produced a long mincing screech. The room was dim, the architecture had managed to slap a window anywhere that would admit minimal sunlight, almost as if intentional. It was larger than it initially appeared from the outside and tables stretched back moderately far with a large bar near the entrance with towering stools and some higher tables. The furniture was surprisingly modern and Eliza's suspicions that genuine effort was being invested into the establishment was satisfied. She noticed that although it looked rather empty, it was due mainly to the size and the generosity of the patrons to not invade the personal space of their comrades. She approached the bar with all eyes, more or less, observing her movements, through conversation, from whatever angle they could manage with discretion. Her movements were soft and her posture perfect, enabling her to glide with ease; her hair seeming to blow in the nonexistent wind. The man behind the bar was as generic a man as Eliza had ever seen. A thick bushy mustache and black hair split in the middle that was slicked to each side; he wore a plain white knit and an apron over top, the apron having a poor frog outline upon it. Eliza decided that his appearance was an intentional attempt to be further inviting and familiar, which she could respect and therefore made an effort not to judge this particular man on his appearance.

The man behind the bar nodded, very subtly, and addressed Eliza.

"Hello madam, what can I do for you?"

Eliza's dark blue eyes lit up almost as if in a frenzy, causing the man some alarm; she determinably placed two flasks on the bar. The once discreet eyes became less so and a few turned to observe the scene.

"I don't see any wine, only the masculine beverages... Who are you to not have wine?" she began with an air of frustration, "and I had such high expectations from the appearance of the place and you have let me down. I am in distress and it is your doing sir, yours personally." She wiped the corner of her eye before continuing, "Whiskey is it? Pour a glass, quickly now and fill these flasks and go away."

Her appearance was so dejected that the man almost began to grow emotional himself.

"Yes, of course... If I may inform you... though... there is a wine cellar just this way," he said, sheepishly.

Eliza's brow furrowed and, turning red, she spoke with such a quarrelsome tone that it left no suspicion that it was not out of embarrassment.

"Well sir, why didn't you say so! But first fill a glass, that glass there, and then fill these flasks. And bring what you have, my friend Simon will be in to deal with the expenses and reception and so on..." She paused, taking a moment to look around before continuing, "but do not move quick I am very fond of this place and love these small town bars, yes, very fond and I like your appearance, it fits the place. Yes, point to the cellar for Simon when he comes in but do not leave."

"My apologies..." the man said while pouring a glass of whiskey, careful to select the exact glass that she had pointed to. "We do not receive many ladies here, and wine is not very popular in these parts."

"Yes yes, and no need to apologize, I suppose as long as you do have it there is no issue." she said, receiving the glass he pushed toward her and taking a gentle sip.

"May I ask if you're planning to stay the night? If so, we do have plenty of rooms."

"I'm afraid I haven't decided yet. I tend to give places one or a few drinks to catch my attention."

"I don't mean to doubt your constitution mam... Do you think maybe you've had enough for a while?" he said, filling a flask.

"You small man! What a tiny world you live in! Why I was just in the English court not three years ago and would you believe it the women had a bottle of wine with each meal! A bottle each mind you, a bottle each!" Eliza said, wagging a raised finger, "and you should see the French. Oh how I was chastised for my lack of fortitude. Of course they were quick to compliment as well, because I am quite sensitive. They said, 'She looks like Mary Queen of Scots… and drinks like her as well,' Mary being notoriously sober and especially boring even for a ten-year-old! Mary Queen of Scots they said! Ahah and there was a large painting I saw, and the resemblance was legitimate and she was indeed beautiful but with these types any compliment is an insult you see because they are bound by decency to declaw anything vicious."

The slow whine of the door signaled the entrance of Eliza's friend Simon. Eliza had grown to calling anyone who served her "friend," but Simon was indeed a friend. Approaching Eliza she handed him one of the flasks, now filled, which he placed into his jacket pocket.

"Your charity is limitless my dear friend Simon, now sit and have a drink, for we are staying the night, and then prepare our rooms. My dearest Simon, before all that, you must retrieve the wine from the cellar. No no, not to load yet that can be done tomorrow. Retrieve it for here on the countertop. It is unforgiveable that such an establishment does not have it here for the ladies to see. Yes, I am quite vexed about it because I had such high expectations for the place. Look around Simon, do you see how well oriented the room is? And can you believe that it has no wine out for the ladies? It's distressing and I cannot remain here without an assortment of wine to distinguish the atmosphere."

Simon looked to the bartender who shrugged his shoulders.

"I suppose she's right," he said with a sigh, leading Simon down a short hallway to the cellar.

Eliza, imagining how the wine should be arranged to adequately satisfy her faculties, sipped her whiskey periodically, until a young man, only slightly older than her, approached and sat near.

"What a tall glass madam, there may not be enough here to fill it again, whatever will you drink tomorrow?" he said maintaining a serious expression with impressive ease.

"Less, I imagine, as I will encounter a town with more bravado. You see bravado is the only exchangeable asset for drink." Eliza said, allowing the man to become the sole recipient of her gaze.

"Well unfortunately you'll find no such bravado with me."

"Surely? Do you possess no talents? Bravado can take many forms my dearest friend."

"Alas would it not be hubris to claim myself talented?"

"Aha! So the play begins, here enters the philosopher? No no, I embark to see my dearest philosopher and you are not him. Well maybe you are? Let me ask you, do people say you are capable of great things?"

"Indeed they do."

"And how do you respond?"

"With enthusiasm I suppose, although restrained."

"Aha, again! The correct answer my beloved friend is the following: you must respond with a stern inclination towards proving them *wrong*."

"Prove them wrong?"

"Correct. It is your responsibility to prove all those who say, 'You are capable of great things,' wrong. Hubris is to say, 'Would it not be hubris to claim myself talented.' Yes! So you do possess bravado! but bravado makes me sick, I do like my drink after all." Eliza raised the glass to her lips, tilting it just enough to allow a hint of whiskey to touch her lips. "That said, I forgive you. I am quite a forgiving person; I have never once held a grudge. So let us continue if we may. I feel it is my great calling to meet everyone who's ever had it said of them, 'He is capable of great things,' and my duty to investigate such claims. So let me ask you a question if you may be so oriented, how does a man like yourself become great?"

"Great men are men of virtue, as Aristotle posited. To Imagine the type of person we want to become and work for that. You see we all are born with certain peculiarities of character, some more than others. It is the task of life to shift those peculiarities and irregularities to the furthest and most desirable conclusion. And it is the object of every human to fully realize where they stand in relationship to the great virtues. Indeed, he must enter the world and be a man of action, it is only through this that he can adequately place himself and become great."

"I see, but Aristotle himself imagines the purpose as being to obtain happiness, or something called 'flourishing,' I myself see no reason to imagine this as the goal and so the whole of Aristotle is nothing but recreation." She took a formidable gulp from her glass, emptying it.

"I see... It's perfectly alright to dismiss him but I'll claim that it won't last. Sooner or later you'll rediscover him and probably without even knowing it."

"Perhaps you're right Sir." She nodded, reaching her hand curiously over the counter towards the bottle of whiskey just out of reach. Leaning her entire weight on the bar top she stretched her arm as far as she could, knocking several glasses over as her elbow jostled to and fro.

Simon emerged at the sound and taking Eliza by the elbow began ushering her upstairs where the rooms were.

"Forgive me Sir, but this talk of virtue... And whiskey does make a lady tired no matter the time. And with all the travel... I'm in desperate need of a nap. Au revoir, dearest friend."

"Au revoir, Madam."

THE ROOMS BEING ABOVE THE BAR AREA, ELIZA MADE HER WAY down the stairs feeling refreshed and level headed. The steps began to give way and the bottom of the stairwell seemed to glow in vibrant hues of red and white. Reaching the bottom, she looked upon her habitat with glimmering eyes. The windows captured perfectly the setting sun and managed to thwart any attempt of a stray ray to escape. The quality wood tables, polished to a gleam, imitated the red sky making the room appear to be filled with blushing clouds, swollen with passion. The floor, being of a darker orientation, vanished among the illusion, the distant door floating on the horizon. There was a man sitting at the counter talking with the bartender, Eliza approached and sat down.

"Excuse me sir may I have some water with Ice?" She looked at each man and blushed, without knowing why.

"Certainly Miss." the bartender said, twisting one side of his thick moustache as he collected ice from a formidable chest below him with his other hand, placing it in a glass.

"Hello again, I was hoping you would not vanish for too long." chimed the patron sitting next to her. He was a blooming man with medium length brown hair, parted to each side. His face was clean shaven although the outlines of growth attempted to emerge. His brown eyes gleamed with the hue of the reflected sun. The cool breeze that rolled in through the open doors and her rested state made the setting comfortable, especially with the addition of his soft deliberate voice.

"Again…?" Eliza's face replicated the room, turning bright red.

"Oh…?" the man said with a calm surprise, sliding the glass that the bartender had filled with Ice water closer to her.

"And I worked so hard to gain your affection, what a pity." he said with a smile, his voice managed to glide with each new word. Eliza remained silent hoping to be the recipient of longer and longer sentences. After some seconds he began again.

"Well I suppose it's for the best, Indeed, for I now know the answer to the ever-important question. The deciding one in which a beautiful woman can calibrate a man's intellect and decide his worthiness." He let out a short burst of laughter. "Although now that I've told you, it won't be attributed to my cunning mind. I've never been good with mulligans... I confess I have been thinking about you these past few hours and have played out this conversation in every way I could Imagine, none of them coming close to this."

Eliza smiled, her blush had receded although her cheeks still remained pink, and looked at him with warmth, her head tilting slightly with smile, a giggle lingering at her lips.

"Anyone afraid to be a fool is a bore, and so there I was and here you are. Fool looks good on you in all honesty, but what a shame that I enlightened you."

"Indeed, but I still have much to learn! If I may ask though... As I feel it my gentlemanly duty, and seeing now that it may have been out of character. What induced you to drinking so much?"

"Let us go for a walk, the sun has set and the chill is perfect!" Eliza smiled and taking him by the hand pulled him toward the door and out into the town.

Only a gentle glow from the sun remained, illuminating the horizon, the fragrance of summer greeted them as they left the doorway of the inn. Her hand clasped his with a surprising strength that he imagined unbreakable. Whether it was a physical strength or an emotional one he could not tell, either way he embraced the journey.

They continued for some time. Eliza's grip had slackened and they walked hand in hand down the street without saying a word for some time.

"I know you expect me to apologize monsieur for my drunken behavior earlier, but it is not in my nature, I've grown to accept the pain that accompanies an unapologetic woman. It is with a flowery girlhood sentiment that I allow the ideal of the quiet burden-ridden wife to tower over me. It is true I imagine a husband who stumbled from grace and whom the sharp talons of vice clutch every appendage. I would surely have to find some admirable work as a seamstress or a prostitute to provide for us and would come home every day to find him in the same place as he was when I left. I would urge him awake and he would turn only to reveal the growth of his beard and the darkness under his eyes. I would wonder how the bags under his eyes remained so black despite his constant rest and would come to the conclusion that a drunken sleep only provides a suppression of consciousness to his looming failures but they remain in his soul and so no rest will be had." She sighed, tightening her grip on his hand, noticing that he stepped with a slower cadence allowing her to face him slightly as they continued, his demeanor, although hardly visible in the late evening, remained warm and she sensed that he was not condemning this fantasy.

"Any children?" he said, calmly.

"Yes of course, one who accepts the pain mentioned understands that they have an obligation not to suffer alone. When I arrive home after a noble but humiliating day, my children will run to hug me. My little daughter will reach me first because she has more energy due to my slightly older son giving her the brunt of his ration and I will wipe the dirt off her cheek. It will be formidable and I will have to spit on my finger to help break the dirt up. My son will come next and we will all three hug and our stomachs will growl and we will all laugh, my husband joining in as he was stirred awake by the commotion." She spoke, turning slightly towards him as they walked, a gentle swaying of their clasped hands, her free hand animated. Her elaboration had increased in volume until the pitch acquired a certain quiver. Containing her tone to more reasonable means, the quiver remained and her complexion stiffened to prevent tears. They walked in silence for a while, until she felt coherent.

"In any case." she said, a light inflection returning to her voice, "I am sorry monsieur, for my drunken behavior earlier."

"It's not in my nature to judge." His voice retained its characteristic warmth, he let go of her hand placing his own inside his pocket. It was clear that the nighttime chill was the culprit. Eliza did the same, continuing at the same pace except moving a step closer.

"But it's in my nature to be judged... I wonder if this paradox is reconcilable, one side surely has to give. Maybe I will make it my mission to make you judge me. If I may ask, how long will you be staying here?"

"I have been here one week already, and intend to stay another."

"Fantastic, so I have an entire week." An unrestrained laughter burst from Eliza, her head thrown back, her pale face catching the moonlight.

After exploring the town to each participant's satisfaction they returned to their point of origin, the old although newly remodeled inn. Eliza led the way to a modest swing that ordained the porch of the inn and they took a seat side by side, swaying gently.

"I'm here to visit the local pastor. I gave a sermon yesterday and will give one on Sunday, and be on my way. And so you see, it's my profession not to think less of people and so I have an advantage. That said, I don't doubt your social flexibility, and so for my own sake I have to ask that you rescind your mission."

"My social flexibility?"

"You had asked me before if anyone has ever said of me, 'he is capable of great things,' and where most would find this admirable, it is more admirable for me to have it said, 'he is not capable of terrible things.' Being applied to me the first is a miscalculation of sorts, a malfunction of one's taste buds, one who hasn't experienced greatness. The latter is much more applicable. It's humility that gives me peace and with it comes no expectation of grandeur. When one closes the door to evil they also close the door to good. To be humble is to be not good or bad but to do that which one views as right, as godly. And what is godly is always modest. You on the other hand possess a capacity for greatness. I don't doubt that people have said that you are capable of changing the world and I imagine that they were serious. And with that capacity you could do base things with as much grace as accompanies your cadence. Yes, I could not help but judge you if you willed it, but I have become so enamored by your beauty that it would cause lasting damage. Heartache that would be welcome assuming that it was not intentionally afflicted."

"And so I am effected! Monsieur I predict that you will come to love me or hate me and it will be my natural proclivities that dictate one way or the other!"

The calm swinging slowed and each sat in silence. Eliza had edged closer until a serene contact was made. This lasted until too tired to remain, she took his hand in hers and pressed it to her cheek, kissed it, and went inside. He remained a while longer.

EIGHTEEN

———

THE MORNING CAME QUICK, ALMOST INSTANTLY IT SEEMED TO ELI-za, as if she had closed her eyes only a second before. She lay in bed allowing the soft blankets to remain enveloping her; the room was more comfortable than most one would find during an extended journey. She noticed the construction was immaculate and large beams remained purposely visible protruding occasionally from the walls with an immense few stretching across the ceiling. The room remained with its original wooden tone and sporadic gold framed artwork acted to accentuate the natural color. A lean and modern dresser sat near the bed with a mirror attached. The window opposite the bed was slightly open allowing a cool breeze to roll in. Although the sun had just rose, it did so on the other side of the building, producing in Eliza the sensation of evening. The town outside begun stirring and slight clatter could be heard, increasing in frequency the longer Eliza lay. 'This is a nice town.' She thought to herself, pushing the covers gently out of the way she turned and sat up, a casual yawn escaping her mouth. Her arms extended to their fullest length and a gentle sigh accentuated her lips. She rose and danced towards the window, her chin extended and long neck acting as an expression of her proper posture.

The town remained still except for, as Eliza observed, the occasional patron that hurried quietly by. A child's exclamation could be heard in the distance, although not coherently enough to understand. Eliza imagined that it was a child who had been reunited with a friend. She smiled imagining two children running and hugging each other, with an infinity of decisions and opportunities ahead of them. The day could unfold however they desired it to.

The stillness was broken by a loud screech that Eliza identified as the door of the inn, and she watched as the man she had met the previous day propelled himself into the street. Instinctively she crouched down, almost falling, to eliminate any possibility of being seen and lunged for her shoes, slumping to a sitting position she rushed to tie them and hurriedly stood up and ran out of her room. Her eyes focused on the stairs in front of her she lacked any appreciation for the structure that had inspired her the night before and, reaching the bottom, doubled her pace. Still wearing her night gown, she couldn't help but attract the attention of the few patrons gathered around the bar for breakfast, although she paid no attention. A loud screech preceded her induction into the street and nearly hugging the wall she followed in the direction that the man had been observed going.

The road was a dry dirt that acted well to muffle Eliza's frantic steps and she moved so quickly that every third stride turned almost into a leap. She remained as close to the shops and homes as possible, occasionally retreating into a corner until finally she found Monsieur. He walked at a slow but deliberate pace. Eliza identified it as the gait of a man who had an objective but was in no rush. His charm was especially apparent in those fringes of the day where one is expected to be less formal. His flowery outfit matched the weather and he moved comfortably with his hands perched behind his back; for how early it was he presented an admirably energetic image. Eliza's eyes remained fixed on him, she tried to decide if he looked better from the front or the back and came to the conclusion that she could not decisively answer.

Eliza paid no attention to the town around her, now bustling with people, shops coming alive and storefronts illuminated with the sunlight. The temperature rising with the sun, she began to sweat; thick droplets accumulating on her forehead. Monsieur, retaining the same pace, only stopped to greet the occasional acquaintance, and even then, only for a few seconds. He was easy to follow. Finally, he came upon the door to a large church situated on the opposite end of the town and entered. It dwarfed the buildings surrounding it and its garden demanded the town to make way for it, giving it a secluded appearance despite the close proximity of other structures. A formidable tower stretched to the sky above the entrance that climaxed with a cross. Eliza waited a few minutes then opened the door, peering in. The expansive ceiling added a gravity to the room, making the air seem heavier. Rows of empty pews allowed one to imagine a place for every meaningful person they had met throughout their life. Stained glass windows invited the sun to express itself more adequately and even tell a story. Eliza recognized it as the story of Adam and Eve. A single lit candle in the distance added to the array of light and near it she witnessed Monsieur on his knees near the altar, deep in prayer. Seeing how serene he looked and feeling ashamed at the thought of disturbing him Eliza reeled back as if waking from a trance, allowing the door to slam with such a violence that she imagined birds springing forth from a tree in the distance. She sighed and lifting the bottom of her night gown, which by now had been covered in mud, she started back in the direction of the inn, her posture returning to its usual elegance.

Eliza's hands, dirty from crouching, transferred the contaminate to her forehead each time she wiped it free of sweat. Her white gown had also become almost entirely brown; she trod on unapologetically with eyes fixed forward and a casual smile on her lips. The town was awake now and the busy streets kept her walking at a quick pace. Feeling a tug from behind she turned revealing an equally filthy child who looked up at her affectionately.

"Ay der miss. Like ta play a game?" the boy said making a circular motion with his hands.

"Rounders?" Eliza responded, crossing her arms and placing a hand on her chin, looking up in thought.

"We've got na bats miss." He pointed to a group of similar looking kids on the opposite side of the street. They all waved in unison noticing Eliza's gaze, she waved back.

"Do you know the One Frog Inn?" she asked, deciding to sit down on the ground to be eye level with the boy. Her arms lazily wrapping around her knees.

"Ye, I know it."

"Would you meet me there in ten minutes, and I will see if I can borrow one?"

"Ay miss Rounders would be good!" His face lighting up especially after Eliza had sat down.

"I'm Eliza, and what is your name my dear friend?"

"Hampton, miss Eliza. Hahm-Ton. Yoor very pretty miss."

"And so are you Hampton." Eliza smiled and as she stood up she hugged him, patting him gently on the back. "I'll be off, meet me shortly dear Hampton!" And she began walking, watching him turn and run back to the small group that awaited him. As she turned the corner children's cheering could be heard behind her.

Throughout Eliza's life rounders had been a casual outlet for competitive energy. She had found that physical activity was a good source of calibration, the sharpness of her mind in studies translated almost directly to rounders and intellectual progress correlated with physical confidence. It was a tool she had learned in the French court as a girl, where everyone regardless of age or station enjoyed the game.

Approaching the One Frog Inn she was reminded, seeing her reflection in the window, how filthy she was. Her night gown almost black, dark hands, and a few streaks of dirt across her forehead which had also dripped downward with her growing perspiration. A loud screech announced her entrance and she approached the counter behind which the bartender stood.

"Do you have a rounders set? Bat and balls?"

"Good morning, yes, yes we do. It's out back in the shed, if you'll just give me a moment."

"Perfect. And sir a shot of vodka, to warm me. And I will take what bread you have."

He nodded and poured a shot which Eliza took gracefully, and proceeded towards the back. Eliza hurrying up the stairs quickly stripped and began scrubbing her face with a wash cloth. Her fresh skin revealing itself from under the mask of dirt, almost glowing. Although her features were delicate, on closer examination, especially when completely bare, Eliza's figure had qualities of strength. Her fragrant neck gave way to pristine collarbones. Proper posture accentuating her breasts allowed, assuming her dark hair was up, one to observe a thin but defined back. The narrowness of her waist emboldened the thickness of her hips and together with her dimpled bottom they exclaimed an artful fertility. Opening her travel chest, she dug through, transforming a pile of folded clothes to a heap of cloth, grabbing a pair of white riding capris and put them on quickly, they grabbed her legs revealing her form more adequately than a dress would. A simple, excepting a few frills at the neckline, blue shirt was put on and she rushed back down and out the front door. Hampton and his group were waiting.

"Miss Eliza is that yu?" he said, his eyes glowing at her drastic change of appearance.

"My dear friend Hampton, it is I!" Eliza exclaimed, her breath short from rushing. "And who are your friends?" She added.

There were five others in total of varying age and who all looked entranced at not just Eliza but more particularly her posture. She noticed this because they all attempted to emulate it. Hampton, putting his hand to his forehead in order to block the sun looked as if he was saluting. The other children giggled as Eliza addressed them.

"Hello everyone, I am Eliza, I am a child like you, although I am older I am a child and so I would like to be your friend. Will you play rounders with me?" As she spoke they moved closer, and at the invitation for friendship they all began to hug her.

"Yes! And we can be friends!" They all shouted, patting each other on the back.

"Then let's first have a bite, inside, inside my friends!" Eliza motioned into the One Frog Inn, and all the children looking at each other, smiled and skipped in, accompanied by the occasional high five, and hug.

As they entered Eliza grabbed two baskets of bread that the bartender had put atop the bar before he searched for the rounders set, and placing them on a table she spoke,

"Sit, sit, one can't play on an empty stomach. Eat, my friends!"

Eliza, going behind the bar, took several empty cups and brought them to the children who had begun to eat, and using a pitcher, filled each glass with water and one with wine for herself.

The merriment of the children relaxed Eliza and she sat at a different table, allowing them to be themselves for her enjoyment. She noticed the endearing but peculiar way that they drank, which was to take the cup with both hands and put it to their mouth, almost as if drinking out of their hands, although one child managed to master drinking with one hand but the technique established itself more out of necessity, that being so bread could remain in his free hand allowing him a large bite between sips. The occasional laughter accompanied one child's glimpse at another, in which the whole party would giggle and take another bite in unison. As she sat, pressing the wine to her lips, she felt a small hand on hers, picking it up Hampton kissed it gently with tears in his eyes.

"Thank yuu Miss Eliza, thank yuu."

Eliza nodded her head affectionately and noticing the bartender walk in she averted her eyes to him. Initially worried that he may not have the necessary equipment she was reassured after she saw his arms full with a netted bag, bats sticking half out.

As if making a decree Eliza stood and placed one hand on her heart and the other in the air,

"Aye my friends, I told you I would find a Rounders set!" She pointed to the man entering and all the children cheered.

Eliza took the sack of items into her hand and allowed it to slink to the floor dramatically.

"Finish eating friends and come outside when you are ready." Eliza said, allowing the children to smile and nod before she turned and exited, deciding to sit on the entrance step instead of the more comfortable swing only a few feet away. Hampton came and sat beside her.

"Miss El-lie-zah. Wer seven now and cud use one more. I'll run and fetch Mister Thomas."

"Mister Thomas?" Eliza said, her voice remaining soft.

"Do u no him miss? He stays just in here as well. Shud be jus up tha rode."

"Yes I know him." Eliza said, a smile growing on her face. "Go fetch him and we can meet at the park."

By now the sun had begun shining with serious vigor and the sand of the field accompanied with the expansive green outfield radiated heat. Eliza noted how along with herself each child had a stiffness which she associated with anxiety. This was good as she imagined the importance of a competitive spirit as significant for living a proper life. Competition allowed one to express a universal

thirst while in a partitioned environment, afterwards enticing normal social functions to flow gracefully and without tension. Those,
she noticed, who didn't engage in games had an unbecoming rigidness to their form and were inevitably shunned by everyone in a position to shun. She smiled at one boy, Lucas, who was warming one
of his shoulders up by swirling it in large circles. He nodded with a
determined grin on his face. Minutes after arriving they all noticed
the two figures arrive. Hampton who stood with a grand posture,
no doubt due to his successful retrieval of Mister Thomas, waved as
they approached. Mister Thomas was holding his jacket and had his
shirt sleeves rolled up, light sweat on his forehead, he walked beside
Hampton with one hand over his eyes to block the sun. He smiled
scanning the children standing beside Eliza.

"Nice to meet you Eliza." Thomas extended his hand for a
shake. "I was quite startled this morning with the loudness of the
church door."

"Yes Thomas, the pleasure is all mine, and it's a shame that
church has such a startling effect on me.. Now kiss me on the
cheek like a gentleman." She embraced him allowing him to kiss
her on each cheek. "Shall we begin?" Everyone present nodded.

It was decided that each adult would be a team captain and team
pitcher, essentially allowing the children to decide the outcome of
the game. Whenever the children urged Eliza or Thomas to bat,
they would simply remind them how tiring it is to pitch and that
would settle the matter. The game raged on for several hours and
each child conveyed the proper intensity for a hard fought, thrill-
ing victory, or an agonizing defeat. The score remained tied until
Eliza's teammate Hampton urged her to bat, causing the rest of the
team to join. Eliza nodded and took her place on the mound with
bat in hand. Noticing this, Thomas's decorum changed and he
straightened, taking some sandy dirt from the ground he rubbed
a bit on his hands, presenting an intimidating specimen. The

children in the outfield perked up with determined faces. Thomas, throwing the ball with genuine intensity exhaled loudly as he strained every muscle to propel the ball at a ferocious speed. Eliza kicked her leg and swung the bat with such enthusiasm that her teammates shouted as the wood made a booming crack sending the ball flying high. The children in the outfield expending what little energy they had remaining, managed to relay the ball inward with a vigor lacking in the previous innings and with the threat provided by an uncorked Thomas, they miraculously held Eliza at second base until obtaining another out and ending the round.

The next inning Thomas came to the plate and clenched the bat in his hand, motioning with his free hand to his ecstatic bench to quiet down. Eliza crouched low placing the ball on the ground and took a handful of sand and dirt, rubbing her hands together vigorously. She recollected the ball and stood up, tossing it gently into the air and catching it with as little effort. After a few tosses she tightened and instantly upon catching it she kicked her foreleg extending her body fully and sending the ball rocketing towards home plate. The children recognized that the speed was faster than Thomas's throw, but even so he clenched the bat and swung with such a deliberate arc that the ball exploded upwards with a velocity so quick that everyone lost sight of it until finally it appeared far beyond a hay bale which had been designated the home run threshold. Thomas's team erupted and rushed him, hugging and patting him graciously. Eliza put her hands behind her head and sighing waved her team to come in, where she apologized. They hugged her and explained that her throw was amazing and they would win next time.

ELIZA SAT ACROSS FROM THOMAS, A SMALL TABLE BETWEEN THEM, gently blowing a cloud of heat from the top of her coffee cup. He reclined as much as was possible in the sturdy chair and looked relaxed as he stared out the adjacent window. They hadn't spoken since the game had ended an hour or so earlier.

"You know, rounders was originally an English game. For the game to survive the revolution, and just as impressively a transition to France is surely a testament to its quality. It's fascinating how a silly game can endure despite prejudices and overall ill will. Then again, all one has to do is play to understand the efficacy of the endeavor. I remember as a young girl how seriously it was taken in the courts, obviously under a façade of recreation, and how accurately it expressed one's individual character. I think it is a vital instrument to learn about oneself, and a society that doesn't engage in it will inevitably become sick. How could they not? To go without games is to forgo a dive into one's soul. This is why children tend to seem the most wise, they are constantly learning about themselves, they lack the audacity to say 'I know myself.' I wonder if an adult can be wise if he does not occasionally play games? Is he not claiming something undoubtedly false?"

Thomas rocked forward and leaning on the table in front of him, placed his hand on his chin inquisitively.

"Every sentence you say Eliza… I would have to contemplate for a week to properly respond." He returned to his previous position, relaxing back in his chair and looked out the window. Eliza's eyes followed each subtle movement.

"Oh of course, that's why I speak the way I do dear Thomas. Maybe I want you to think about me for weeks and weeks, that is why I lace my sentences so." She delicately motioned her coffee cup upwards and blew on it lightly, although it was no longer hot. She sipped; her eyes remaining on Thomas.

"I'm leaving on Sunday…" he said, searching for words, "Would you come to mass to hear my sermon?"

"Yes."

NINETEEN

THE REST OF THE WEEK PASSED LIKE A DREAM. ELIZA WOKE UP EAgerly each day and walked Thomas to his morning duties. Hampton and his troop occupied the place of offspring and once Thomas rejoined them the merry family spent the days laughing and exploring. They had played rounders several more times but although Eliza and Thomas both played heartily she could not remember the scores. Often Thomas would wipe the sweat from Eliza's brow with a thumb and the pair would smile. Eliza would occasionally and without thought remark, "Oh, Thomas." A gentle laugh accentuated each interaction, and a smile adorned her face always.

When Sunday finally approached Eliza, reflecting in the mirror, imagined that she had never looked so beautiful. The day-time strolls had given her cheeks a pink hue and although her ivory skin remained perfect, the activities of the week had given her a limber appearance and her figure appeared toned. She dressed in a flowing sky-blue summer dress that rushed forth from her hips. The material waved among her precious frame and her youth brought the elements to life. She did not carry a purse and would not allow anything but the warmth of a companion to occupy her hands.

Thomas received her at the bottom of the stairs, as was custom, and taking her hand they left the inn, a loud screech emanating from the door behind them.

"I know you don't like churches Eliza, and so it means even more to me that you are coming."

Eliza smiled and they walked slowly until reaching the church. The Sunday service was beginning to take shape but being early they were only greeted occasionally by acquaintances of Thomas. Eliza noticed that they viewed him with a certain reverence. Sitting down, Eliza was comfortable, it seemed almost instantly that Thomas was addressing a full congregation. The words were inaudible as Eliza watched his noble frame move wherever attention was desired. She was fixated on his lips as he spoke. She decided that it didn't matter what he said and that she would follow him regardless. Looking around and acknowledging the captivated audience she wondered if they were listening, or just watching as she was. Occasionally he would look towards her and make eye contact, causing her heart to throb. Smiling, he would continue on and she would for brief seconds hear single syllables through the deep thronging in her breast.

She was exhausted by the time he finished and quickly removed herself to the fresh air outside the church. He joined her moments later and took her hand in his as they leaned against a wall.

"Was it that bad?" he smiled, both staying relaxed in each other's grip. After a moment she sighed.

"It's worse than I imagined..." She sat down and he followed. "You're not as boring as I thought." She brought his hand to her lips and kissed it. Thomas's slackened hand followed gracefully in Eliza's grip and he felt her softness against his skin.

"I'm leaving today." he said, staring into the distance. An occasional obfuscated exclamation could be heard from inside the church whenever the stationed pastor made some surely important point.

"You should come with me." he added, wincing subtly almost as if expecting a blow. Eliza's face reddened and the pace of her heart quickened. She noticed that Thomas glowed as he asked. Something had stopped Eliza during the prior week from asking the question, 'what's next?' it had been her experience that asking 'what's next?' only made 'what's now?' seem less real. She wanted to fully experience the week with Thomas, and now finally she was confronted with, 'what's next?' and it was obvious to her. As he had opened his mouth to ask the question, Eliza already knew the answer. She would go with him wherever he went, and they would be together. Eliza sat quietly, waiting to regain herself so she could speak.

"I'm on my way," Thomas continued, for once not being able to tolerate silence, "To a far-off town called Wilheimer Falls."

Eliza stood up, dropping Thomas's hand in the process. Her breathing remained quick but acquired a heaviness. Her heart dropping into her stomach.

"Where…?" she said, her brow was furrowed and she asked with such a seriousness that Thomas would have been alarmed if he hadn't been too nervous to pay attention to anything more than 'yes' or 'no.'

"Wilheimer Falls. It's one of my old teachers. He has been moving around so much that I can never seem to catch him. Finally, he is in one place."

Eliza, painted with frustration, shook her head violently and raised a hand as if to slap him as he rose. He began attempting to apologize for what he assumed to be a response to him crossing some line. Eliza began laughing.

"You are more boring than I thought!" she laughed. "I have no time for boring."

As she turned Thomas attempted to grab her arm which she jerked away emotionlessly. Thomas noticed that even in her frenzy she moved with grace.

TWENTY

LOUD BELLS RANG IN THE DISTANCE BRINGING WITH A BREEZE, THE sad, solemn funeral toll. A childhood Alexander sat some distance away watching the simple flow of a stream. The water shimmered and danced with the gray mournful sky. The ground was wet with dew and licked the lower portion of his pants, staining his bottom where he sat. He heard light steps and the bustling of a bush signaled Eliza's entrance. Her movements were the most mature feature about her and without them she appeared to be missing something, as if she was born for movement. She sat next to Alexander close, their hips touching.

"I thought you would be here." Eliza said reflectively. "Look at the water, isn't it nice?" Tears began to form in Alexander's eyes. Eliza scooted closer although being so close already she only managed a slight rub. Looking away his hand instinctually covered his face and a few heavy breaths escaped.

"It's okay to cry ya know?" Eliza said, placing her hand on his and, while retaining it in her grip, she moved it comfortably between them, although there was hardly any room. Alexander felt the warmth of her hand and her body pressed against his. A few lingering tears emerged and he felt okay. He felt like the troubles he had to face, could be faced. He looked at Eliza and her deep eyes peered back. Eliza inched closer and placing a hand on the side of his face kissed him deeply.

"I love you Alexander, shall we go?" she said, standing up. Her black dress, if any other color, would have been ruined from the ground.

"Yes." Alexander sighed deep and stood up. He felt light, a large burden seemed to be lifted, he finally felt like he could survive the funeral.

ALEXANDER SAT FACING A SMALL STREAM, IT WAS SHIMMERING AND dancing with the grey sky. 'That was a long time ago,' he thought. I wonder how it would have turned out, if I hadn't made such a mistake. He broke a small twig in between his fingers and took a moment to reflect on his own sentimentality. 'Was I looking at the same stream back then? I've become emotional these past few months... I wonder. There are three possibilities as I see it: either I've regained something, lost something, or have acquired and am experiencing something new. In the first case it would imply that I had lost something initially, and remembering back, the stream did seem beautiful and my heart does beat with the same ferocity, thinking about her, as when I was actually with her. In this case I clearly lost something when we separated. Maybe that side of myself was unearthed when...' Alexander's thought paused for a moment and changed course. 'The second possibility that I've only now lost something, I need to be careful with this thought because it is certainly the most favorable. In the first instance I would have to admit to a large mistake and so obviously I will unconsciously prefer reaching this second conclusion where no mistake is admitted, also on account of the fact that I as a general rule do not like change. This explanation would conclude that I gained something when separating from Eliza all those years ago and although I feel physical pain when I recall the event, still it was a necessary action to arrive where I currently reside intellectually. It would further imply that I made a mistake a few months back and could imagine it as something like a lapse of judgement. Or I could even suppose that it was absolutely essential to experience such a possession in order to arrive at a more thoughtful position. Maybe if one is shut off entirely to such flights of fancy they are following the correct intellectual path only by coincidence. A man traveling down a path who reaches a fork in the road and flipping a coin follows one path as opposed to another. He then continues until finally reaching its conclusion and exclaims, "I've finally arrived at my destination!" "But you had no destination when you embarked," I would say, "You decided only after you arrived." Or maybe someone traveling down one path opposed to another would say, "I've spent so long on this path that I might as well follow it to its conclusion," and upon arrival they, too tired to make another trek, exclaim, "I have arrived!" No, my current predicament, if it was the case that I lost something, would be defensible I think. The important thing is to stop at the fork and consider one's destination before pursuing one path over another, which I believe I have done. It's only these last few months that I have glimpsed in the distance, through a clearing in the trees, or perhaps from a mountaintop, the faintness of the path that I declined. And where I sit, tired, weary, and burdened I linger and observe the path that looks so stirring. How restful it looks and for a moment I notice a narrow and steep path almost straight down the mountainside that I have to imagine leads to that path. And so I have been put in a position again where I have to consider my destination. And although it is clear, I linger. But using this analogy of a path, how could the final proposition make sense?' Alexander sighed. Standing up he brushed himself off. 'I will have to think more about it.'

He walked through the cemetery and past the church, slowly arriving at and making his way through town. Alexander had lost what he initially thought was a blossoming love for a bustling town and walked generally with his eyes pointed downward, looking a few feet in front of his face. His long strides suggested that he meant to pass through the busy streets as quickly as possible. Occasionally passing the Dancing Sheep his heart would beat and a terror filled him that he might run into an acquaintance. It hadn't happened recently but whenever approaching its vicinity he felt his face redden and his pace hurry. On the stark occasions that he allowed his eyes to wonder to the establishment his curiosity piqued at its occupancy. Each time it seemed to be packed tighter and tighter and the lively fellows he saw constantly walking in and out did not look like the standard Wilheimer Falls resident. His thoughts wouldn't wander far though and he would pass it and slacken to his normal self.

As the sun began to set Alexander concluded his long trek home and entering, he walked into the study where Luther sat, occupied by a book. Placing a bookmark to keep his place he laid the tome in front of him and greeted Alexander in his customary fashion,

"Hello Young Sir, how was the town?"

"I didn't stay long," Alexander said with a sigh. "Although the air was nice, and the clouds managed to retain the sun adequately. I do prefer it gray after all."

"Yes, gray is always agreeable, it slows the otherwise rambunctious man, and rain best of all."

"Ah but implicit in rain is time. The pitter patter of it ticks like a clock and so I find it hard to lose myself. It's the gray stillness that for me operates as a proper canvas for thought... Any news for me?"

A smile flashed across Luther's face.

"A friend of Benjamin Mills came to call on you this morning and I must say he did look to be a proper scholastic. Anyway he left that for you." Luther pointed to an envelope on a bookshelf near the door. "He said Benjamin would like to invite you to dinner and he expects a response."

"Is that so? It was only briefly that we did meet, and I had expected him to leave as abruptly as he came."

"Indeed. Have you not heard? He has currently taken responsibility for the Dancing Sheep while Wilbur grieves." Luther said, self-assuredly. Alexander felt offended at the word 'grieve' and decided it was indeed a rude way of phrasing.

"I have noticed it rather busy there." he said, curious as to why Benjamin opposed to Wilbur would result in such a drastic change. "But isn't it for the most part unchanged?" he added.

"No! Of course not, the timing is indeed perfect. As you know, although I'm personally unsure exactly why, Mr. Mills has quite a following. And has been out of public life for years."

"And so what? So people are especially hungry and dine at his establishment?"

 Luther laughed although Alexander wasn't joking.

"Yes hungry indeed, but not for food. They make him lecture and ask him questions all day. The whole restaurant apparently listens. It's all just what I've heard obviously."

"That sounds excruciating." Alexander noted.

"As I said the timing is perfect. He just recently published a paper that has angered some and I imagine that he intended to continue in his quiet way of life and not hear anything about the stir it caused. But now he is trapped." Luther appeared excitable and continued, quickening his manner of speech, "The general theme was that society has reached such a despicable tone that we have surely incarcerated Jesus Christ in a lunatic asylum. That one cannot go against the grain or be critical of anything with substantial vigor and those who do are locked away forever. He goes on to say that if everyone inside an asylum was freed and everyone outside put in, that is: a reversal, society would go on functioning with the same efficiency and outcomes. I have to say I liked it, if for nothing else but its provocative nature."

Alexander felt, to his own confusion, a pang of emotion that almost prodded him into defending religion, something which he had never done or even had the urge to do. As he had decided during childhood in what was probably his very first intellectual declaration, along with many others who as children are forced to either accept or reject that religion was unbelievable.

"I would think... That if Jesus Christ was indeed alive today... That he would belong in a lunatic asylum." The initial phrases lingered in his throat and he for some reason felt difficulty in uttering them. Although he eventually regained his usual ardor. "There would be nowhere else to put him. Suppose that he did come back, from my perspective it would prove nothing. I don't see and won't accept a correlation between performing miracles and being the son of God. So then, it would be too dangerous to allow him free because he could mobilize his supposed followers, and there is no telling what they may do. And what other proof would he have besides his miracles? Perhaps crucifixion scars on his hands and feet, but that too is hardly compelling. We could probably walk into a sanatorium down the road and find someone with those, who inflicted them on their own body for some reason or other. Maybe if something truly startling occurred... I wonder... Let us try to imagine! The sky fills with light, and in all its splendor the clouds open up and a golden chariot rides down to the figure of Christ who waits patiently as it pulls up beside him. Again, that would not satisfy me. My main criticism is that nowhere in the universe is it written that 'only the Christian God can summon chariots.' And this criticism holds true for any conceivable proof. Suppose amongst the shimmering sky a cloud descends and Mother Mary emerges. Let us go further, suppose that she has proof that it is her. Some ancient document or some item that was known to be hers. Even if she could convince me with absolute certainty that she was in fact Mother Mary, I still do not see it written that 'only the Christian God can revive Mother Mary.' I find the whole thing tiresome. It would be more trouble than anything if Christ returned now, and as he would have no convincing proof, it would be in our best interest to lock him up before he could do any true harm."

Luther, sharing a similar conclusion, could only help him to concretize his thoughts.

"The question then becomes what would convince you?" he asked, rubbing his beard thoughtfully.

"I suppose that nothing would." Alexander said with a sigh. "I really cannot imagine. I would have to be wholly restructured, that is: my current conclusions would have to be thoroughly unsettled one at a time and each one would have to be delicately replaced by a more sympathetic position. This is obviously not ideal, because one would like to think that a simple proof would be enough for one to change his opinion. An initial criticism of my lugubrious intellectual movement might be something like, 'suppose the question was related to fairies, would not the sight of, or interaction with, be an adequate proof of their existence?' And I would say yes that would be sufficient! And so too would I believe in Jesus Christ if I saw him, but the question is not about belief in him it is about belief in his 'parentage,' which is not proved by his simple appearance, just as seeing a fairy would not prove that that fairy's mother is Cleopatra and so on."

Luther taking on an adversarial role began,

"Well why assume that his parentage matters? Suppose that the question is not hinged upon his divinity, but instead that his divinity is a derivative of his character. In other words, the divinity comes second! Firstly, one must ask not 'is he the son of god?' but 'would I follow him?' If one is convinced of the character of an individual, the proposition that the individual makes, 'I am divine,' might be easier to swallow. And using your analogy, if a fairy's existence was proven to you, would it be entirely far-fetched to believe that fairy who then said its mother was Cleopatra? The proof of the fairy proceeds and makes easier the second claim. And so it would be with Jesus. If you were truly enamored by his greatness, and the proof of his existence, perhaps it would be less amenable to rational proof. The great figure of Christ would tower before you! You would have no choice but to believe."

"Maybe" said Alexander, looking down to collect his thoughts, "But I cannot imagine a figure so powerful and with such charisma. I suppose that if my absolute trust in the individual is *assumed* prior to the pronouncement of divinity then I would have no choice but to believe. Yes, I believe you may be right, and it is an interesting thought and if it were the path that most Christians take then I would be more sympathetic. It implies a rational view of buildings one's religiosity slowly, and becoming first enamored by the figure of Jesus before any motion is made but too many do the opposite. They first accept the divinity and then read about the divine figure and this view seems flimsy because without the divinity everything is then lost. The prior view would require, like my own view, to be slowly degraded in order for a change to occur." He finished, glancing back at Luther who had a loose smile on his lips. "Let Benjamin know that his invitation is accepted." he added.

TWENTY-ONE

"HE HAS CONSENTED!" EXCLAIMED PHILLIP. "YOU WOULD DO ME great injury to deny me this opportunity to accompany you."

"You know very well Phillip, that I have never once made any consideration in regards to your injury. In fact, I often move with the intention of doing you harm in every way possible." Ben said with a smile.

"And here I stand! Yes, you cannot get rid of me so easily. But do let me come." Phillip responded, emulating the smile of Benjamin.

"It's impossible. The phrasing of the invitation had the implication of a solitary meeting, and he accepted on those grounds. To spring another guest would be a transgression against propriety! You will meet him soon enough."

"Very well, I will bare this injury Benjamin, only because it's you who's inflicting it. I suppose I am just becoming so bored of these academics. It's as if the very institution meant to educate actually disintegrates something. When one signs on the dotted line to attend a university they should be forced to accept the terms currently absent from the contract. It would say, 'we will educate you on the condition that you never say anything original!' It was initially a promising enterprise but students of all ages became too enamored by their teachers. The teachers amidst the worship conveniently forget to mention that it is only their age that makes this gulf between teacher and student. They bask in it and allow the

students to raise them so high that now every fame hungry ego-
ist pursues an academic position. And so the generations go and
the most persistent and unoriginal thinkers are hoisted to the top.
That is why I think we are entering the age of self-education. In
this sea of academic illusion, it's business as usual, while the true
breakthroughs come from outside, from that small circle of the
disenchanted and the autodidacts who say, 'fine, fine, do whatever
you want. Real work is being done over here.'-"

ELIZA WALKED AT HER NORMAL PACE, A QUICK SAUNTER, UNTIL
some distance from the church. Unable to resist looking back she
saw the vague figure of Thomas sitting where they had been together. A light blush forming on her cheeks she continued on into
the town that was now bustling. She was dressed elegantly for the
occasion and drew any eyes that weren't preoccupied, although she
paid no attention. 'I've been here too long.' she thought, 'How did
I get so caught up in this to delay myself an entire week!' A subtle
giggle formed on her lips and danced on the breeze until erupting
into a laugh so uncontrollable that Eliza had to stop and support
herself against a wall. 'You silly girl... Oh well.' she thought after
finally regaining her composure. 'No more delays.'

Determining the best procedure for leaving occupied her
thoughts. She had unpacked a lot of clothing and it was strewn
across her room, but other than that she was confident that she
could be on her way within the hour, if she worked with haste. She
heard a faint voice from behind her.

"Eliza!" the voice exclaimed, turning she saw the origin. "Miss
Eliza!" the voice again exclaimed, and Hampton appeared from a
small clump of townsfolk. "Miss Eh-lie-zah, gud day!"

"Hampton! Dear sweet Hampton, your big sister is leaving and I must kiss you goodbye come here, come, come." Eliza said, bending down on one knee as Hampton approached. Tears began to fill his eyes.

"But Miss Eliza, why?" Hampton said and as he reached her she grabbed his face and kissed each cheek. Her hands remaining on his face, she looked into his eyes and said,

"Hampton, love impels me onward. Dear sweet Hampton, always follow love. Promise me you will my friend, promise me!" Tears streamed down Hampton's face and he struggled to keep his eyes open to remain within her gaze. Eliza's eyes were watering as well.

"I promise Miss Eliza." he said. She kissed his forehead and hugged him.

"You must never let anything get between it." she went on, "No matter what Hampton, even if the whole world is against you, even if you must wait, Hampton you must follow your heart." Standing up, she wiped her eyes and continued onward.

As she approached the One Frog Inn, she noticed her carriage parked just outside, and getting closer she saw Simon sitting on the porch, swaying gently on a rocking chair.

"All set Madam," he said, standing up as she approached. She nodded and entered the carriage. Simon climbing atop and urging the horses onward they slowly picked up speed until a gallop signaled a sufficient pace.

Eliza opened her window allowing a swift gust to disturb the otherwise serene velvet curtains. She noticed a flask on the seat across from her. Unable to contain herself, booming laughter escaped her lips and grabbing the flask she took a sip. 'I can't wait any longer,' she thought resolutely, noticing her own elation.

TWENTY-TWO

As they approached the church young Alexander was guided by the lofty pace of Eliza. Hand in hand they walked until the funeral bells thundered in his ears. Each loud ding seemed to squeeze Alexander's heart until finally he broke grip with Eliza and stopped before the church doors. Eliza, who had been partially up the small flight of stairs that accommodated the door, turned around and hugged Alexander. She looked into his eyes and smiled,

"Come on." she said solemnly, "It's time."

She took his hand and led him onward. With each step Alexander could more clearly hear the light chatter of a full church, and as they opened the door he was plagued by a serious concern that they would have nowhere to sit. He sighed, thinking, 'Maybe I should have come sooner.'

"We've come at the perfect time." Eliza said, looking around.

Macey, who was the owner of a small shop in town called Antique de Macey, approached with a smile, although Alexander noticed that her eyes remained melancholic. She bent down and hugged him. Her hair smelled nice, Alexander noticed, like fresh cut flowers. His mother loved gardening after all and had often encouraged him to help, especially when it came to the important task of deciding which flowers smell best. She was warm and sincere, hugging for what seemed like the perfect amount of time to convey such sentiments and taking Eliza's hand in the midst of it the three of them were connected. She rose and stood in front of them, with her hands on her hips like a proud parent might, allowing a few seconds of silence to pass.

"Do you like my dress?" she said, smiling. Eliza's eyes followed each subtle emotion that flickered across Alexander's face, and understanding that the question was directed at him, she remained fixated on his face. From the side Alexander looked as well as he did from the front. His small nose proportioned well with an adequate chin and thin, intimate lips. His face made few unnecessary movements, and Eliza couldn't help smiling whenever she watched him. His eyes were the true feature of his face and sparkled like the ocean might, as the sun rising early in the morning glitters off it. She watched as his face displayed pleasure at Macey's kind gesture, and noticing that Macey, making the question about herself, allowed Alexander a certain relief.

"It's very nice Miss Macey." he said, smiling.

Eliza's father Charles noticed them entering and, excusing himself from a conversation, came to them who remained standing near the entrance.

"I think we are about ready to begin." Macey said as Charles approached prompting him to nod in response.

"You look good Alexander." he said, careful not to allow any emotion to tinge his compliment. "Come now." he added, "There's a seat here. In the front."

Still holding hands, Alexanders grip tightened as if to hold Eliza in place, although she pretended not to notice and pulled him onwards. Charles led them to a row in the front where only Eliza's mother and his father's best friend, Luther, sat. As they settled Alexander released his grip and placed his face in his hands, beginning to cry. Eliza noticing this sat back lightly rubbing his back. Luther placed a hand on his knee,

"It's difficult Alexander. And that's okay. It's okay for things to be hard. It's okay to cry."

Alexander felt as if time was distorted. He wasn't crying but managed to maintain a state of perpetual tension. He imagined that crying would help but could not promptly induce it. His cloudy thoughts were punctuated by a sporadic and swift inhale followed by a deep and precise exhale which he could not control. Each successive inhale he imagined losing control before the breath had finished, although it did not happen. His thoughts focused on the gentle hand gliding up and down his back. The pressure was light, focusing on it Alexander felt that probably only three fingers were all that produced the sensation. Despite them being no more than a gentle breeze, the warmth they omitted restrained him. He acknowledged that he would have lost control a long time ago if not for those three fingers. When he regained his breath, he looked up and his distorted feeling of time was confirmed. Where Luther sat before, now sat his uncle Charles. The previously noisy room, despite the solemn expression of the noise, was now silent, and Luther was addressing the room, from behind a podium that was ordained with a large cross on its front. He looked to Eliza, whose eyes waited patiently before her, reconciled to thought. As he straightened she looked to him and smiled warmly. He smiled back and taking her hand in his, he reluctantly followed the instruction of her eyes, who fixed their gaze on the speaker, Luther. The words danced off Luther's tongue and he kept his audience sympathetic. Although Alexander couldn't make out what he was saying, time seeming to move slowly after all, he could occasionally decipher the names James and Anna, his parents, which sent a tremor of despair through his body until it eventually reached his head, causing his vision to tighten. He imagined the world closing in and would feel claustrophobic for a few seconds, until noticing in his hand, the hand of Eliza. The world would open back up and he would feel a calmness overcome him, until he recognized the names again. This continued for some time and Luther seemed to transform into one person after the next. And each fresh person spoke words that were just as jumbled as the previous, except for those painful names of course.

This proceeded until Alexander felt that intimate hand pull him upwards, and looking around he noticed that everyone was standing. Alexander followed Eliza until reaching two open caskets that contained his parents. The week prior to the funeral had given him some time to process but probably not enough, he realized. 'You know I don't like change.' he thought, addressing the bodies before him. 'Why would you think something like that?' he scornfully followed with, to himself. He sighed, 'it's only natural that I think something like that. It's only natural... My parents are dead and I am broken. They left me and no one loves me and I will grow up alone. And it's my fault.' He sighed again and put a hand on his mother's hand who laid closest to him. It was clean, and delicate and retained more softness than he imagined it would. As a drop of water plopped down on her hand he realized that tears were rolling down his cheeks. He bowed his head and looked to Eliza who was a few feet away. "It's not your fault," she said as they continued outside, her hand taking his.

The loud bells rung determinedly and managed to keep Alexander's thoughts reined. Each successive throng brought him back to the present and he watched as the attendants, with their grieving satisfied, began their trips home. Home had been a delicate concept of thought lately. After his parents had passed, one week ago, Luther and Charles had taken charge of all the arrangements. Luther being closer had managed the affairs of the Climicus estate and made most of the arrangements, while Charles accumulated the affected. Although he himself had only arrived the day before, his wife Mary, and daughter Eliza had reached Wilheimer Falls three days earlier. Luther was an energetic replacement and miraculously kept everything more or less in order, while making

Alexander feel the most at ease that he possibly could. Alexander felt a contentedness that week, especially while watching Luther. He moved quickly but Alexander suspected it was out of necessity more than anything else. His theory was proven whenever he asked a question or made an inquiry, or at breakfast, lunch, and dinner, when Luther made a point to completely halt and give relaxed attention and realistic answers. Alexander was impressed with Luther for how well he framed harsh words without seeming insensitive. When he asked in a prodding manner, 'will everything be okay?' Luther replied, 'I imagine so, but that is partially up to you. Isn't it?' And several more questions of that sort.

When Eliza arrived, he loved her instantly. Despite being unsure how, he was positive that she understood him fully. They shared everything with one another, and she knew exactly when to be bombastic and when to be sincere. Alexander felt as if he had been thrust into a play surrounded by magnificent characters. She was pretty like an actress too, piercing blue eyes and flowing black hair. Pale skin and a delicacy that was unacknowledged as intimated by the occasional bruise from rough play. She acted as a perfect counterweight to Luther's occasionally over honest approach, wrangling and pacifying any woe that may be running rampant in his head.

Eliza and her family followed Alexander back to the Climicus estate, with Luther staying behind to finish whatever arrangements were further necessary. The ride back was silent. The emotions invoked by the articulation of his parents' names had exhausted him. He sat with his head slumped and staring at the ground, looking out the window, he decided, would be nauseating. He occasionally looked up at Eliza who reclined back sleeping, her serene expression led Alexander to the conclusion that she was having a nice dream. His eyes would linger before transferring to his Uncle Charles, who sat upright with his eyes closed, clearly just focusing on his thoughts. His wealth was apparent from his attire and his appearance was overall majestic. He hadn't said much to Alexander but was vigilant to make sure he never felt out of place. Consistently including him in things, and moving him around to be occupied as much as propriety demanded. Alexander appreciated it and however badly he wanted to feel alone, the people around him wouldn't allow it. Alexander sighed, 'I can't think clearly.' he thought, 'I need to be alone.'

Alexander's life prior to the tragedy was ideal. He decided when he was young that happiness wasn't precisely as important as people made it out to be. His father was an intelligent man and although he never expressed his actual beliefs, choosing instead to instill in Alexander the tool of mental flexibility, Alexander decided that his father had a similar view. He much preferred contentment. A vigorous mental life full of reading and ripe with writing punctuated only by new intellectual insights. Since then, he hadn't felt like himself.

Dinner was had in silence, except for the occasional polite comment by his aunt Mary, 'that was a nice service,' and so on. As everyone prepared for bed and the day was over, his uncle Charles, hearing Alexander's footsteps in the hallway, called to him from the study where he sat behind a desk, papers strewn about in front of him. Alexander entered,

"Can we talk?" asked Charles.

TWENTY-THREE

THOMAS SAT AND WATCHED AS THE FIGURE OF ELIZA FADED INTO the distance. He could feel how dry his throat was and his face burned in a way that signaled to him that it was a shade of light red. A feeling of lightness animated his heart and he felt happy, the breath he exhaled he imagined to be cool and refreshing. His shoulders slinking back luxuriously, he focused on the subtle sound of the church procession taking place on the other side of the door and closed his eyes. The peace came not from the outcome but because he had expressed his soul adequately, and Thomas believed that there was no better mode of living. There are constant difficulties when maneuvering through social situations which are by definition inundated with webs of culture, civility, empathy and so on, and one often muddles ceaselessly through these weeds caught on one or another, misrepresenting themselves at every juncture, or perhaps they master them and use them to their advantage, and for recreation. But, the truest salvation is realized when one cuts the weeds, even for just one sentence, and conveys what is inside their soul. Thomas believed he did that and was content with wherever that path led.

After some gentle reflection, more so on the beauty of the town around him than his inner workings, he stood up and reentered the church. The door was heavy and Thomas felt that church doors must be heavy so that one cannot walk into church by accident.

He sat in a pew near the back and listened while the ceremony closed. He stood as the congregation joyfully dispersed, individuals often stopping to talk with him and thank him. A sincere smile graced his face and after everyone left he approached the pastor who nodded to him.

"Shall we talk in the office?" Pastor Nick said, smiling. He stood up and politely motioned for Thomas to lead. They entered, Pastor Nick sitting behind a simple desk with some papers on it, and a few candles on a stand next to it. Thomas sitting nearest the door on a comfortable chair facing the desk.

"How did it go with Eliza?" he asked.

"Well enough, in terms that I am relieved, but not so well in that I was refused." He sighed and continued, "I'll cherish the week we spent together and our friendship. And this town bathed in sunshine will remain forever dear to me, but I confess that it was impossible not to imagine a vibrant life together and that is something that I have not experienced before. I will definitely miss her... I am not willing to put any more thought then that at the moment. Forgive me for my brevity."

"I see. Well enough then! You have no obligation to share, my friend. Let's move along to the matter at hand. I understand you're traveling to Wilheimer Falls next? I wrote to Father Richard the pastor there and he is willing to install you in a position effective whenever you arrive. And as you know there is always an excitement that follows a visiting preacher and generally they are welcome wherever they go. I've acquired sure lodging for you, if you wanted to stop on your way in Grant Creek. You are of course willing to stay here as long as you want, and surely there." he said, smiling with his hands on his desk, double checking some papers as he spoke. "Whenever you are ready, and whatever route you take, the Church and God is always behind a man such as yourself."

"Thank you, Father. And as for Grant Creek, I'm just too eager to see Benjamin again."

Thomas smiled and stood up, Pastor Nick following him.

"We are fortunate that you spent an extra week with us Thomas, it was an honor to host you. Will you be leaving today then?"

"The honor was mine, and yes I think I will be on my way." Thomas said, stretching his hand towards Pastor Nick who embraced it sternly and shook it affectionately. "You'll take care of the children?" he added.

"The arrangements have made. Safe travels and send me word from Wilheimer Falls!" Pastor Nick added as Thomas proceeded through the door, nodding as he went on.

Thomas continued through town at a leisurely pace, and very much enjoyed the winding streets. He loved long walks and took them whenever possible, allowing his mood to direct him. He had no preference between a townscape and a forest setting, as far as he was concerned each had their own charm. Walking now, he looked at each passerby with a smile loosely animating his face. Each person, he recognized, was a magnificent example of God's grace and creative capacity. Everyone he passed had a grand significance in the eyes of God and Thomas did his best to acknowledge that trait in every individual he saw. He felt immense joy when someone would smile at him and say 'hello.' In the busyness of the world, Thomas noticed that some people were preoccupied, although through no fault of their own, and one of his missions was to show them an alternative: to be always present. This was best done through Christianity. Once one gives up their life to God they acknowledge that the world unfolds as it must, and faith that things will work out for the better, and one can enjoy whatever life brings.

Approaching the One Frog inn, Thomas noticed Hampton sitting on the bottom step of the porch solemnly poking a stick lazily into the ground in front of him. Seeing Thomas, he leapt up dropping the stick and ran to him, hugging a leg and beginning to cry. Thomas began lightly patting him on the back and Hampton remained locked for a few moments until finally he looked up at Thomas with tears in his eyes. Thomas took his hand and led him back to the steps, sitting down next to him and put his arm on Hampton's shoulder.

"What's wrong Hampton?... Do you want to talk about it?" Thomas spoke lightly, his voice barely audible.

"Eliza's gone!" Hampton said, sniffling. He rubbed his eyes.

"Is that so?" Thomas replied, hearing the name so soon unexpectedly illuminated a wound that he imagined was smaller. Like one who, in a brief intermission, might forget exactly how to describe the pain to a doctor until it returns fully. 'It's natural,' he thought, 'yes, natural, natural, natural.' He continued internally to avoid his thoughts drifting to the ache, 'perfectly reasonable.'

"She left!" Hampton picked up the stick he had dropped and began prodding a clump of dirt in front of him. "I did ent want her ta go!"

"You liked her, didn't you?" Thomas said, looking into the distance.

"She was my fav-or-ite!" Hampton exclaimed.

"Mine too Hampton. Maybe she will come visit you some day! Yes, I'm sure she will."

"You think so Mr. Thomas?" Hampton stopped playing and looked imploringly to Thomas.

"Yes. So until then we just have to remember how much fun we had. What was your favorite memory Thomas?"

"I liked wen we were all together. It was like... It felt like... A family..."

Thomas put an arm around Hampton and pulled him close.

"Everything will work out Hampton. I'm proud of you, you know?"

Hampton smiled, wiping tears from his eyes and off his cheeks.

"I'm afraid, I'm leaving today as well... I'll return soon Hampton. Can you forgive me for leaving?"

"I can forgive you Thomas!" Hampton embraced him once more and stood up triumphantly.

"You're my friend right?" he added.

"Of course!" Said Thomas.

"Then I can forgive you! We are friends!"

Thomas nodded and stood up, patting Hampton on the head and ruffling his hair. He went inside and began packing.

TWENTY-FOUR

BENJAMIN SAT AT A TABLE PATIENTLY LOOKING AT A MENU. HE HAD been to "Rene's," often enough to know what it entailed, but viewed it more to pass the time. Alexander would be arriving soon and Ben knew that whether he said it or not and whether he wanted to come or not, he would appreciate the location. What it lacked in familiarity it made up for in seclusion, although it's vast space was taken up entirely on Sundays, during the week it seemed virtually empty. In addition, it was far enough from The Dancing Sheep, that if someone did recognize him it would be obvious that he was not currently partaking in 'public life,' and despite anything negative to be said about the popular intelligentsia occupying the town there is a clear and impassible line made between public and private life. In other words, Benjamin was sure that they would be unbothered.

Alexander entered and seeing Benjamin strode towards him, pulling out a chair and sitting across from him. Benjamin nodded to him and although their eyes were locked Alexander seemed lost in thought. Underneath his eyes a subtle blackness persisted and despite a wide open and energetic gaze, Ben perceived a tiredness as if he hadn't slept. Sitting back, and feeling no pressure to engage, Ben retreated into thought for a moment. He had been unsure of what they would talk about and reconciled to let the conversation flow naturally, which he now realized as an oversight being that

Alexander was perfectly capable of maintaining silence. He looked at Alexander and sighed,

"I often think about her…" the words slipped from his mouth, he even felt a moderate blush pass across his cheeks. He watched as Alexander's eyes flickered and a depressed, almost agitated grimace appeared on his face. Alexander spoke quickly and his voice trembled with irritation,

"I personally refuse to think about her. Yes, you mean Angelica of course, the name even seems foreign to me. I am tormented because I know you mean her and who is she? She is someone who I've spoken a few sentences to, and no more, and therefore it makes no sense for me to think about her. And forgive me for perhaps being insensitive, but she is dead. Although you began the topic so I think I am within civility to be blunt…" Taking a deep breath he looked downward and allowed his tone to soften, he spoke much slower. "But no, never mind, I am being rude, and I apologize. Let me start over. Yes, it is natural for the grieving process to last longer in those who were of closer proximity. I can't imagine what you may be going through, so I will pose this question: is it a good thing or a bad thing that you still think about her, about Angelica?".

Despite sensing that Alexander had more to say, he acknowledged that the conversation would be situated on his side of the table and continued.

"I imagine it to be a good thing. The spirit of an individual is kept alive by those who think about them. It remains in all those who that person influenced. Take for instance a counter example, imagine that someone lived without ever having contact with another person. That no one will ever discover that they have lived. What could be said about good and bad in such a circumstance? I contend that it would be neutral to dwell on the thought of a person in such a situation." Benjamin took a sip of water from a perspiring glass that sat in front of him. "So by saying that thinking about her is a good thing, I have to propose that the thought is affecting me positively. I don't think it would be suitable to say it would be good unless I was willing to make that statement. Because if I said, 'I would rather think about her than not.' Or, 'thinking about her allows her spirit to live on,' I am still absent of the element of goodness."

"And do you not despair when you think about her?" Alexander asked, his voice low and his eyes fixed downward.

"Of course! And so my heart throbs and I exclaim that despair and emotion in general is goodness itself! To think of her stirs such powerful forces within me that I would be a shell of myself if I did not know I possessed such a force. And furthermore it is because of this that I have learned something substantial about myself. Each time I recall her image I learn more and more... And you who refuse to think about her. Maybe you came to the opposite conclusion?"

Alexander looked up, and seeing the grin on Ben's face, he smiled back.

A waiter approached and, bowing, he refilled the water in front of Benjamin and asked the duo if they were ready. Ben began and ordered an elaborate meal, making small talk about the freshness of produce and so on, allowing the unprepared Alexander to glance at the menu. As he did Ben expanded on whatever caught Alexander's eye and made recommendations accordingly until finally a choice was made and Alexander passed a pleasant glance to Ben who nodded happily.

"I do not think about her." Alexander said solemnly, "But I do still dream about her." He stopped, as if collecting his thoughts. Ben decided not to interject and allowed the silence to linger. Alexander eventually continued, "It was initially so often and vivid that we built a rapport. And so realistic was her figure that I did not allow myself to question it for months, we were intimate, it's as simple as that, there ceased to be a distinction between being awake and being asleep, except that I preferred the latter..."

"But the dreams have lessened? And you refuse to engage wakefully?" Ben asked.

"You were right when you said that I came to the opposite conclusion. Being beholden to emotions is the enemy of reason, and anyone who has ever accomplished anything which I consider noteworthy has done so via reason. One learns this as a child. Any child who is worth their salt will test the waters of authority and act out, break rules, etc. In other words, they enter a social world of emotions and use reason to calibrate accordingly based on the push back, punishment, reward and so on. And when inevitably they reach the limits, a point where an antiquated or incoherent rule is so entrenched that it cannot be transgressed, they experience the most potent form of anger. They may thrash for a time but eventually in their futility a question is arises, 'Is it actually reasonable to be angry?' and whether the answer is yes or no, a follow up question emerges making the first one almost obsolete. And from the skies a transcendent and eternal being called reason whispers, 'is it useful?' And to the question, 'is it useful?' there is only one answer, no. The profound child will realize that in no situation is it ever useful to be angry. Why? Because an individual can act angry without experiencing the emotion of anger. So in the rare circumstance that displaying anger would be helpful, one could do just that, display it! And spare themselves the recklessness that accompanies all emotions. This profound understanding manifests itself among each distinct emotion. And so it is in the case with these fond remembrances of Angelica, who I only gazed for a moment, which are complete fabrications. That is, the question which I have through great lengths habituated to accompany new emotions and that echoes constantly if neglected to be answered has recently and finally demanded an answer. The question being, 'Is it reasonable to feel this way?' and in the case we are referring to the undeniable answer is no. And the following charitable answer, 'will it help?' can at best be answered with 'for a time.' but that time has now passed and I have pulled myself up by the bootstraps of reason in order to move forward, and the emotion which was a novel one is now properly domesticated to reason."

Benjamin enjoyed the exposition, although a slight pang of shame pricked his senses. His interest in exploring Alexander's mind had manifested itself in the conversation and despite the conversation beginning with Benjamin's thoughts as the topic, he had forcefully changed the content to Alexander. He noticed this after a slight and subdued irritation had returned to the boy's voice.

"I think this conclusion is natural," Alexander continued, his voice relaxing and an approving softness applying itself to his pronunciation. "For someone who is born with a reasonable temperament like myself. I'm still unsure what to make of individuals unlike myself."

"Do you have someone specific in mind?" Benjamin asked, feeling that this was a topic that Alexander invited purposefully.

Alexander laughed, which Ben felt was uncharacteristic despite the naturalness with which it proudly marched from his lips. "It seems I've hijacked this conversation. The blame isn't entirely on me though, is it?"

Benjamin laughed as well, "I gladly accept my portion of the responsibility and would have preferred nothing else. And as I've never been especially fond of rigid decency and willingly and constantly transgress it with my favorite mistress called sentimentality, I again admit that this conversation is going precisely how I would have wanted it." Ben noticed an unfamiliar lightness to Alexander.

Alexander smiled, "Aha! Well I won't give you the pleasure."

"Okay, Okay, fine! I will resume with a shameful civility and reply to your oration. Let me try to address the position presented in such a way that would apply to everyone regardless of temperament. The child who you're presenting is asking the wrong question and therefore coming to a wrong conclusion! Is it reasonable? Are we to suppose that this is the primary question of life? Imagine an old man lying on his death bed, would he whisper as his parting words, 'if only I had been more reasonable?' No! No dying man will say this, not one. Why? Because the question that life presents is not so superbly rational. Imagine the child instead asking, 'am I experiencing what it means to be human?' It makes me giddy to imagine how drastically the child will flourish. And maybe the clever child would respond, 'rationality is what makes one human,' and I would pat him on the head! I would say life is more complicated than that, for things can have functions as well as qualities and people too have many dimensions. Like a ship that everyone agrees is the most well-constructed ship ever made, I would ask the boy, 'would you like it blue or green?' (assuming it would have no effect on function) and the boy would try to say, 'it does not matter,' but to me it does! The most well-constructed ship ever made should stoke the imagination of other shipbuilders! It should seize the eye of onlookers! It should inspire awe in the hearts of the public! It should flourish. In every sense possible."

Just then, the waiter arrived with several dishes of food and both men ate in amicable and thoughtful silence. Not another word was spoken.

TWENTY-FIVE

——————

AS A YOUNG ALEXANDER ENTERED, HE WAS GREETED SOLEMNLY BY Charles Climicus who sat on top of his father's desk. Leaning down on one knee Alexander's uncle pulled him close, hugging him. He smelled pleasant, like the woods but without a tinge of sweat that Alexander noticed normally accompanied men who smelled like the woods. Alexander sat and Charles dragged a chair closer to allow more intimacy, although Alexander's eyes remained scanning the desk which was covered in miscellaneous papers.

"You know this desk is yours now Alexander."

"I know." Alexander responded, although he didn't know. In fact, Alexander could not recall a time before seeing the desk that he had ever attributed specific ownership to anything.

"The house too. Everything."

"I know." Alexander again lied.

"Anything you need; you still have a family."

Alexander felt an uneasiness emanating from his uncle's words and could tell he didn't know what to say either.

"I know." he replied, again, acknowledging that he has to say something else eventually.

"You know..." Charles began, "We are leaving for France... Next week."

Alexander stirred, sitting straight up as if struck by a blown to his chest. Turning pale, he stammered,

"Leaving…?"

"Leaving." Charles said softly.

"Eliza?" Alexander whispered, his voice shaking.

"Leaving…" Charles sat forward and placed a hand on Alexander's knee. "And you?" he added.

"What…?"

"Would you like to leave with us?"

"To France?"

"To France."

"I…. don't know."

"Think about it Alexander, the choice is yours. You will be taken care of no matter what you decide, you have a family. Think about it. We will remain here for a few days but I will need your decision sooner or later. I know you have a lot to think about. I will leave you to it." Charles stood and left the room quietly, leaving the door open.

Alexander stared at the desk. Not particularly out of interest but to suspend his disorientation. The desk was his, and with that insight a gruesome reality thrust itself upon him and his heart beat quick. He looked at a picture of his mother that hung behind his desk in father's study. A picture that hung in his own study, he realized. Her eyes were soft and he could feel her gentle breath against his skin after she kissed his forehead. "I cannot leave." He thought.

PART THREE

Eliza's Journey

TWENTY-SIX

THICK DROPLETS PUMMELED THE PARKED CARRIAGE, THE RAIN surpassing its earlier neutered preponderance. An almost black sky lingered overhead with only brief tufts of white occasionally in the distance, although nearly invisible, lingering similar to how a lonely oasis might appear in a desert, so distant and precious that an onlooker may presume it to be a mirage only to quickly dash the thought. It is too necessary to be a mirage and one must act in order to retain their morale and so for all intents and purposes, for the mentioned observer, it does indeed exist. And so Eliza sat, facing Simon. A small negligible light penetrated the carriage where she peered from the window. The air was green, magnifying the lumbering thicket surrounding them and with the enhanced quality the figure of mother nature revealed herself. She stands almost imperceptibly at every threshold where a town ends, or where civil cultivation wanes, hers is a different sort of order that one has to spend a lifetime contemplating, but one recognizes her beauty best in the most remote of places, and every so often she displays her rapturous wonder to those solitary creatures who labor there.

Simon had recommended that they light a candle but Eliza denied the request. She was annoyed that Simon had refused to continue despite the current weather. They had been traveling for a week and, although they only stopped sporadically for a night here or there, they were making poor time. This was because Eliza had changed the destination an innumerable amount of times, so much in fact that Simon was also becoming annoyed and had reconciled to continue at a pace that suited him. This new disposition resulted in many bombastic diatribes where Eliza's voice echoed through the trees, and one could notice birds taking flight, startled, in the distance. She had oscillated between the destinations of Wilheimer Falls and the ocean, which was in the exact opposite direction, until finally deciding on the ocean. Her sturdy declaration thundered with emotion when she made it, vibrating in the wind and dancing with her previous loud words that still hovered in the distance. She had said, "I can't look Alexander in the eyes until I've seen the ocean again!" and with that Simon, although remaining lugubrious, no longer outwardly protested.

"I'm going to get some fresh air." Eliza said calmly to the figure Simon who sat resolutely in the shadow across from her.

"You can't be serious! It's a downpour, just wait it out, don't be unreasonable."

"Unreasonable? Simon I'm bored. I've wasted too many days in my life. I'm going out."

"In this weather? You're joking, it's dangerous."

"I've been keeping an eye on your watch, it's been over an hour since we've heard any serious thunder anywhere close. Besides, a walk sounds pleasant. Is that reasonable enough for you?" Eliza said with a smirk, "What's more reasonable than doing what sounds pleasant?"

"You'll get sick!" Simon pronounced, knowing full well that it was futile.

"Start a fire to warm me."

She dropped her dress revealing a tender frame shaped by light muscles. Simon watched in disbelief but expressed no surprise. The cool mud licked her foot as she stepped from the carriage, nearly swallowing it. She gently freed her hair from a tie and took a deep breath as if it had been suffocating her and as the rain washed it backwards behind her she smiled. She stood with perfect posture as the water glanced eagerly off her figure and closing her eyes she angled her chin upwards, allowing the storm to kiss her lofty face. Thunder could be heard in the distance and the constant barrage of water gracing the forest drowned out everything else.

"How am I supposed to find firewood in this?" Simon shouted from inside the carriage, causing Eliza to erupt into laughter. She attempted to open her eyes towards Simon but the frequency of impediments made it impossible. Finally, she put a hand to her forehead as if blocking out the sun and looked to Simon, who had stuck his head out but quickly regretted it, he was laughing heartily in response to the situation.

"Figure it out dear Simon!" she said with a smile, turning and beginning to walk.

She walked slowly, reflecting on the refreshing rain that cooled her naked body. She had listened to Simon's protests all day and his continuous promises that the rain would stop. 'But why would I want it to stop,' she thought. Water gathered on the ground softening it for her bare feet but she still remained careful and followed a thin reservoir that accentuated the hilly terrain towards the tree line. The woods were dark and despite the sky remaining ominous, they felt inviting. The healthy canopy redirected much of the rain and as she entered, the sound emanating from the water gliding off the leaves seemed distant and the pitter patter that was a second before so close to her was replaced with a vibrant orchestra of wildlife. Birds called to their prospective suitors with enchanting melodies among the dimness, occasionally greeting her for a moment as they flew by. Crickets chirped hello from hidden dens. And the rain itself, now subdued, managed a gentle and welcome sprinkle, keeping her just wet enough to remain ecstatic.

The subtle flow and gentle babble of rainwater accumulating on the ground led her onwards through the thicket, trusting that it knew the clearest way forward she followed it eagerly, extending her hand to brush against the pretty shrubbery at her side, her feet gingerly stepping forward, treating each new foothold as a novel experience worthy of notice. The rain singing overhead, changing its tone every so often, called forth a flood of new emotions with it. Distant memories sprang forward: she was a young girl in stable France, she stood upright and cleverly in a field outside her host's estate, her plain dress blowing in a gathered breeze, and Count Leopold explaining the threshing machine to her anxious ears. "One must understand how people labor," her father had once said. Her eyes, though, drifted to the towering pines across the plantation and a darkened cloud that crawled across the sky. She interrupted Leopold, who was entranced in his task, with laughter as an abrupt and powerful wind kicked them both out of their thoughts, accompanied by a downpour that soaked them both instantly. "Damnit!" the Count had exclaimed with a frightful face. Eliza remembered his face in that moment, and was glad that she had seen it, she felt like she had known him better after that. Their relationship evolved from that single experience and despite his popularity and noble position he would always bring her cookies when returning from a trip abroad. True enough, he brought many gifts to many people but that delicate flaky confection was always reserved simply for her.

The shrubbery eventually gave way to a modest clearing, carved by the intricate hand of time, and the canopy opened briefly to admit a greying sky. The juncture was only so wide to allow a small stream to saunter through, likely expecting to remain unnoticed forever. Eliza sat, the cool grass pampering her skin. Her legs crossed, she watched the stream. Eliza shared a similar feeling with the stream who due to the weather had grown and flourished. She allowed her mind to drift, but no further than the elegant vista before her. The stream carried with it a variety of fallen flower pedals that Eliza observed welcomed the journey. Imagining that she could smell them, she smiled as the fragrance reached her nose, thanking the flowers as they sailed by.

❦

As time passed, Eliza cooled with the sloping temperature, and the quieting rain kept her just wet enough to remain muddy. She stood and placed her feet in the stream, cleaning them, despite knowing that it would not last even one step. With the fading storm the wildlife sang with a renewed vigor and their voices led Eliza back towards the carriage. As she approached, the light scent of smoke captured her nose and she remembered a feeling called warmth. Her pace quickened and emerging from the woods she was greeted by a fire. She rushed to it and hunching near it she rubbed her hands together, freeing the last bit of dry dirt that clung to them. Simon appeared, smiling, from behind a dense collection of brush with wood in his hands. He triumphantly dropped the wood into an existing pile under the carriage and, throwing Eliza a small blanket from inside, he approached the fire.

"Thank god the rains finally stopped," he said, wiping some sweat from his forehead. "How was your walk?" he added.

"Well. Thank you… I'm sorry if I've been short with you Simon."

"Oh Eliza, how long have we known each other?" Simon said, laughing. "Since you were a little girl! And how far have we traveled? Around the world!"

Tears began to accumulate in Eliza's eyes, she spoke softly, "Who was that little girl Simon? Who am I, sometimes I don't recognize myself…"

Simon fanned the fire, allowing the flames to grow, the damp logs that he had added catching light, and sat back down in silence. Eliza smiled and he replied with a subtle nod.

"Thank you." she said.

TWENTY-SEVEN

———

THE SUN ROSE SLOW AND THE THICK TREE LINE MAINTAINED THE
darkness of the camp. Eliza had slept deep sprawled within the
carriage but the emotion of the day had left her too tired to dream.
Her eyes opened in the dim shadow of a pine, sitting up she allowed her senses time to orient themselves. The familiar chirps
rang seemingly from every tree and twigs could be heard snapping
every so often in the distance. Her nose eventually took command,
guiding her senses to the fire where a light sizzling was accompanied by the smell of pork. Simon occasionally tussled a modest
pan, and Eliza, noticing the smoke the fire exuded, followed the
serene gray apparition to the sky where it revealed a drastic change
from the day before. She joined Simon at the fire and, with tired
eyes, smiled. After flipping a few sausages, he offered Eliza a flask
which she declined.

"It wasn't too wet was it? How did you sleep?" she asked, holding her hands to some embers that adorned the fire's outer edge.

"As well as I could. The bugs are the problem, yes the bugs. I've
always had trouble sleeping with my face covered. Thankfully once
I'm out, I'm out."

"I'm glad! I was worried that the rain may start up again and
your tent would leak."

"Ah, fate wouldn't have that miss Eliza." Simon said, handing
her a sausage that he had grabbed with a sturdy fork.

Eliza sighed. "Simon don't use words like that! Especially not this early." Taking a bite of the pork she annunciated her satisfaction with a content moan.

"Yes, early for you, but not for me." he said with a grin, taking a piece of sausage for himself. Silence permeated the camp until, finishing her meal, Eliza spoke,

"I think... I won't drink any more Simon." she said, sheepishly.

"That's good Miss Eliza." Simon responded.

"You said we traveled the world, but when? And where was I? Present? Who knows. I think about that young girl in France and why she started drinking. It was because of custom, to fit in, but who am I trying to fit in with now? Now it's become a peculiarity! Which is a good thing. Peculiarities are good things, but only if they are an actual expression of one's desires! I am unique because I have the characteristic of being traveled and the qualities of France, where I spent my youth, but am I just a French girl? I won't allow it anymore! Am I just doing it to fit in here? No Simon, No. I am changing because I, myself, want to. I'm tired of habit Simon, I'm exhausted by this life we've lived. I want to become who I am. That said, I won't accept the word fate Simon. I will take responsibility..." she paused for a moment, thinking about what to say next. "Did you know... That even though I was younger, Alexander looked up to me when we were children? I never did forget how he looked at me. And now... I'm to return to him as what? A French girl? No... I think he needs me... Me and not a French girl."

"Eliza." Simon said, softly, "That's who you are. I know... That isn't very helpful is it?" he laughed but quickly recovered a concerned expression. "I remember when your father passed. And how slow the weeks progressed afterwards... How solemnly the shadow of the window frame etched itself on the dusty floor of my room. And how the household remained gray until finally Count Leopold informed me, with a glimmer in his eye, that you had accepted his offer to stay. You grew so quickly and I watched as you mastered the French culture. How thrilled I was that the Count brought you along as he traveled. Each time you returned you were that much more cultured. But Eliza, you made those cultures your own. You did those things not just to fit in with society, but to see how society fit in to you. You will see that, I promise. And I will always be here as your humble servant and friend. You are Eliza and you are loved. You are *that thing which is loved*."

Eliza laughed at Simon's last sentence, which he had fumbled to say. "I'm 'that thing,' huh?" she said smiling, to which Simon self-consciously furrowed his brow. "Indeed! Then that shall be my starting point and I will build from it." She paused for a moment and continued, stammering and uncertain what to say, "One day Leopold will come to America and he will be proud of me, for becoming truly myself. And my father? Simon it's too early to be sentimental, let's be off." Simon nodded and began preparing the carriage.

The long days passed mostly in silence. The rugged path occasionally jostling a comment out of Eliza as she was startled by the creaking of one wheel or another of the modest vehicle. Simon, who was primarily occupied with maps, remained in one of two states, either he was intensely focused on the road and direction ahead, or completely distant as if in thought. Eliza had once inquired what exactly he thought about when seemingly entranced and had received an unsatisfactory response, 'I'm not sure Miss Eliza,' he had said. She observed later that this quality was especially necessary for any serviceman who at the whim of his or her master was consigned to a whole range of mundane tasks. Although she appreciated this quality, she often wondered and imagined, recreationally, if she could do it. The realistic conclusion was that it was impossible, she acknowledged that her impulses, no matter how small, required immediate satiation and it would be impossible to subordinate those to anything but, she imagined, the most furtive passion she could conceive. 'Maybe for someone special.' she thought. 'Am I maybe that special to Simon?' she was comforted by the sentiment and appreciated him even more every time she noticed him in such a state.

The dense forests gave way to sparser vegetation. Eliza kept the window open, viewing the distant trees which was preferable, she thought, when contrasted with greenery in a closer proximity. The expanse between her and nature allowed a more static view. Each tree stood still and provided ample time for pleasantries. Eliza greeted those who smiled at her and listened to their stories told from trunk to canopy. Occasionally yawning she joined them with their brilliant appendages yearning for the sky, reaching higher and higher until accompanied by a new breed of wind, unhindered by the bustle of everyday life. With curiosity she imagined what the vantage point would look like at the tippy top of each tree. The interest grew so quickly that she began desperately surveying for a tree that she perceived as climbable. The branches beginning relatively high up on the trees made it an exercise in imagination for Eliza. She struggled to conceive of a mechanism for reaching the top and the spectacular view that such an endeavor would reveal. Breathless, she placed her hand on her head in frustration as the trees became rarer and equally as unclimbable, eventually giving way to fields that lacked them all together.

THE DAYS AMID THE FIELDS WERE LONG, AND DESPITE AN INITIALLY appreciated gravitas the once expansive vistas grew monotonous. Eliza decided it was because if she fully immersed herself in the passionate contemplation of one part of the scene she could not, no matter how hard she passionately contemplated, draw anything additional from redirecting her gaze. Even attempting to view the fields from a different existential perspective, which she saw as a last-ditch effort, like a farmer, or a lord or a cow, no mental gymnastics after a certain point could restore her interest. She sat with arms crossed and her knee bouncing for so long that her legs became sore from the exertion. The boredom mounted as she considered stopping to stretch her legs, only to be confronted with the thought that it would expand her time in the setting. She reconciled to accept her soreness to expedite this portion of the journey.

Just as Eliza was starting to lose count of the days she was startled out of resignation when Simon, with a nearly frantic voice, shouted "Trees!" signaling a welcome succession to the quiet stillness of the American plains. A smile grew on her lips and the fragrant wind prodded tears from her eyes as she leaned her head out to see what had caused Simon's outburst. "Trees!" Eliza shouted back with pent-up hope. The hues of green exploded from the mundane golden tint of wheat that had been her tormentor for a duration that she refused to dwell on. Drawing closer a distinct sound emanated from beyond the thicket of salvation, which made her heart cry out in joy. "River!" Simon shouted in a frenzy. "River!" Eliza exclaimed back as they both started laughing as if broken free from a dungeon and feeling the sun for the first time.

They stopped close by the river and the mid-day linger allowed the duo much needed rest. It was, of course, a rest from rest itself and finally being able to stretch their legs free of guilt, Eliza, with Simon abreast, strode, elated, along the river. The quick current churned the emerald water and shook awake those emotions which stagnate in a traveler's heart while in a particularly plain country. Their steps bounced as gentle mist occasionally sprinkled their features. Eliza laughed and removed her shoes as soon as the rocky path gave way to a sandier composition. Her pale feet sunk slightly with each step, saying hello to the water that greeted them from just under the ground. Her dress dragged on the wet rocks that required her to briefly climb over them to maintain a view of the river at her side. Welcoming the cool surface against her hands she vaulted over them whenever obstructed, dirtying her dress further.

"Careful Miss Eliza, that's your last clean dress!" shouted Simon, who was now falling behind Eliza's youthful pace.

"Who cares!" Eliza shouted, prancing out of the eye line of Simon, who had given up trying to maintain a quick pace. He stopped for moments watching the river flow just down a small slope.

Eliza glided on, giggling with joy at her new environment. Her muddy feet sliding as she hopped around obstacles and swung with any tree branch that protruded into the natural path along the river. Coming to a steeper slope she slowed down, observing her best way to maneuver down closer to the water so she could dip her muddy feet. Her best option, she decided, was to rely on a modest plant that eagerly jutted from the bountiful ground so close to its sustenance, just atop the slope. She clung firmly with one hand on the plant and the other bracing herself as she leaned back, her curled toes buried in the mud below her. Steadily she placed one foot in front of the other, burying it with care before continuing. She moved confidently, inch by inch, until the wet mud gave way and the plant whom she had placed so much confidence in leapt from its origin and she slid down the entirety of the slope and so quickly that she only realized the folly when she felt the brisk water on her feet. She lay flat on her back in a shallow overgrowth of the larger body of water a few feet away. Her eyes drifted to the sky and the pristine white clouds that crawled across it. Without sitting up she looked at her muddied hands, one of which had a gnarled root in it, 'I shouldn't have used a plant,' she thought with a sigh, 'sorry, little friend.' She dropped it to her side where it was invited by the gentle current to see the country. Her ears, just out of the shallow water listened intently to the lively splashing accentuating in her mind the exact path that the river carved through the area. Grasshoppers chirped in the distance, occasionally increasing in volume as the wind elevated and perpetuated those modern sirens.

Noticing her dress completely soaked, she sat up and glanced around. She peered at Simon who was sitting calmly at the top of the slope. She observed the path that her body had taken and the sheen of the mud that she had polished, with her back, on the way down. After a few moments she began laughing and attempting to splash Simon with the water at her side, he joined her expression readily, and remaining in laughter, she stood up.

"Help me up Simon, I'm stuck down here." she said, merrily.

"I don't know if I can Miss Eliza, with that dress soaked you've gained twenty pounds! I'm not as strong as I used to be you see."

"Simon you've always said I needed to gain weight, well I've done it! This is my compromise; I'll wear muddy dresses until the end of my days." she said, attempting futilely to climb the slippery incline on her own, careful not to uproot any clearly inadequate shrubbery.

"I think you made that decision long ago." he said laughing, "Hold on a moment, let me find something to pull you up."

Eliza watched as he disappeared further along the higher ground and she sat down patiently. Yawning, she observed closely the tiny pond she found herself in. It was shallow, only about two inches deep and as she sat partially on the slope only her feet remained in the water. Judging by the state of the path they had followed and the condition of her current location she decided that during heavy rain this was the path that the water had chosen. She imagined the river doubled in size amidst a storm, swallowing where she sat. As her eyes drifted she noticed the plant that she had accidentally uprooted caught on a rock perched just before the main body of water. Surefootedly she stood and moved the few feet necessary to free the plant, and tossing it into the river she watched it float away, it's visible leaves waving thank you in the wind. She turned to view Simon atop the slope approaching with a large fallen branch. With a smile on his face he drew closer until, losing his footing, he fell backwards, the colossal branch flying high into the air and landing behind him. The mud, previously polished slick by Eliza, all but yanked him downwards and his weight along with momentum provided such speed that he discovered new depths to the pond that Eliza's light frame couldn't penetrate. Sliding into it he was almost fully engulfed in water and reeling his heels he only narrowly avoided plunging into the actual river along with her friend, the plant, who had left her moments before. His face was covered in mud unearthed when his feet collided with the soft substance just below the water's surface and he sat up frantically clearing it the best that he could.

Eliza laughed as Simon, stammering curse words, splashed water on his face, clearing the debris.

"That wasn't what I had in mind." he said resolutely, accepting his fate and remaining sitting, partially under water.

"It happens to the best of us." Eliza said, reaching a hand out to help him stand. A giggle escaped her lips, "Why Simon, you're even muddier than me!"

"And who wears it better?" Simon said, looking upwards at the slope he had just fallen down. The indentation where they had both slid was even better defined and looked almost like an intentionally created avenue.

"Well it's grown a bit stale on me whereas you look like a new man, just this once I think you win." she said, smiling. After a brief silence she continued, "Now how do we get up that?"

Simon with his eyes darting around was calculating many options. They could if necessary wade a bit down the river to find easier access up the bank but the most straight forward way was to commit to returning from where they had fallen. As Eliza watched on, Simon took a few steps back and attempted to run up the slippery mud and grab a tree branch that hung just above his destination. Barely missing he slid back down on his hands and knees despite clinging to whatever was in his reach.

"Try again Simon! I'll help." Eliza said, posturing herself as high as she could on the unforgiving terrain just to the side of where Simon had made his attempt.

He again ran and propelled himself upwards with all his strength. As he began losing speed Eliza lunged behind him, her hands on his butt thrusting him upwards. He lingered for a moment, held in place by Eliza who was completely committed to success and thus was sprawled face first just under Simon, now entirely covered in mud. Using Eliza as a foundation he clambered up slowly, eventually standing back up in triumph at the top.

"Well done Miss Eliza!" he shouted, posturing the branch that he had gathered previously down the slope, this time remaining much further back. Eliza brushed some water on her face, clearing it slightly, and grabbed on as Simon yanked her up.

"Wasn't that fun." she said, slapping Simon on the shoulder as he caught his breath from pulling her up.

"Yes. Let's do it again tomorrow."

TWENTY-EIGHT

ELIZA AND SIMON APPROACHED THEIR CARRAIGE EARLY IN THE DAY, both filthy and hungry but in good spirits none the less. Coming closer they noticed from around the bend a small smoke stack where they had parked. They hurried with curiosity and eventually noticed two individuals sitting by a small fire encircled in rocks that had a pan crackling over it. One figure looking up from the pan shouted in a friendly tone, noticing the confusion on Eliza's face,

"Howdy!"

"Howdy." she replied as she neared.

"Wasn't sure how long you'd be gone, sorry to alarm you, it's common courtesy in these parts." He said, shaking the pan on top of the fire as he spoke. "Not many ladies in the back country." he added.

The man was just old enough to be called a man, Eliza attributed the wrinkles around his eyes to extensive travel and other than that his face was clean and his hair well kept. His clothes were modest but fashionable with a pair of glasses protruding from the front pocket of his light jacket. His boots were rugged and looked silly with his fashionable attire, his fresh pants tucked inside them. He looked up from a log he was sitting on with poor posture, his back hunched and his hand clasping the pan handle tighter than necessary.

"We're in no rush. So we take the less traveled paths when they present themselves." Eliza said coming closer to the fire and sitting down lazily, dried dirt falling from her dress as she moved.

"Well enough mam, I didn't mean to presume you owed me an explanation. Me and my brother just saw your carraige and thought this was a good place to stop, especially after such a droll stretch. You don't mind if we share a camp for the night? It's boring just the two of us sometimes." he said, with a relaxed and slow tone. As Eliza was beginning to talk he interrupted her, "Oh! It's done." he added, shaking the pan again, "Here, have some bison." He maneuvered some meat into a crude bowl and handed it to her. As she took it she began,

"Of course, you can." she said, delicately easing a portion of the meat into her mouth.

Silence protruded as Eliza ate slowly, the man who had spoken wore a labored smile on his face. Some distance behind them the other man, who not noticing Eliza approach, had left and could be heard rummaging for firewood in the thicket.

"You speak French mam?" the man asked, breaking a silence that had become prolonged.

"Not in this country." Eliza answered reproachfully, identifying the question as an obtuse and unflattering attempt to show off, and therefore necessary to rebuke.

"Aye but it's one of my only talents." he said with a smile, "all well, the question served its purpose I suppose."

"And what purpose is that?" she asked.

"To show that I am civilized of course."

"It's well known that there are none who are civilized in the back country. Civility is for civilization... For the city." she again rebuked, this time merrily.

"What good is knowing French then, if I cannot use it to prove my status?"

"You can use it to prove your status sir, just not here! No... here one uses it solely to communicate. With who? The wind of course, or if you should encounter a sparrow by chance, they know French as well."

"Yes and the bees as well, is it?" the man replied with a smile.

"You dirty boy." Eliza said with a laugh.

The man prodded back, "With all due respect mam just look at your dress, you're the dirty one."

Eliza leaned back on her hands and sighed, looking down at her filthy dress,

"How can I argue with that? I'd almost forgotten! You've brought me back to reality sir, and I was just getting comfortable." she added with a wink.

"Was not my intention, although I can't help it, delivering reality is my trade, that is, journalism. The name is John."

"Eliza." she replied.

The other man approached with a collection of wood clasped in his hands and added a few modest branches to the fire before noticing Eliza.

"Oh. Howdy." the man said, startled.

"This is my brother Jarvis." John said, poking the newly added branches with a branch of his own, in response the fire expressed a renewed vigor and sent embers high into the sky. "Jarvis this is Eliza." he added, nodding to Eliza who nodded to them both.

"Man I'm exhausted." Jarvis said, setting the wood a few feet behind John. "I have a whole heap over there." Jarvis pointed in the general direction that he had arrived from and continued, "I didn't even do much per se, but it must be on account of being on that horse for so long."

"Well think about it Jarvis, what would we do out in those fields? The best thing for us was to just ride through." John said.

"I know that! I'm just saying…" he shrugged his shoulders, "Let's go have a look around man, I need to stretch my legs some."

"Alrighty, since you did get all that wood." John said, standing up.

They walked in the direction that Eliza and Simon had emerged from, where the river could be heard in the distance. Eliza watched as John lumbered next to his brother Jarvis. Jarvis had many similarities of his brother, although much younger. His cool brown hair hung to his sides, with a meek ponytail dangling loosely in the back. His once fashionable clothes looked as if they had not been changed for a while and any attempt at tucking anything into anything had long been abandoned. His smile was brighter than his brother's and his teeth were nice. A smooth face made Eliza assume the boy was young but he moved with a maturity that made one unsure exactly how young. John had similar qualities although he, being older, displayed the characteristics one would expect. Everything about him was tidier and his hair, being short was just simply combed to the side. His face didn't appear to accommodate a beard very well, but a few whiskers managed to color his appearance ruggedly.

"They seem nice." Eliza said to Simon, who began stoking the fire.

"Yes, nice indeed, John and…?"

"Jarvis." She said, to which Simon nodded. "If they are gone for a while, we should start supper. To surprise them you know? That would be the proper thing to do."

"You're quite right Miss Eliza."

THE THICK WOODS THRASHED TO AND FRO IN THE COOL EVENING wind and the low whoosh occasionally lifted from the leafy canopy, calling out in a howl. Eliza smiled as it rattled her hair, which she had only just cleaned and combed. The stern breeze occasionally, trapped against a rock face, would whip into a frenzy and in its fury a mini vortex of debris would manifest for a moment before dissipating. Despite its quickly neutered character each time the phenomenon occurred a hint of alarm flashed across Eliza's face. The heavy wind recalled to her a particularly charged storm that had frightened her as a child. It had happened while crossing the Atlantic to France. She was very young when it happened but certain circumstances impel her memory with vividness to recall the distressing apparition that had appeared, that day, in the distance. Wandering onto the deck of the *La femme de Paris,* she viewed the lonely specter that hovered miles away. Never had the captain shouted so loudly or had the crew moved so quickly, never had anyone for that matter. The unusual silence of the water confused her and only briefly did she manage to glimpse the tearful determination painted on the faces of the now unrecognizable crew. Her friend the cook Francis Levian, who never before left the kitchen, was amongst those fumbling with the ships apparatus. She looked upwards, to the sky, and witnessed the slow, calm, circulation of clouds juxtaposed with the franticness around her. Watching without understanding the culmination far in the distance she felt a gentle breeze blowing at her dress. Curiously observing the crew as they moved quicker and quicker Eliza waited for an answer. Watching ever so closely, her haze was replaced with alarm when she came back to her senses and noticed that the gentle breeze had never once halted its swell and her dress now snapped back and forth violently. Not the briefest hesitation accompanied the winds ferocious growth and feeling as if she may fall over she clamored to one of the cabin's support beams and wrapped her arms tightly around it. Burned in her mind is that feeling of a perpetually growing wind. The gale threatened to rip her free from the thick wooden pole. Her shouts vanished among the deafening wind. Only when her father found her and grabbed her, almost aggressively, Eliza remembered, and burying her face deep in his chest, was she finally relieved from the nightmare, for the frantic crew managed to avoid any closer acquaintance with the apparition.

Occupying her attention with supper, Eliza's mind found relief. Jarvis and John remained absent during her labors and so she hurried to have it ready just as they arrived. Along with Simon, their mundane culinary skills matched perfectly with what they had left to cook. Any elaborate delicacies never lasted long and so they usually resigned to rotate between salted pork and salted beef, occasionally dragging a few chickens on a small trailer that could conveniently be rented for a trip from one town to the next, supposing properly made connections from the lender. Fruit and vegetables were kept in a sugar crate but were eaten quickly until only a few remained which were sparingly rationed. Eliza had decided to make a stew using almost everything they had on hand. This was partly because she wanted to treat her new friends well but mostly because of Simon urging her to, knowing that they would reach a new town sometime tomorrow. With Simon's help she meticulously spiced and boiled the water, and covered beef and vegetables to simmer and moisten in it. She imagined that Jarvis and John must be able to smell it no matter how far from camp they had traveled. Eliza, now relatively clean, and free from her muddy dress operated carefully to avoid being splashed by the hearty stew that bubbled in a welcoming manner when her spoon visited. An occasional sip from the wooden instrument that garnished her delicate hand filled her with delight and Simon seeing her pleasure demanded a sip as well,

"Give it here!" he called affably.

"Just one sip!" she replied, handing him the spoon, "Then you have to wait until our company arrives."

"Ah, I hope they come back soon, it's just about ready. Really delicious. I'll sleep well tonight with this to warm me." Simon said, handing Eliza back the spoon.

As Eliza placed the spoon down, they heard a stirring in the woods from where the men had left earlier in the day. Jarvis emerged followed by John,

"Well I'll be damned if I couldn't smell that the moment a boil set!" Jarvis shouted, drawing closer. John was a few paces behind them, they both moved without the bouncy decorum maintained while they had left. As Jarvis approached, she noticed that he was covered head to toe in mud and she immediately observed further back that John was coated similarly.

"Come sit! It's just about ready." she replied loudly. Jarvis came and sat, while John digging through his saddle bag arrived and joined them with two bowls in his hand. As he sat dirt erupted from his joints.

"How the hell did you get up that thing?" John said looking at Eliza.

"We took a right proper slide, ha ha," Jarvis added.

Eliza unable to control herself any longer laughed uncontrollably and with Jarvis and Simon joining in they all gasped for air, Eliza even falling to, and clutching, her side. Eventually regaining composure, and noticing that John sat shaking his head, she captured what air she could and returned to her natural self.

John handed her his deep bowl and she scooped the bountiful stew into it. The stew sparkled in the sunset and provided a welcoming warmth to the modest wood bowl. Eliza handed it back, John's eyes lighting up as the fragrance drew closer, and as he took it anxiously from Eliza, all watched as a clump of dirt from his shirt fell directly on top of the vibrant dish. They all stared in silence, the bowl almost hovering in John's grip as he held it exactly where Eliza had passed it, as the lone but formidable piece of dirt slowly sank. John's brow furrowed as he placed the bowl down in front of him. Eliza's chest tightened as she struggled to remain composed. An almost silent giggle escaping from her lips sent John, instantly, into rabid laughter and the party continued where they left off, Eliza falling almost immediately to her side clutching tightly at her exhausted abdominals. Jarvis kicked rapidly, falling backwards from the stone which he had occupied next to Simon who had his head buried in his hands, his shoulders bouncing up and down.

They continued, comfortable in each other's presence and despite pleasantries accompanied with necessary but genuine compliments the party ate quietly. John had insisted on eating his stew regardless of its extra ingredient and maintained that the deliciousness of the stew may have actually been enhanced by the mishap. He recommended that they should try adding the same bountiful element to their own meal, and when no one conceded he shrugged his shoulders saying, "fine by me," before taking another spoonful into his mouth. When he finished, he wiped any residue from his lips and sighed in satisfaction,

"That was welcome Eliza, many thanks." he said, "We'll be heading out early tomorrow, and we haven't met anyone who heads out as early as us."

"It's been a pleasure." She smiled, knowing that her and Simon typically left camp relatively late.

"We're going to Maplewood, there's an art festival there that should be lively, especially considering the state of the youth. I take it you're headed there as well?"

Eliza looked to Simon who began, "Indeed, that's the closest town but I wasn't aware of any festival."

"The state of the youth?" Eliza curiously interjected.

"Ah sorry Eliza, I assumed you were one of those rabid anti enlightenment types. I'm documenting it for posterity, or so I like to think. There's a stir among them, the university types, about this place called 'Gray Town.'-"

"What's Gray Town?" she asked inquisitively, feeling that he wanted to be prodded forward.

"It's like anything else, an idea run amok. It's claimed to be the most sorrowful place on earth. Always gray... Beautiful women go there to die and time stands still they say. And of course, what is more Christian than sorrow? It's being hoisted up as the home of, as the new beacon of religious thought, but that new kind of religious thought. In this age we've left behind those old celibate cranks and now our religion is blossoming with romance and responsibility rather than revelation and duty. In the gray a pillar of light is most visible ha ha ha, that's what they say. I personally think the analogy doesn't make sense, but I've been answered by believers. Grayness is actually more hopeless than darkness because in the gray you can still see, that's the logic I was told and that darkness swallows the image but grayness disturbs and drains it. I suppose there's some sense to it."

"Why would anyone care about where?" Eliza exclaimed, "The importance is *who*! That's what's most significant. Surely it is!"

"I think I understand." John said, "There is no place without people after all, and who are people? Are those making the so-called pilgrimage, people? Ah it's all very confusing to me. But I will add that there is a messiah waiting for them there. Well he's not really a messiah but he's one of the world's leading intellectuals. Benjamin Mills is his name, and I will say it could be worse because Benjamin Mills is at the very least honest and he doesn't proclaim anything great about himself. He's speaking a whole lot of what he perceives as truth. I myself can't understand a word of it, but I can catalogue the effects of it and that's what me and Jarvis have set out to do."

"I'm just here so some of your smarts will rub off on me John." Jarvis said with a laugh, "Journalists are the smartest folks after all." he added, slapping John on the shoulder.

They both stood up and bowed to Eliza, thanking her one more time for the meal and preemptively saying good bye for the next morning. She, being inclined to go to bed much later, sat watching the fire, next to the unnecessarily large pile of wood that Jarvis had accumulated, and thought. As her eyes slowly shut, she slumped back sprawling on the cool ground, tucking her hands under her head and exhaled deeply.

When she awoke the sun was out and John and Jarvis were gone. A few mosquito bites colored her exposed arm a pale red and she grimaced for a moment to avoid scratching. Simon had packed away their belongings and reclined himself against a tree stump beside the now smoldering embers. Eliza rose and began pacing back and forth occasionally thrusting her arms in one direction or another, as if she was arguing with someone. She pushed her hair away from her face and with her hand still on her head she looked to Simon, "I want to see Alexander now." she said sheepishly. "We will go to Wilheimer Falls and that's where I will live out the rest of my days."

"But…" Simon began but caught himself. After a few seconds he started calmly, "Miss Eliza we've been on the road for longer than I can take."

"And you will never have to be on it again, once we reach Wilheimer Falls." she responded, resolutely.

"I'm telling you now that I won't turn around again after this. I've had it with turning around. I'll continue on alone if you try it, I'll do it Eliza, I will."

"We won't turn around again after this. It's a deal. I promise."

"Okay then. And no more pressuring me so much, we have to go at a reasonable pace." Simon said, his voice cracking as if he had been wanting to say it for a very long time.

"Yes Simon, we can go at a reasonable pace."

"All right then." he said, satisfied.

Taking her place, Eliza sat merrily as Simon prodded the horses onwards.

"You're going the wrong way Simon!" she shouted, sticking her head out of the carriage.

"We've no food Miss Eliza, we have to go forward to Maplewood before we can turn around, it's only a few hours ahead."

TWENTY-NINE

LUCY LET OUT A NAY AS SHE STRODE FORWARD GALLOPING DELIBER-ately on the well-maintained path. Jarvis patted her gently, "You're doing great girl." he said gently, leaning forward as he rode. Jarvis was never fond of waking up early but came around when he felt the cool morning breeze that preceded the sweltering heat of mid-day. That and his older brother John tended to be more agreeable when they made quick progress. They rode at a moderate pace and as the sun rose they watched as the poor back country high-way transformed into a pristine and ornamented trail. The brush was trimmed neatly wherever it intended to encroach the way and modest trees were occasionally planted parallel on each side, acting as a mile marker. "Must be just up ahead!" John called to Jarvis who responded, "We've made great time aye?"

Just as the sun had delivered herself, Jarvis and John stopped in front of a well-made sign that read 'Welcome to Maplewood.' In the simple valley sat the elegant town, whose church, despite being the furthest building in view, dominated the horizon. Its tower stretched to the sky and a large bell, yearning to ring, adorned its climax. The sheer size invited any onlooker's imagination to fan-tasize about entering, similar to how one might view a mountain in the distance and almost be mentally transported to its peak. Buildings sprawled out before the church but never seeming to in-validate the natural green inhabitants that sprang pleasantly from the earth. The hues of animate and man-made balanced delicately without one overcoming the other, both dancing in the sunlight that acted as arbiter and caretaker. "Ain't that something." Jarvis said, to which John nodded. They continued at an easy pace towards the town.

Despite the earliness with which they arrived the town seemed more awake than a normal town should be.

"The early morning aristocracy?" Jarvis said with a smile, "Isn't that the phrase you used in Boston?"

John laughed, "Yep, so my smarts are rubbing off?"

They continued onward amidst the slight but unexpected bustle. A woman carrying a basket of fruit lumbered by, wearing a frock and hair net.

"The market must be that way." John said. And as a woman carrying a canvas covered with a sheet marched the other way Jarvis chimed in,

"And the proper festivities that way?"

"Indeed."

Greenery engaged them at almost every corner, and the town being built in the modern fashion of blocks spoke to its planning. Occasionally a residence that presumed wealth would have a modest yard with a welcoming bench facing outwards, yielding a view to the shops adjacent it. The maintained road was pleasant and the ride was comfortable, Lucy strode with ease over the soft, level dirt, a nay escaping her lips every so often. Eventually coming to what appeared to be a boarding house, with a sign in the window reading, 'rooms for rent,' Jarvis jumped off his horse and approached.

"I'll take the horses." he said.

"Meet back here at two?" John replied, to which they both nodded, John walking away afterwards.

Jarvis, after tying up the horses and making arrangements for the night, patted Lucy on the side, letting her eat a handful of oats from his open palm. She was well kept and her coat glimmered. The care Jarvis provided in her livelihood was a stark contrast to his own and he often looked out of place riding her. None the less she adored him and the relationship showed as he rode and they became a single unit. Rather than Jarvis, with his dirtiness, dampening the pristine horse, Lucy managed to improve his appearance while retaining her perfectness. Additionally, his humble horsemanship paired well with the domineering presence of her figure and allowed the horse to express itself as much as the rider. "I'll be back girl." he said, walking in the still early morning coolness towards the center of town.

The sun spoke quietly and the heat bounced furtively despite any reservations as it crested the hilly horizon. The warmth provided prodded the early risers awake, leaving only the artists who dwelt in those passionate and intellectual landscapes asleep. Often unaware of earliness and lateness they arrive to their beds at an hour that suits their ill health and only in so far as it does not inter their trade, waking up sporadically, and distressingly, to scribble one thing or another before all but collapsing back into a tentative rest until the heat of the day and brightness of society spurs them awake. Jarvis had slept well and walked on. He let his mind remain loose and open to the new environment. Shop bells jingled in the distance as doors swung to and fro revealing the happy faces of travelers who spilled out onto the road, swelling slowly and greeting those already situated along the main street. He felt comfortable in the bustle and the jolly voices that echoed from every direction relaxed him. Smiling as he walked he nodded merrily at anyone who entered his gaze and even laughed with a gentleman whose voice boomed unexpectedly.

The church rang eleven as he approached and he halted before the mighty bell and bent his neck to look straight up at the instrument that could no doubt be heard all throughout town and even for miles outside of it. 'Ten already?' he thought after counting the continuous chiming above him. The church was the landmark he wanted to see most and so decided that he could rest while the congregation of artists finished setting up their booths. He assumed it would be like other events he had attended and was intent on not missing one piece. Art provided a genuine sense of awe that Jarvis had learned to thoroughly enjoy. He disagreed with John who said that art is meant to be contemplated. In fact, part of the sense of enjoyment as he saw it was from the fact that John's opinion on the matter did not sway him even a little bit, as it was bound to do in everything else. What he saw with his own eyes and what he thought was what he saw and thought and no amount of words could change that.

He started walking back towards the hotel now that his inclination pertaining to the church was satisfied and looking down a cross street, he spied a modest tree that provided what he imagined was a perfect cover from the sun which had snuck above him. It stood just outside a cozy home whose yard maintained a small decline giving the space where shade was provided a perfect slant for one to lay on. Jarvis walked over and sat down easily. Hearing a door from the cozy house open and a woman and small child emerge they both waved as they passed him heading for the town, the little girl holding her mother's hand laughed and skipped when Jarvis smiled back. He laid back placing a handkerchief over his face and sauntered into a jovial nap.

HE AWOKE TO THE DARKNESS OF HIS HANDKERCHIEF THAT LINgered over his face, refusing the entrance of any light, and his sleep being an unexpectedly deep one he forgot briefly where he was. He laid for a moment with eyes open in the darkness and let his mind wander to each limb which felt relaxed among the meted grass underneath him and the earth that slanted for his personal comfort. The shade in which he lay remained luxurious after such a long stretch of his trip and only the gentle breeze at his hand, carrying a warmer variety of air, signaled to him that the sun shone brightly. He sat up and next to him lay a young girl flattened in comfort, asleep, with a dirty handkerchief adorning her face.

He observed for a moment her restful posture which sprawled without a care in the world flat on the ground, her delicate hands interlocked over a small waist. Her shoes lay next to her feet which appeared dirty, as if she had been walking barefoot since the first sign of some accommodating grass. Her dress fit nice and hung pleasantly on her motionless frame, and even despite the wrinkled state of it one had trouble imagining anything more flattering. Gravity was kind to her.

"You smell." Jarvis said, almost as if to himself.

"You lie." returned sleepily from beneath the handkerchief.

Eliza pulled the article from her face but remained relaxed on the welcoming slant of the yard.

"It's really a perfect spot you've found..." she said after a brief pause, turning her head to observe his features.

"I can stay a little longer." he answered, in a tired whisper.

"I hoped you might." she replied after a few moments, interlocking her fingers behind her head.

"Did you see the church?"

"My eyes avoid churches lately, was it nice?"

"It was."

"But is it nicer here?"

"It is."

"It is, or it was? I hope I haven't ruined anything." she said genuinely.

Jarvis smiled and replied in a low tone, "Like the silent church before the service begins, better than any preaching."

Eliza remained silent, looking up at the branches that caught the faithful breeze, until Jarvis added,

"It's something my brother says sometimes. He's read enough to where I'm better off just listening."

Eliza smiled at him and he smiled back, until he continued,

"Sometimes it feels like I've just got nothing to say…"

Eliza sat up, "This tree is really perfect shade isn't it?" she said, observing how it sprawled out above them, and after a few moments continued, "I wouldn't have napped in such a splendid spot, it would have never occurred to me. And if I may inform you I think nobody on earth would have chosen this exact spot for a nap. And now you've shown them. You've shown me how magical a nap can be, and I will spend the rest of my days looking for a place like this now that my eyes have been opened. Some people aren't sayers Jarvis, they are show-ers."

Jarvis smiled and laid back down putting his handkerchief over his face,

"A little longer." he said. Eliza emulated his sentiment and returned to her earlier position comfortably, laying with fingers intertwined upon her waist and a dirty handkerchief on her face.

JARVIS STIRRED AND SAT UP IN THE EASY SHADOW THAT BATHED him and he let his eyes wander. The soft grass by his feet danced in the breeze which now did nothing but accentuate the heat and the dirt road looked clean despite occasional debris which blew from its distant origin. The sun just beyond its midway trek through the sky gave him a general sense of the time. He looked over to Eliza and found himself again enamored. The handkerchief was resting near her face which had turned and she maintained a lofty fetal position etching upon the primitive green the lovely shape of beauty. Jarvis felt his gaze appreciate her inch by inch, her hair flowed flamboyantly from her head and her current position tangled it healthily into soft hands, her clean forehead emerging from the foliage. Curious blue eyes hid behind eyelids like someone might peak from the safety of formidable curtains only to retreat at any chance of discovery. Her small nose was cute and fit her face well, her mouth when smiling followed its shape with perfect symmetry, but now hung open, her warm pink lips providing its shape. Jarvis followed the air as it entered her mouth and traveled down her delicate neck and into her robust chest adorned with flower petal fabric.

Amidst his observations, Eliza jerked awake.

"The devil's luck... I swear I just fell." she said, rubbing her eyes.

Jarvis laughed, "You looked pleasant enough!" he managed.

"I suppose that's all that really matters." she replied, throwing some loose grass at him and standing up, reaching down to grab her handkerchief.

"I'll be off then?" he said after a brief hesitation.

"And I'll join you. Where are we going?"

"To meet with John, everything should be set up by three, so we can eat something and then go exploring."

"The only thing I love more than exploring is eating." she said with a smile.

"Shall we?" he said, motioning his hand towards the town. They both began walking merrily.

The restrained streets had blossomed into a crowded vista of curiosity, ripe with smiling faces and ponderous decorum. As they crossed towards the inn where John was to be met Jarvis let his eyes wander down back towards the church, the road now teeming with booths and displays, on the corner some easy to handle food was for sale, and an occasional sign read, 'no touching.' He passed resolutely keeping his eyes on the dirt in front of him and maintained a quick pace in the center of the road. Crowds of people gathered here and there near large canvases, some of which had immense covers over them, not ready for the eyes of onlookers yet. These were the art pieces most famous and in no need of prior recognition, pieces who would gladly share the economy of gazes that heartbreakingly determines the prominence of one artist over another, those grand works which had their time and place and now acted as mementos to an earlier period yet still found appreciation in antiquated spirits who linger outside of any particular age. Music could be heard in the distance but only for brief muses giving one a taste and a calibration of the aura that would eventually permeate the town completely, it operated at a distance to not distract but subtly guide one's consciousness. Like all good music it does not demand attention but operates as a medium for attention to be supplemented by certain emotions. Jarvis felt Eliza's excitement as she all but skipped beside him, struggling to keep up with his quick pace. He looked back to see her eyes drifting from work to work and allowing the scenery to swallow her. She naturally lingered back as if hoping that he might forget about her, which he decided he was more than willing to do if not for his opinions concerning art. He grabbed her hand tightly in his own and pulled her onward through the thicket of folks gathering at particular intervals.

"Not yet Eliza! You'll spoil the whole enterprise." he said in protest to her expression which appeared saddened as he hurried her along. "It's not all set up yet. If one can't experience it as it's intended to be experienced, it's better to just wait, we will see them all eventually, the fair in its entirety."

"I saw a glimpse of the most beautiful woman. And now you rob me of her…!" she sighed, "I suppose I'll trust you but Jarvis if I don't see that painting again I will never forgive you."

"Yes, yes." he said, nodding his head as he pulled her along, "and I will never forgive myself." After a few moments he added almost as if to himself, "Imagine seeing the actress from your favorite play buying bread."

They continued on, nearing the Inn where Jarvis had made arrangements they noticed Simon hurling an apple sized ball through the air, and following it with their eyes witnessed John catching it and cocking his arm back in return. He flung the ball sturdily, arcing it high and slightly behind Jarvis who ran backwards, keeping his eyes fixed upon it, to make a perfect catch. He nodded to Eliza, "Go long!" he exclaimed. Eliza began running with a laugh and made her way towards John who stood a few yards in front of her. Turning, she eagerly awaited the ball which now eclipsed the sun as it approached her from a considerable height and she caught it in her hand gracefully, bending her knees to absorb any potential impact. She tossed, turned, and threw it the small distance that remained between her and John and he rocketed it towards Simon. "Over here again!" she shouted, rolling her shoulder to warm it up, to Simon who obliged. Catching it she called to Jarvis who remained at the spot of his initial throw, "farther back!" Jarvis jogged a few paces back and Eliza threw as hard as she could, dwarfing the previous throws and the ball made it easily to Jarvis who had to shuffle backwards and jump in order to restrain the ball. "What a throw!" he called back, beginning to walk towards the inn, which sat between all parties. Each of them approached, John catching up to Eliza, patted her on the back, "Good to see you again." he said gaily, "Let's get some food."

They sat at a comfortable table just outside and behind the inn which had been set in preparation of the festivities, along with several others, under a canopy. It viewed the procession of spectators who enthusiastically wandered in from distant streets and horses strode occasionally to signal the entrant of an out-of-towner often accompanied by a nay which echoed through the air. The chatter of distant voices gave the atmosphere an energetic countenance and when Jarvis smiled at Eliza, who remained fixated on the menu his eyes drifted affectionately to the town behind her where a diversity of people exuded a uniformity of enjoyment. After they ordered John spoke lightly,

"Did you see the church?" he asked Jarvis, adding "When I heard it strike ten I imagined you must be just reaching it. The bell may be worth seeing in itself, I'll bet."

"It was worth the expedition. They are so much more extravagant on this side of the country. I could hardly appreciate the whole thing."

"Indeed, you'll have to take me there tomorrow? Maybe we could take a day and view it from different vantages. I confess I was jealous I won't get to appreciate it today, when we rode in it was very enticing from a distance."

"Yes that sounds good, I may not have gotten my fill." Jarvis replied.

Eliza watched on as they spoke and her interest from the night before prompted her to ask a question to the long-winded John.

"What a shame John, why was it that you were deprived of such a lovely conquest?"

"Journalistic business of course, along the same lines as what we spoke of last night." he said, adding with a telling smile, "But I wouldn't want to bore you…"

"You must tell me!" she implored, grinning back, "It's no bore at all."

"Right. Well let's see…" John put a finger on his chin, more for theatrical effect than necessity, his willingness to discuss the topic was palpable. He cleared his throat and continued, "We spoke briefly last night of a place called Gray Town, although I didn't elaborate too much on its peripherals and only in passing did I mention

Benjamin Mills. Well if you've never heard of him it's partially your fault but with all his writings I'm sure you've experienced his influence in one manifestation or another, it bleeds into damn near every discipline. Anyone with any particularly deep question in any field will eventually end up at his work and it's hard to trace our popular thought today to anyone but him. Well he accumulated all this work, influence, and writing under the nose of the past few generations and it's only this most recent one that has uncovered his breadth fully and he's quite exploded in popularity the past ten years or so. The schooled masses adore him but they discovered him just a bit too late. He had already isolated himself and only wrote occasionally and ventured to never speak publicly again. The kids were haunted by old newspaper clippings containing small and unnoticed reviews proclaiming him the most eloquent and intelligent speaker the reviewer had ever witnessed. Eventually whispers emerged from the abyss that he had fallen in love. The nature of his writings and the sad state of his upbringing made a whole generation weep with happiness at this revelation and they stopped searching for him, the idea being that they would make the sacrifice of never meeting the man and allow him to live out his days in happiness. They savored his work like they might a dead man's and for years spoke of it and debated it using honor laced phrases like 'the late renowned Benjamin Mills,' or 'the dearly missed Benjamin Mills.' His name emerged for the first time in years when someone witnessed him crying, absolutely distressed, on a red bench in a small gray town. The traveler who saw him made delicate inquiries to those in the vicinity and discovered the cause of the agony, the death of the most beautiful woman who ever lived, Angelica Hamilton. The traveler questioned further and it was revealed that Benjamin was running the operations of the tavern and sobbed quite frequently." John took a sip of water and looked towards Eliza who looked entranced, her eyes prodded him onwards,

"Can you imagine? An entire generation who built their cavalier worldview on the foundation that their spiritual father was living a happy life with the woman he loved. And to have that taken away? Well his work instantly took on a new meaning and it was scoured all over again with this new information in mind and it glimmered with a fresh romantic hue that went previously unnoticed. The town gained an appeal first because of the insinuation that Benjamin had been there this whole time, that fact alone being enough to render it as possessing some kind of beauty, despite the original traveler's description which painted it eternally grey, so much so that time seemed to stand still. And secondly because of the figure Angelica whom was determined to be the most beautiful figure who ever lived and the entire motivation for Benjamin's body of work, which he thrust out into the world gaining infinite renown that was then shunted all for her. The story goes that it's now a purgatory for him and he has resolved to suffer there, in that place where time doesn't move, until the end of his days. Naturally everyone is curious and insists on traveling with haste to Gray Town, not only to witness the historic spot where beauty incarnate died, not only to feel that resounding wake no doubt left behind, but to save the hero Benjamin. So to conclude with this portion of my findings and why the young romantics and serious religious types find it so mesmerizing: in the dullest, dreariest, most melancholy place on earth we have the most brilliant man who ever lived and the most beautiful human who has ever graced the planet. Yes, so you see when I put it like that why the religious see its attraction, mainly the paradoxical element. Like Jesus was the lowliest human but the strongest being, in Gray Town, we have the most beautiful love story in the most wretched of places. A refreshing pairing of opposites in other words, the most attractive thing to energetic minds. And this is the first reason they all flock, despite the many holes in the story." John looked up at Eliza who had perspiration on her forehead, her soft but unblinking eyes remained fixed on him and a dreamy smile had crept on her lips.

"If I didn't have business of equal beauty to attend I would no doubt drop everything and go to this Gray Town, in any case I will have to add it to my bucket list. Although I'm curious before you continue what you mean by holes?"

"Of course, I was just getting there. Although I should warn you that if I expose these holes it may dampen your yearning. In other words, they are significant enough, I think, to cast the whole thing into doubt. So… Shall I expose them?"

Eliza sighed, "I suppose you'll have to now! But I was quite pleased with where it left off. Anyway, I have to know now or I would spend my nights thinking about what they could be."

"Yes indeed, the story is worth discovering in its many stages, and you are in the unfortunate position to be a bit behind the rest in learning of it and will therefore receive the abridged version. But when I publish my work you will be ahead of the rest who have not researched it carefully enough. Well the first major hole is that Benjamin Mills had not been especially hard to find but has only been absent from academia, and being the type who has accrued a long list of companions over the years, travels often. This obviously results in the few who actually pursue to meet him, without the proper connections, find only his shadow. And he being a generally insulated person doesn't even notice the fervor surrounding him, or at least pays it no attention. Secondly there's no evidence at all to suggest that he removed himself from society (in so far as he has) because he fell in love. I would say it's much more likely that he was simply burnt out and had finished the major works that he had wanted to finish. And on the matter of Angelica… It's possible that he was in love… by all accounts I've found there is no embellishment that she was indeed a beautiful woman and records show that she did die near town while he was present. But her young age suggests that she could not have been what made him retire from the academic scene many years ago. Lastly, it's been discovered that Gray Town is, in fact, where he was born and so it makes sense that he would have some affection for the place despite its dreariness, and they do say that bland horizons are the bedrock of great minds, for it forces consciousness to turn inward."

"I see." said Eliza, her eyes gazing upwards in thought. "I suppose the most important part of the story for me remains intact. As I am of a temperament smitten by beauty it makes me very happy that Angelica's figure will saunter prettily through history even despite your scrutiny. Yes, and now I'm quite excited for the artwork gathered here to depict this princess of Gray Town and the melancholy place itself. I understand now Jarvis why you had pulled me onward, if I had not known the history and inspiration of the work, perhaps I wouldn't have been able to appreciate it. In other words, with context the displays should be that much more profound!"

Jarvis began speaking in a hushed tone, looking downwards at the table in front of him before John interrupted with laughter.

"Oh Eliza! I think you've betrayed our dear Jarvis, he thinks the opposite! As far as I can tell at least. I've given up on trying to talk some sense into him but he insists that it's wholly unimportant. Maybe your delicate delivery could persuade him?"

Eliza looked at Jarvis who looked frustrated, she took it to be an offense taken at the nature of John's laughter which seemed to be at his expense. His eyes remained firmly planted down and he shook his head back and forth as John spoke. She thought for a moment, allowing a silence to linger before she began to speak, looking at Jarvis.

"Behave John." she said before continuing, "Although I may agree with you, we shall find out momentarily, and I am more than willing to expound my position, my mission is not to persuade. And I would never betray." To this John slackened his smile which had remained pointed towards Jarvis and nodded to Eliza in a formal manner. She started, conducting her exposition in the direction primarily of Jarvis, "I think I have an example that captures my thoughts on the matter. When I was a young girl in France our steward had significant family ties, particularly Scottish. And one of their most prized possessions, a family heirloom, was a large portrait of Mary Stuart the young queen of Scotland. Now imagine me growing up and everyday seeing that portrait. She was beautiful and I wanted to emulate her and what made the portrait even better was learning of her virtue. When my governess taught me the necessary history the artwork came to life, I recognized the scenery around her, could smell the salt of the sea in the background, feel the wind that commanded her dress. I suppose my point is this, if she had been an unsavory character the painting would not be as inspirational to me."

Jarvis listened intently and peered calmly into her eyes as she spoke, her soft tone talking him down from his momentary but heightened agitation with his brother. "There you have it." he said, his voice laced with frustration and his agitation returning. "It always comes down to education doesn't it? Ha ha. What a shame for me then and how pleasant it must be for those like you and John who are so endowed. Let me ask you this then, how much learning is enough? Let's use the example you provided, the portrait of Mary. Did you learn every detail of her life? Obviously not, such a proposition is impossible. You learned just enough, never encroaching certain possibly detrimental avenues. You did all the work, as you say, and the painting came to life, but what a flimsy life it is! One detail could tumble the whole thing down. Imagine for instance you found out that she had a secret affair? Or that she was whorish despite history's rendition of her. The painting would be tainted and all that 'context' would be useless. Suppose then that I came by, uneducated as I am, and pronounced, 'What a beautiful, noble, virtuous lady and this painting is alive! Truly an inspiration.' Would you reply, 'it's no inspiration sir, she is a whore?' Why not just all start from the same place, one without this stupid context. If she's inspirational let her inspire. I'll tell you why it can't be so, because it's all simply a rouse concocted by the learned to proclaim a made-up superiority. Did you know that there are people who are professional critics? That the public is afraid to say, 'I see it.' and so these charlatans live a life of luxury at their expense. Well, I refuse to be told that I don't understand this or I can't comprehend that. They take everything else, but I won't let them take art."

Eliza looked forgiving despite his biting cadence and looked thoughtfully into the distance. John's posture straightened and he began speaking,

"Well said Jarvis, I don't think you've described your position quite so eloquently before. I don't particularly like critics myself but I think I will defend them briefly, if you don't mind."

Jarvis looked annoyed, "Let's just leave it where it is, I've stated my position. Much to my reluctance and regret but I did…"

"Indeed, but we have an audience today and if we stop now your contribution on the subject will be accepted without proper consideration."

"John, two sides of an argument have been stated, Eliza's and my own."

"Yes… I suppose you're right. Allow me to just finish my defense of critics, since it was not broached by Eliza and then we can continue." He paused for a moment before continuing, "A critic has as you've already dismissed some semblance of context regarding certain pieces of artwork. Now we can in many cases, and which I believe you must find a way to include into your approbation to strengthen your argument, broaden our definition of context to particular styles such as gothic or renaissance. Now a critic has intimate knowledge of these particular genres and so can recognize them in other works. For instance, he may recognize the inspiration for a new painting and can therefore understand what the younger artist was attempting to do. So, for many critics the content is not necessarily important but more so the question, what was the artist trying to accomplish and did he succeed? From this perspective of course he is going to know better than someone who knows nothing about art. And indeed…"

Eliza interrupted, "You're operating under the assumption that what constitutes successful art is 'art which has done what it was intended to do,' and John is saying that art is alone 'that which is beautiful,' or I'm sure he would choose a different word, a better one surely, maybe art is 'that which is contemplative.' 'that which requires no explanation.' Yes, I'm quite sure he would put it much better but he's said what he intended to say and you've congratulated him. So, let us continue this conversation another time, shall we? Where were we before? Yes, tell me more about Gray Town." her voice managed to bring Jarvis back from a frustrated stare which occupied itself with some children playing in the distance.

John, looking around the table, took a moment to gauge everyone's disinterestedness in the argument and an attention that he had noticed dimming since after Jarvis's earlier plea. "My mistake friends. My apologies Jarvis, you know how I can get some times. Let's take a moment and have a drink or two." He smiled warmly which was returned, although with less enthusiasm, by Jarvis.

Eliza sitting between them put a hand on each and said, "Yes… a drink!" Wine was brought and despite a glare from Simon who sat across from her, she sipped it merrily.

A few minutes passed with an absence of words, each member of the party enjoying the company of each other solely through proximity. The cheerful town around them offered lots of vibrant fodder capable to an astute listener of being sifted and an occasional word or sentence could be focused on and tracked to its distant origin, thus unlocking at least one side of a pleasant and simple conversation. Jarvis listened carefully to the echoing and heard a young child saying "wow" in an enthusiastic manner. A smile growing on his lips, he decided that he was happy that children still said wow, that people in general said wow, and that he had said a variation of wow just this morning when viewing the church from a distance. 'Why was I getting so upset at John?' he thought to himself, almost laughing. 'It's just not worth it...' He looked to John whose gaze was following what appeared to be a well-off man wearing a nice suit and proceeding with an equally aristocratic posture across the road. Noticing Jarvis, he smiled and raised what was left of his drink, nodding to him and finishing it off to which Jarvis replied in kind. Eliza's eyes were closed but her face appeared lofty, her cheeks and forehead slightly moist with sweat, her chin perking upward. She occasionally took a deep breath that was audible and exaggerated but retained a rhythm that matched her normal delicate exhalation.

"This town is nice." Eliza said, slowly opening her eyes. "And I think we managed to come at the perfect time, what great luck. And to make new friends along the way."

John smiled and nodded his head. Jarvis leaned back comfortably with satisfaction on his face. Eliza began again, "All right. Your explanation of Gray Town was fascinating but I suspect you have more to say. Would you mind? I'm quite curious... And then we can go enjoy the festival."

"Of course." John said, a grin growing on his face, "It's obviously a point of much interest for me considering I've traveled all around the country for it. Well the second part of the story which was only alluded to, but would never be suspected with the details provided. Benjamin Mills has massive sway as I've already made clear among the younger generation, more so than I think he imagines, and he recently wrote an essay which has thrown him back into popularity even to those few who have been hiding under a rock recently. The essay makes a few propositions that have angered many and captured the hearts of others. Firstly, that the entire field of psychology is arbitrary, secondly that if Jesus Christ returned in this age he would no doubt be in a lunatic asylum, and thirdly that if the roles were reversed between inhabitants of said asylums and the general population society would be just as functional. In other words, if you took everyone who was committed and allowed them all to occupy a town then that town would proceed differently of course but without serious issues."

"Well I'm not especially interested in psychology." Eliza replied thoughtfully, "I'm not particularly fond of Jesus either. Yes, it's my unfortunate view that he lacks divinity altogether and this I confess I was convinced of very young. Still the proposition is worth thinking about assuming we are capable of granting Christ his miraculous details."

"Yes it's interesting indeed, although do we really need to even grant him those to think it through? We can just imagine that he is a great moral teacher and if necessary compel to him some eccentricities. The argument, I think, is that one cannot have any radical ideals in modern society and one must value only what society views as valuable. When one begins speaking, if it is from an ethical vantage point unfamiliar to the listener, the listener's eyes will squint with paranoia and they will whisper that the man is mad. And fate isn't kind to those who it is whispered of, 'he is mad.'-"

"As anticlerical as I am John, for the sake of argument I won't let you remove Christ's divinity so easily and I therefore disagree with your premise. He isn't just a moral teacher... He's the son of God and that's where his authority is derived not to mention if he were in an asylum it would by definition mean that he was resurrected again, or… yes he ascended to heaven didn't he? So that would mean he wasn't brought back to life but instead descended from heaven. Besides, the bible isn't conducting mathematical proofs, it's revealing truth. I'll announce it like this: if Christ was revealed to be alive, it would be those like me who occupied the mad houses and not because I was committed forcefully, on the contrary I would have checked myself in. They would ask me my ailments and I would tell them that I do not see the obvious and that which is apparently plausible makes no sense to me, that I gave all my earthly belongings to Beauty with a capital 'B' and not to God. I don't see it as possible for there to be a simple moral teacher, no matter how radical, who could make me check into an asylum just by nature of their existence. That said despite those reservations I think there's something worth contemplating as far as madness and value judgements. Say for instance someone doesn't value clothing or hygiene, or… Never mind, those will give a coherent enough image, yes suppose someone doesn't value them. Why, after all, do we value them? I would see it as perfectly reasonable for someone to completely shunt the enterprises all together, although I would never associate with them, what would they care? They would end up in a mad house sooner or later no doubt and I imagine that it would be before a very prudent question would be asked, namely: 'what is it that they do value?'-"

"Perfect!" John said, "Bravo, what a wonderful response and a perfect summary of his final conclusion which I will simply leave on the table to chew on while I bring us back a bit and continue exploring the reversal I mentioned and what exactly brings Jarvis and I here. The quote that really characterizes the paper is: 'Madhouses are the churches of tomorrow,' it is this sentence that inflamed the youth and cemented the essay as a lucid and profound tract. A climax to an already provocative enough collection of societal criticisms and religious instructions and made the entire country pick up a pen to defend or rebuke the thought. The young generation of Mills's followers took drastic steps though…" John's expression took on a stifled state of excitement primarily for the sake of suspense and he sat forward lowering his voice as if telling a secret. Eliza, entranced, leaned forward as well. As John paused to let the gears turn, a vague idea flashed in her mind. A mere flicker that she could not grasp lingered like an afterglow.

"You can't be serious." she said instinctively, not knowing exactly what she meant by it. A smile grew on John's lips.

"Serious enough to travel back and forth across the entire country… Yes, they've been given the name 'Mad Mills.' Not my idea, unfortunately someone beat me to it and the name stuck. I think I could have managed something wittier but none the less that is what they are called. Yes, the rabid young academy dwellers are men and women of action, you cannot take that away from them. They actually purged asylums and brought the inhabitants to abandoned old towns. Or I should say they forced their way into nearly abandoned towns and took over. There were six Mad Mills in total across the country each as big as an entire town and many populated by more than one asylum."

Eliza struggled to imagine how such an experiment would turn out but her mind showed very little aptitude for conjuring an image adequate to satisfy her.

"How is that possible? I can't even picture it." she said, anxious for John to alleviate her perplexity.

"It's hardly possible as we've found out… Jarvis and I have been chasing the ghosts of these Mad Mills. Of the six, two had the enterprise called off after just one night. I'm sure it was quite a reality check to those proud students when, that first morning, they woke up to discover more than a few suicides by hanging. Would you believe that they faced no criminal charges and the whole thing was essentially swept under the rug as 'youthful effulgence' and 'unfortunate but admissible psychological experimentation?' It really shows the sway that Benjamin Mills has, that at every level of society people were genuinely curious if what he said had some meat to it… Two others collapsed within a week, one due to a fire that burned half the town to ashes and the second when a flu broke out. So, Jarvis and I being at a crossroads had only two options. And as I found out earlier today, we chose the last and correct one, the other being shut down after a few of the patrons were refusing to eat due to trust issues and so after three weeks the authorities who had allowed the scene to play out finally decided to step in. The one we are heading to now is just outside of Richmond and from all accounts it has been described as stable."

"I told you Richmond was the right choice!" Jarvis chimed in, seeing that Eliza's eyes were wide and wanting of some brief attention for himself.

"Indeed you were Jarvis." John smiled. "It's been over a month now and it's still functioning although really there isn't much information to speak of. After all, not many people go flocking to what amounts to a town of lunatics. That's precisely why we are going, it's a duty to document what goes on from an objective standpoint otherwise the only accounts will be from the students themselves or long time admirers who romanticize anything related to Benjamin Mills. We will go and make a proper catalogue of the situation."

"How truly interesting." Eliza said, yearning to know how the town must actually be functioning. "You really must write to me when you've found out more… I would really like to know all the details, and from where I sit you seem to be the foremost expert on the subject at hand." she added.

"Oh now don't go calling him an expert it will go right to his head." Jarvis protested.

"No, no." John said with a competent grin, "Just a humble servant of the people… Fulfilling my function and adding what I can."

"You've done it now!" Jarvis said. They all laughed in response.

The town by now had climaxed in terms of density and people crowded the streets with enthusiastic determination. All moving at different speeds allowing themselves to be stopped by anything that caught their eye and demanded attention. Those of different tastes hurried by, trying diligently not to impede the contemplative individual who was stopped dead in their tracks. One could look around and see many of these sentries standing still staring into space and generally in the direction of some piece of artwork in the distance. Such expressions presented on canvas or formulated in sculpture often offered pontification from many angles and distances, and in those circumstances the appreciative onlooker approaches slowly and in a general, roundabout way. The portrait that Eliza had seen earlier but had been pulled quickly away by Jarvis returned in its vague shape to her mind.

"Shall we go explore this pretty town?" she said.

THIRTY

———

IT STOOD LARGE. SIMPLE FRAME, A DELICATE WOODEN STAND; THE figure stood with one hip lightly slanted and a serene gaze peering into the distance. Her eyes, due to the nature of the town, danced towards the church down the road. The smirk her mouth possessed was determined and made one want to smile in reply and cheer for the figure. 'I believe in you,' was what came to one's mind on viewing how her sad eyes mingled with resolute and striving features. Eyebrows slightly slanted and tan cheeks all angled towards an active life. Her blonde hair clean, almost white, tied tightly to one side. Her feet, sandaled, stood on a small island green with grass. Surrounding her and encompassing most of the painting was a sea of gray waves. Every shade imaginable sought to sully the protagonist and the last remnant of greenery. She stood fast. Strong calves gave her lofty expression life. A flowing white dress prompted feelings of levity and grace, one wanted to watch her move. Her bare shoulders defined by youth and her neck pristine and commanding. She stood. Despite her gray surroundings she was optimistic. As if the exact final brushstroke was the one that possessed optimism. Like any slight alteration would undo the entire work.

The town faded out of existence as Eliza's eyes surveyed the woman with admiration. John spoke to Jarvis and Simon behind her but nothing reached her. She felt as though the woman represented the polar opposite of herself and sought to grasp exactly what made her feel this. They had different complexions obviously, Eliza being of a paler origin, but in terms of activity Eliza was as adventurous as they come. She lingered over each limb and sought to fully understand one before moving on to the next, attempting a reconciliation of parts. An amalgamation of individually significant parts to create a sublime whole. She decided that what made the figure so beautiful was a tenseness that manifested itself only in the parts of her being necessary for action. In other words, the figure radiated no proclivity to intensity but was, more so, impelled to it. She was patient by temperament and it showed in her soft features. Eliza could imagine her in the most trying situations, baring the calamity until the time came to proceed to a solution. Sitting in church the figure had a model appearance of those who genuinely appreciate the preacher's words. Eliza saw this as the significant difference. Church was impossible under anything but the most sentimental and sincere motivations, sitting still contrary to one's will was just impossible for her and because of this she saw herself as lacking a decorum resplendent with the serenity of a soul filled with sermons.

Eliza noticed the bland wooden frame that accentuated the grim gray profile that distinguished much of the painting and, with the frame, civilization strong armed itself back into existence. In an instant the town shuffled back to a similar spot that Eliza had left it and the shuffling of feet with the chatter of distant voices garnished her environment.

"Wow." Eliza muttered, pleasure coloring her tone.

"Incredible, isn't she?" John replied with eyes remaining fixed on the artwork in front of them, "I was just saying that this is one of the primary pieces that struck me as worth making the trip to this side of the country as opposed to the other."

"She's just so... Beautiful..." Eliza said, "And I cannot make out exactly what it is. She just seems to be alive!"

"I like to think it's what motivates an artist to create that dictates exactly how much life their work imbues. This is a truly inspired piece, so that grace itself has guided the artists hand. Art is unique to the human being and therefore it is where God most potently reveals himself to us. It is where he can give us signs, nudge us in one direction or another, set our souls free and so on. Yes, I think it lives up to the whispers that I've heard."

"This is the young woman from Gray Town?" Eliza asked, hoping he would elaborate more.

"Indeed. The painting is called, 'The deprived bride of Truth: Angelica.' Angelica of course, being the young lady from Gray Town who was loved and in love with Benjamin Mills. The title then makes reference to him as 'truth' itself."

As they continued, the energy of the town acted to enhance Eliza's experience. Those of all ages and walks of life accentuated the streets and appeared reverent and enthusiastic in relationship to the content. The overall theme, Eliza noticed, was not only Grayness and the Gray Town but sprinkled throughout the many encompassing vistas of desolate and mundane scenes (which invoked serious emotion to be sure) were powerful and beautiful women. The most recognizable to Eliza, and a welcome surprise was the portrait of Lucile Dupan, an influential writer explored in her youth, 'There is only one happiness, to love and be loved,' she had written under the pseudonym George Sands. John noted a similarity between Dupan and Eliza which flattered her. In the portrait a blue dress brought empathy and understanding to identically blue eyes that surveyed any onlooker with kindness. Pale skin matched Eliza's and curled hair invited her to imagine a similar style gracing her own raven locks. "The similarity is uncanny," John said, adding, "You could have been sisters." Eliza let herself daydream on the topic of an older sister and smiled as they went on.

John explained those who Eliza did not know. "Theodosia Burr, one of America's daughters." he identified. "She disappeared at sea in the prime of her beauty. Rigorously educated and a promising bright star that now only reminds the young women of this nation that sometimes providence fails to protect even the talented among us. A regular stoic too after her father Aaron Burr, whose life was one hammer blow after another. Little girls carry her picture around in a locket. She represents a strong and independent spirit while illuminating the necessity of motherhood and motherhood at all costs to be sure, for she sacrificed her health in the end for it."

"Sally Hemmings, one of America's mothers. Clever, cunning, and gorgeous. She won the affection of our third president with her stunning profile and surely her wit is what kept him infatuated. Her lineage will bleed into every corner of America for as long as this great country stands. Yes, a true inspiration to all."

The day went on. The sun eventually tucking behind the hilly horizon reminding the towns occupants of its fleeting presence with a cool breeze announcing its departure. The texture glowed among the blue sky above it and the ever-present moon crept subtly into view. Accompanying the climactic event and, in a sort of answer back, the volume of the music emanating from the center of town increased in pace and volume. The chatter echoed as words that needed to be said had to be almost shouted to ensure notice. The paintings remained out and folks danced in the streets among them. Vendors celebrated a profitable day by giving out what stock they had left, wine and spirits included. In the crowded streets Eliza laughed as someone handed her a drink and clinked his cup against hers. Simon, as well, had a large flagon that he drank feverishly, smiling as it emptied into his stomach and partially down onto his chest. John cheered and Jarvis holding his arm out for Eliza to grab let out a "yippie," as they danced around to the upbeat music. The artists protecting their work watched on with joy and despite having to ensure their work survive the night they, none the less, felt involved. For once they could seemingly enjoy society and the fairy tale festivities with fireworks in the distance, and the town would honor them by staying awake until the early morning hours, each person supporting the spirit of the other, until the time came when every single person went to sleep together. And in one moment, where the streets were once crowded now they were empty.

ELIZA AWOKE, PUSHING THE THICK COVERS OFF OF HER, LETTING A deep sigh escape her lips. The open window allowed a gentle gust to occasionally enter, rattling her closed, but slightly loose, door. Movement could be heard in the town outside and lying back she wondered what time it might be. She slept deep and felt well rested, doing the math she calculated that it was probably around noon. Shimmying towards the edge of the bed she sat up allowing her feet to hang over the lofty edge for a moment before hopping down and yawning sheepishly. Approaching the window, she first saw Simon harnessing the horses and making sure everything was fitting properly. Her eyes wandered towards the town where she noticed many people bent over, large pouches at their sides, picking up garbage that had accumulated from the festivities. She watched as individuals of all ages energetically went from one trash item to the next and she enjoyed imagining that it was for the sake of the town's visitors, so that they may wake up to a pristine town despite the chaos the night before, that they may think the whole night was a dream. Eliza hurried to get dressed, wanting to help the townsfolk.

She felt vibrant and alive, one would be shocked if informed of how much she had drank the night before and impressed with the vigor with which she sprung from the door of the boardinghouse.

"Simon!" she shouted, twirling around a support beam and down the modest porch steps.

"Good morning, Miss Eliza." he said putting a hand to his temple as he spoke and wincing slightly.

"Ah just about ready I see? Perfect! We will be off soon enough; I will help the townsfolk beforehand. Find me when you are ready."

"Will do." Simon said, holding his oat filled hand to one of the horses now harnessed to the carriage.

Eliza nodded and continued onward. She found a little girl whose bag was nearly full and dragging heavily behind her. Eliza walked beside her and with a firm grip on the satchel relieved significant weight from the little hands struggling earnestly to pull forward.

"Mind if I give you a hand?" Eliza said smiling. The little girl smiled back and responded,

"Not at all mam."

They went on both stopping to pick up small items that had accumulated near the edge of the street, leaving the bag open in between them.

"Did you enjoy the festivities last night?" Eliza asked.

"Why yes mam. Did you?"

"Yes I loved them. Honestly. The blonde girl who stood right there, she was my favorite." Eliza pointed to where the painting once stood, although they had been removed earlier, the displays still burned in Eliza's mind with such significance that she could point out any that was referenced.

"Angelica." The girl smiled. "Have you heard about her?"

"Would you tell me?" Eliza asked with a soft, low voice.

"She came down from heaven! To light the darkest places... But she had to go. She came to remind us! That things can be pretty no matter where they come from. She's the prettiest but she invites us, like I said, no matter where we come from. To believe in ourselves. To point to things that are pretty and say, 'That is pretty.' Even if no one else sees it. She's my favorite too, she's all our favorites!" She skipped around with joy and trash in her hand as she spoke, putting it into the bag.

"Thank you for sharing darling. That was beautiful, I shall remember her story for as long as I live."

Eliza and the girl danced back and forth picking up garbage as they went until the pouch was full. The girl seizing it in her grip strained to drag it to no avail. Eliza laughed.

"I can take it darling. Why don't you go run along? You've earned a rest."

"Thank you, mam!" she replied, skipping away with a giggle.

Eliza tied the bag shut and hoisted onto her shoulder, nearly falling over backward as she flung the weight from her hip. Regaining her balance, she walked on. It was heavy enough to tire her and she was breathing heavy with each step but was, none the less, in good spirits. The sun was shining overhead without a cloud in the sky and the only sound was the rustling of trees that graced the areas between the road and sidewalk. The vibrant green contrasted against the stone buildings behind it and the glass windows reflected what they could. In the distance one could smell bread baking and the perfume of cooking meat tantalized the imagination. She occasionally passed someone like her dragging a bag behind them half filled with garbage and as they met each other, both parties smiled and nodded. She rounded a corner and saw John standing there looking through some papers that hung from a board. As he noticed her his stern expression softened and he approached merrily.

"You look fantastic this morning Eliza!" he said, adding, "I must admit my head is in a bit of turmoil, but I've been given a concoction by the host and she assures me that it will cure this headache. And a good thing too because the day is beautiful so it's really a shame that I'm not able to enjoy it in its entirety. That said, I'm planning on going to the church to have a look. I assume you'll be off soon? I spoke with Simon earlier, before you were up I believe, and he was in the final stages of preparation… My gosh Eliza put that bag down for a moment and catch your breath."

Eliza laughed, forgetting that it was on her shoulder and lurched it forward with a thud and noticed how out of breath she was, "Whew." escaped her lips and she brushed her forehead with a dirty hand, leaving a streak where it traveled, and realizing her mistake wiped it clear with her cleaner hand. "Thank you John, I feel great." her face was glowing. "Yes we will be off soon. I can't wait." she paused for a moment. "…I mean I've had fun but I'm ready to go is all." She smiled.

"Say no more, fun is fun but we all have destinations, don't we? I'm glad I caught you before you left. I know it may sound strange but may I ask where you are going, and if it would be alright if Jarvis corresponded with you…?"

Eliza's face took on a new level of radiance. Her cheeks glowed and the light sweat that had accumulated around her face glistened in sunlight that shone on her pale skin. "Where am I going?" she smiled affectionately. "To the Climicus Estate. Finally, to the Climicus Estate. It's been so long, now that I think about it. I went all around the world but I think that it's the place where I truly belong. I just think back to that little stream and the church bells. The past and the future!" Her gaze drifting as she spoke, imagining she was somewhere else.

John, waiting for more, eventually realized that she was done talking and added timidly, "It sounds quite lovely, and where is the Climicus Estate?"

"Wilheimer Falls!" she blurted, in excitement.

John took on a perplexed look and peered to his sides, almost theatrically, in confusion. He stood in silence for a few seconds but Eliza, elated and in her own world, didn't notice, instead looking towards a chirp that echoed from a tree above John's head.

"Perfect." he finally said, "And would you mind if Jarvis wrote you? I only ask because he occasionally gets quite bored with me. I see it that I'm teaching him a trade... Some way to earn bread. He's cleverer than he lets on but would be much too shy to ask himself... And he likes you a lot."

"Oh... What? Jarvis?... Yes, I would love that! It would be great to have him write me and I would take equal care to write him back. Yes, I'm glad you caught me before I left, I would really like that."

John smiled and lifted his hat to her, afterwards helping her maintain balance as she heaved the pouch onto her shoulder. She walked resolutely, John watching her as she went, with a fur-rowed brow.

Exhaustion setting in, Eliza was happy to see rows of similar bags near a pavilion. Approaching, she tossed it down and brushed her hands together in satisfaction. She looked down the street to Simon who was waving from a distance. Her smile grew larger and she waved back, hopping in his direction. He nodded and as soon as they reached the carriage both parties took their respective places and then they were off in the direction that they had come from, the direction of Wilheimer Falls.

THIRTY-ONE

Jarvis combed Lucy's mane with one hand while petting her lightly with the other. The pristine horse neighed in response. "There there, we'll be off soon." Jarvis said. The sun shone overhead and he noted mentally that the weather is perfect for a long ride. Trees swayed overhead and the energetic chirping of birds could be heard emanating from branches near and far. As John approached Jarvis perked up, his heart gaining in rapidity.

"Did you ask her?" he said, almost out of breath.

"It seems we have another reason to go to Gray Town." John replied thoughtfully.

"Really? That's where she's headed? Why wouldn't she mention it to us." Jarvis asked, dumbfounded and trying to muster an adequate reason.

"It would appear she's unaware that that's where she's actually headed." John said.

"Why didn't you tell her!?" he replied, laughing.

John laughed with him for a moment but quickly stifled it before responding, "I'm not sure... Maybe I didn't want to deny her the slow realization. The conversation felt weird to be honest."

"Weird how so? She told you I could write her right? What's weird then?" Jarvis asked in a serious tone.

"Yes... She said you could write her... Jarvis you know unsolicited advice is my specialty. Contain your affection to a friendly and brotherly variety. I can see on your face you're already annoyed but I'm going to continue anyway. When I spoke to her, her mind was already far away. Distant. This town was already in the past and with it all the people she had met on this little part of her journey. The way her face lit up when she spoke of her destination. It is no doubt love that draws her onward."

Jarvis took a big bite of an apple and let Lucy take one. He sighed.

"I'm bored of this adventure John." He said, genuinely. Mounting his horse, he looked calm but his eyes remained low, knowing that what he said would displease John.

"What if you meet me in Gray Town?" John said almost tearing up at the honesty of his little brother. "I'll check out the last Mad Mill on my own and venture over when I'm satisfied."

Jarvis smiled. "Really?"

"You're not a kid anymore." he replied, digging through his bag and handing a modest sum of money to Jarvis. "Just be careful on your own."

"Will do." he replied. "I'll be waiting."

Jarvis motioned Lucy to go. In a slow trot she began towards the edge of town where they had entered the day before. John watched with a fatherly air and prideful demeanor. He looked at the newspaper in his hand that only had the vaguest description of the Mad Mill he was headed to and tucked it into his jacket before mounting his horse and going off in the opposite direction as Jarvis.

THEY HAD BEEN TRAVELING FOR A FEW DAYS, ONLY STOPPING WHEN absolutely necessary. The time spent in those mundane fields which tortured them earlier in their journey was cut in half, although Eliza didn't mind them much anymore. Now that they were traveling *to* him, she was happy. His faint image lingered in her mind always and when the translucent specter faded substantially she recalled it back to its vivid beginnings, tracing every line that must have accumulated during her absence. The process went thusly an incalculable amount of times. To start she had to call forth her last memory of his face, which she had seen just before leaving for France and in an intermittent period between sobs resulting from his cold denial of her father's offer (that she had taken as a disavowal of his affection for her) on one hand and the reality that he really was not coming on the other. The latter realization was affectionately decreed as incomprehensible and condemned her to a long and traumatic boat trip all alone, despite her parent's presence. His young face in that moment she recalled as being conflicted, his eyes uncharacteristically still as he spoke, prodding one to imagine him thinking 'don't look around too much,' to himself, in order to present a strong decorum. Her departure from Wilheimer Falls was burned into her memory and she had reflected on it a lot. His touch was warmer than usual in that moment and he kissed her cheek with a delicacy, and the way he stepped back reluctantly made her think that he regretted the vulnerability that hovered in the air between them. He stood frozen before her with a modest smile on his lips that betrayed his sad eyes. The green of them glistened and she thought that he would cry, in turn, eliciting a few tears onto her own cheeks. This was the face that she used as a canvas to add a few years here and there, thinning the jaw and providing some rogue facial hair that she assumed would be shaven momentarily (he was in such a state with her approaching arrival that he clearly hadn't the capacity to shave). Maybe she would say, "Oh go on Alexander, don't neglect your hygiene on my account." and maybe he would laugh. 'Yes if that's the first thing I said he would probably laugh. It would be a brilliant sentence to not only show my sophistication, humor, and wit, but also that I've grown. He will expect a sentimental reunion on my part, undoubtedly, and so I should probably take on the role of a society lady attributing to myself all the manners that come along with that. And then afterwards after he laughs I will give him a sincere hug and cry in his arms.'

Out of the window her luminous gaze lingered, inattentive to what it observed directly. The mundane fields had transformed without her notice into a lush green tinged with golden streaks of sunshine. The windy sound of flatland was replaced by the chirping of birds and scurrying critters, occasionally gallivanting into view. Her content thoughts only briefly returning from deep within her to more material surroundings, as if exploring those transcendent under water caverns and only returning to the surface for a fresh breath of air before plunging again. Her head breached the surface and a hearty breath brought her shoulders upwards, her chest expanding slowly with them. She looked out to see a squirrel approach the thin path and take an upright posture on its hind legs, a nut in its hands. Its demeanor suggested that a parade was passing, Eliza smiled as a gesture of well-wishing. The carriage stopped and Simon hopped down from his perch,

"This seems like a good place to stop for the night Miss Eliza. There's a river just down there." he said, opening her door as he spoke.

"Okay Simon." She smiled, joining him on the dirt path and observing some nice clearings through the thicket, perfect for camping.

THE AIR THAT FILLED JARVIS'S LUNGS WAS LIGHT AND HIS GRIP WAS loose but comfortable around the Lucy's reins. His hat hung behind him and the sky overhead stretched blue as far as he could see. A subtle anxiety permeated from within his chest and despite its initial discomfort he was beginning to enjoy it. Never being this far from John, and used to following his lead, his actions took on a clumsy character and when he did things like start fires or set up a camp it took several additional minutes in order to remember exactly how to do it. The freshness of the solitary air purified a feeling of foreboding that initially accompanied his excursion as well as the sensation of forgetting something. He traveled slow, debating on what roads Eliza would have taken and additionally, if he should even pursue her. His lonely mind wandered to a distant horizon and there found a life occupied by him and her. He imagined a middle of the town home and a small front yard, ripe pears falling from the native trees. Townsfolk walking by and waving to Eliza while thinking, 'that Jarvis is a lucky man.' Stirring from thoughts flavored by a life together, he always felt genuinely stupid. 'They make no sense,' he reprimanded himself, 'She was just being nice, she's already forgotten about me.' The cycle went on and on, pleasant thoughts followed by personal reproaches aimed inwardly, his travels speeding up and slowing down with his train of thought.

Traversing the mundane wheat fields had taken a quick few days but his occupied mind didn't even notice. He reached the vibrant shrubberies that signaled the closing proximity of his destination. The inviting greenery swept his conflicting thoughts aside and after slowing down he hopped from Lucy as he entered the entanglement, keeping an eye out for a decent clearing and noticing the sound of a river in the distance. His hands clearing foliage that inhibited the most direct avenue to the river. A thorn greeted him from a bush causing a drop of blood to appear on a recoiling hand but he pushed onward with his shoulder until he emerged from the densest thicket. He moved slowly, looking back to Lucy occasionally to keep his bearings, and when Lucy was out of site he chose one tree after another to help maintain his internal compass. The subtle anxiety that lingered within him crept to the forefront, flaring ever so often before dissipating into a dull throb. He heard the river near and peaking his head from behind a tree to what was observed as a clearing, his gaze came upon a churning river, which, despite all evidence pointing to the contrary, he was beginning to doubt the existence of. It was wide, a bubbling and rapturous white amidst a teal hue, Jarvis nearly fell in and joined the append-ages of land bound greenery which dangled fruitfully into the wa-ter. He felt a sprinkle of moisture on his face and it acted as a salve to his anxiety. He watched with solitary awe the strength of the current, occasionally carrying a log through the rapids and only gracefully deciding not to condemn it to its own depths forever. The opposite shore looked as pretty as his, the trees hugging the water and roots making up a wooden wall. His eyes sought a safe way down and his mind turned clearly and deliberately, looking where the steps were that he could follow to ensure his own safety. He meant to at the very least refill his water supply which could be boiled at a later convenience. Eyeing down the coast, the cur-rent was gentler and the hard roots gave way to cool mud. Slight movement caught his attention and he viewed in the distance a pale figure, naked, sitting in the water, a slight swirling of the foot no doubt to feel the sensation of the current from every direction.

Jarvis ducked his head timidly back behind the tree before tee-tering forward again to confirm the mirage. She was there. Eliza sat nude in the water, leaning back so her hair could be cleansed by the current. Her torso caressed by the flowing water while her ex-posed upper body basked in the sunlight. He felt his heart beating from his ears and his face was red. The anxiety that had lingered was almost unbearable now although he refused to move until he sensed that her eyes were beginning to open to which he replied with a dive back into the safety of nature's canopy. He began the trudge back, following the path that he had taken and determined to find water at a less embarrassing moment, until he saw through the woods a small fire at some distance and imagined that it must be Eliza's camp. He approached, unsure of what he might say, and wondering how he could explain his appearance. Should he explain Wilheimer Falls as Gray Town and reveal his assignment? Yes, he decided, it would be the only way to make proper sense of his wanting to join her on her travels.

He approached, his cheeks still pink with embarrassment, and saw Simon sitting near the fire. Jarvis nodded at him as he looked up quizzically from his seat.

"Howdy." Jarvis said, to which Simon returned with a confused look. Jarvis continued, his voice beginning to tremble, "Is Eliza around…?" he mumbled.

"Not at the moment…" Simon replied, intentionally leaving little room for Jarvis to maneuver.

"Oh it's just… I'm actually heading the same way as you. And I thought it would be pleasant to share the road." Jarvis annunciated. He was not expecting the cold reunion that Simon was offering, although, thinking more, he was not exactly sure what he was expecting, after all, he had completely forgot about Simons existence.

Simon stood up and walked towards Jarvis, putting a hand on his shoulder, his eyes softening and his warm touch directed Jarvis to walk with him. He followed, walking slowly side by side until Simon began speaking, "Oh Jarvis… I think you have the wrong idea. I know why you're here. Yes, I'm sure it's possible we have the same destination but I know why you're *here* and you're mistaken." Simon turned to look at Jarvis who appeared to have been shot in the midsection, but Simon continued speaking anyway, "Because of this mistake you've made it would not be a pleasant journey for you. We are headed to Wilheimer Falls because Eliza is in love and despite her behavior and wide-reaching affection this love that she is pursuing is where any similar sentiments flow from. In other words, she is perfectly willing to explore anything that reminds her of this first of hers, but it is always only a substitute, a replacement, a temporary relief until her true thirst is satisfied. She would be happy to see you but you would misunderstand…"

Jarvis stopped walking and his face grew pale. His eyes glaring at the ground until Simon added, with a sigh, "I think you should go…" to which Jarvis nodded sharply and hurried away. As he put his hand up to clear a path back to where he had emerged from, a sharp prick stung his palm causing tears to burst from his eyes. He wiped them and continued on using his elbow to brace against the foliage. He felt tired and for the first time since he began his trek he noticed the soreness of his muscles, no doubt caused by riding. He made his way back to Lucy who was waiting patiently. A nice pat on the head prompted a nay in response and Jarvis smiled. A sigh escaped his lips and putting his hat on his head he mounted the saddle atop Lucy and paused. 'Well there's no way I'm going back to John… The only choice is to continue on.' He motioned Lucy onwards and she began a merry trot. 'I'm actually relieved.' He told himself.

THE GENTLE WARM AIR WAS REFRESHING AGAINST HER COOL WET skin. Her black hair hung back and the water rushed to wash it clean. The sunlight overhead shone brightly against her reddening chest, the water glistening against pale breasts and muscled shoulders. Lightly haired forearms accompanied pristine hands splashing water occasionally over areas growing hot to the touch and she turned slowly to avoid discomfort. A smile on her face she examined carefully for places where dirt had accumulated in a way that the simple current would not clean. She rubbed her ankles softly under the water and in between her toes as well. The sky remained blue while the water around her maintained a teal hue that contrasted a color perfectly situated between the green of the forest around her and the aqua above. She took her time, allowing the energetic path of the river and the noise it made to keep her in the present. The weather was warm enough for her to remain comfortable despite the briskness of the water. She sat for hours until hunger prompted her to ring her hair out one last time, and find her way back.

She stepped onto the overgrown path that had led her there and moved with care, allowing her body to dry so she could fling her light white dress back on. It fit loosely and she preferred it for traveling as it did not hinder her movement in any way and could be yanked off or thrown on with ease. It also dried moderately quick as she had learned the lucky way on a previous excursion. She entered camp to see Simon sitting with a furrowed brow poking a stick into the fire he had made within a small circle of rocks.

"What's the matter Simon?" she asked.

"Jarvis came through while you were away." he replied.

"Jarvis…?"

"Yes." Simon laughed, "Did you happen to see him? He had that look particular to men who have just seen a naked woman."

Eliza laughed, "No I did not see him. Behave yourself Simon. Has he gone?"

"Indeed, I sent him away."

"Good."

"Yes I let him down easy… I think. Who knows? Maybe I was a bit harsh but he caught me rather by surprise. We pushed pretty hard the last few days so I was in my own head when he sprang from the brush."

"I'm sure it was fine Simon. He's still young, he will get over it. A valuable lesson, no doubt. Although maybe it would have been better if I was here to make sure there was no confusion?"

"No, this way you at least maintain him as an acquaintance, a friend. Let those thoughts linger in the back of his mind if they give him pleasure. Why not?"

"I suppose you're right." She sighed, "Although I really don't like unresolved things."

"Aren't they though? Resolved that is."

"Resolved for me of course. They were resolved when we left Maplewood but he came for the specific purpose of resolution and he only received it partially… Yes, I'd rather have burned what there was of a bridge, it would have been easier that way." She said, sitting down across from Simon, "Oh well." She added, "Acquaintances… friends… okay."

They continued on, after a small meal, determined to use what daylight was left and the journey felt much more agreeable. The sounds of the forest paired with beautiful scenery, hills in the distance accentuating wherever a clearing manifested, allowed the days to move quickly. They had risen into a traveler's rhythm only stopping briefly when the horses needed it and snacking lightly until dinner when they stopped for the night. Eliza would start the fire and cook while Simon used what tiny morsel of daylight was left to set up a quick camp and get the horses settled. They operated like this for two weeks, restocking with whatever was accessible without hardship in the small towns they passed, the horses being pushed to their limit.

"We're only a few days from Wilheimer Falls, Eliza." Simon said, smiling, "Finally some rest."

"A long rest." she said, smiling back. "Thank you for really moving quick this last month."

"Of course." he returned.

Entering the last town before Wilheimer Falls they decided to spend a night at the inn, allowing themselves the opportunity of freshening up before the reunion.

THIRTY-TWO

———

THE SKY HAD GROWN GRAY OVERHEAD, ELIZA AND SIMON BEGAN the last section of their journey. Wilheimer Falls could be reached late that day if they hurried. The solemn posture that the nature around her took brought flooding back to Eliza memories that she had forgotten.

The modest hilly landscape called forth a polite invitation to nap but Eliza's heart beat quick. 'I haven't seen him in years, oh god!' she thought, 'I'm not where I should be mentally, spiritually, intellectually... He will laugh at my dress too. I cannot do this, no, I'm not ready. I will write him a letter and go back to France. Yes, these skies remind me of Leopold's estate, I will return there...' Her knee bouncing up and down, she opened the carriage window allowing fresh air to replace the polluted anxious air that occupied the space around her. An outward gaze noticed in the distance a single tree outside of a small country house, with a bright red bench facing it.

"Simon stop here!" she shouted, gathering her breath. Simon obeyed despite the rush they were in, he began reconciling himself to stopping for one more night and imagined it as a coin flip.

Eliza stepped from the path onto the green fields that occupied her entire surroundings, everywhere except the small house. She approached slowly, the gentle wind mingling with the grass around her. The unceasing gray sky gave the impression of an approaching storm which would never come and the smell of the air conveyed the same message. Supple red apples blossomed from the tree accentuating the bench that shone brightly against the mundane backdrop of the horizon. She noticed fresh flowers placed just a few feet away. Nearing the apple tree, she plucked one and continued on, drawing closer to the bench and the flowers beside them. She sat down, the well-maintained seat was comfortable, embracing her and removing the anxiety that had been building. She took a bite of the apple and smiled, looking down, a few feet in front of the bench. Between it and the apple tree lay a flat stone, etched upon it were the words that Eliza curiously read, thanking the name for the apple which she enjoyed: "Husband, Friend, Uncle : Wilbur Hamilton."

PART FOUR

THIRTY-THREE

————————

THE SKY HAD BEEN BLEAK FOR SEVERAL DAYS AND JARVIS NOTED the accuracy of the moniker "Gray Town." Traveling under the plain unchanging canopy, and in the solitary manner that tinged his trek, he felt as if he was in a sort of purgatory. Time crawled along and morning and afternoon had no distinct characteristics. He awoke lugubriously and hoped that it would be a long time before blackness enveloped him, it coming instantaneously as the sun vanished. Lifeless leaves danced across the trail in front of him but it happened with such mechanical frequency that he couldn't help but think, 'Is that the same leaf?' referring to one that had moved with a similar cadence earlier in the day, or even the day before. Despite a weary management of time, he made good of it and leaned forward consistently, moving quickly through the part of the country where Wilheimer Falls was the epicenter, and finally made it there, unsure of how long it took. He approached the sign with delight on a widened and frequented path that read, "Welcome to Wilheimer Falls, Founded by Alfred Wilheimer." John had mentioned the name before and Jarvis recalled what he had said, "Surely a drunk," came to his mind, echoing in John's voice, "All midwestern towns are named after drunks. It's just simply the case. In early America you had our revolutionary heroes allowing the east coast to be decorated by their names, and then after the fighting was over, the adventurous among us traveled west and so the west coast takes on the names of adventurers, but the Midwest is where those who got tired of travel ended up." Jarvis wondered what John must be up to before he read on, to a sign that was hammered just below the welcoming one, it read, "No formal vacancies: See sheriff for lodging."

From Jarvis's experience traveling he had discovered that the town priest would be a more worthwhile visit than the sheriff, no matter the circumstance, and decided to visit the church first. Not to mention his fascination with the architecture that was unique to such buildings. He entered the town eagerly, excited to finally have reached his destination and smiled as he rode. There weren't many carriages or horses occupying the street and most of the people traveled on foot. It was around noon when he entered, a genuine bustle remained consistent wherever his gaze fell and many street corners had young fellows seemingly in the midst of an argument. Energy permeated everywhere and the crowded walkways moved quickly, voices clattering boisterously among them and laughter springing forward occasionally and often accompanied by similar cackles echoing from the initial sources. He asked a young well-dressed man where the church might be and the man looked up to the tall figure Jarvis, who sat on his horse, with his hand above his brow to block out the hidden sun and pointed a finger south, saying, "Why on earth would you want to go there?" and without waiting for a response hurried along. Jarvis continued and saw a modest building after following the uninterested finger that was offered him. The church was impressive in size but offered no opulence, the stone statues crafted into its side alluded to no eye-catching hues against the mundane sky that stood behind them. One had to struggle to notice the detail and the entire building seemed to fade into cloudy patchwork. Approaching from a distance Jarvis imagined an emptiness where the church stood and almost chalked up his apprehended senses to the effects of a mirage. The one thing that appeared powerfully were the doors. Jarvis gave them their due as architecturally formidable and as he dismounted Lucy he approached with reverence. They stood massive, larger than any he had seen before and appeared ancient forcing one's mind to recollect the age of the town before, in confusion, having to conclude that the doors must have been, by divine decree, imported and the church erected around them. He lingered for a while with the pleasurable thought, 'It's only a church that can start with a door and have everything cater to it.'

Jarvis pushed hard with genuine effort and one of the lofty doors opened obediently. The pews were old but clean. The immaculate wood shone vibrantly and the stain glass windows nearly convinced one that the sun was bright outside. Tinted uniquely they brought to ones senses the flavor of a youthful mass. Jarvis viewed the altar expecting for a moment to see his childhood pastor, who as a matter of fact he did not particularly like, but seeing that he had a few fond memories from his younger days which sat distant and stagnant in the back of his mind, he was willing to accept the weary monotone manner that the old celibate had employed in exchange for a transference back to simpler times. Jarvis looked to the altar where a young man was lighting candles, the sweat on his brow informed Jarvis that he had been speaking, probably the service was nearly over. The man returned to the podium, wiped his eyebrows only, allowing his forehead to remain adorned with droplets, and continued with what he must have been saying moments ago. His voice thundered on, unperturbed by the new entrant, and Jarvis took the first available pew he saw and listened to the ensuing sermon. He wasn't particularly interested in the content, at least the theological content, and so he observed based on other criteria. That the speaker had a nice voice was the first thing he noticed. Deliberate sentences constructed cleverly showed expertise in his craft and one listened as they might to a musical number. A particular rhythm established itself in a comforting manner to one's ears and then a sudden juxtaposition, a surprise, goaded one's attention anew followed by a bountiful flurry of provocative thoughts which were then diluted into the previous consistent manner of speech. Jarvis looked around and the church wasn't as occupied as he had expected. By all accounts from John a serious religious pilgrimage had taken place in the past few months and the busy town and timidly proclaimed vacancies had led him to assume the worst, or best depending on one's vantage point. All in all, he appraised that at least he would have an easier time talking to the priest than he had imagined. He actually regretted not getting there sooner so that he could more adequately grasp the speakers train of thought. He caught only snippets and without context they didn't mean much, "Every man is on his own path." Was a key theme, "Some are led astray only to return with stronger faith."-"Do not worry so much about the emptiness in the seats next to you but worry more so about the emptiness within the heart."

Jarvis listened lazily, allowing his mind to wander. Before he knew it the voice had stopped, the twenty or so individuals had thanked the preacher and left, and Jarvis sat alone in his pew, the preacher's eyes smilingly fixed on him. He instinctually smiled back letting out a deep breath of relaxation. The man approached warmly and sat next to Jarvis, extending his hand which Jarvis shook firmly.

"My name is Father Thomas," the man said.

"Jarvis," Jarvis replied.

"Is it pain or pleasure that brings you here?" Thomas inquired empathetically.

"Honestly Father... I'm not sure I know the difference."

"I see... You've been talking with the New Lutherans?"

"Who?" Jarvis asked, quizzically.

"Oh my apologies."

"Not necessary," Jarvis replied, "I'm here to ask about accommodations."

Thomas laughed, "The sheriff isn't the most civilized man is he? Well in his defense it has been a bit hectic for him lately, what did he do this time to send you fleeing here?"

"I haven't seen him. My brother taught me that the first place a man should visit when arriving in a new place is the Church. The Church is a measure of the town. And the first person one should see is the priest."

"Your brother sounds like a smart man Jarvis, and you are wise to learn from him." Thomas smiled, continuing on, "No matter where one goes the church is home and one's father waits with open arms. And when one returns home who is more proper to see first but their father? In terms of vacancies, yes, I can arrange something, supposing you don't have an aversion to being put to work here and there."

"Sounds fair enough. I don't mind. Thank you, Father."

They sat for a moment, Jarvis revisiting what he saw around him. Despite the boring architecture the church displayed outwardly, from the inside the opulence was two-fold almost to make up for the former plainness. 'Like a metaphor for a man of virtue?' he wondered. It was indeed intentional and although Thomas wasn't fond of extravagance he was not a man to make drastic changes, especially at the risk of alienating his new congregation. He left everything more or less as it was, offering only his opinions on Faith to change the atmosphere. Attendance had been swelling as everyday more and more of the younger generation flocked to Wilheimer Falls to listen to Benjamin Mills speak and, enthralled, they found themselves at Church to further spurn their development. Thomas arrived at the near climax before a stern and quick drop had prompted him to question his style. He had felt revitalized since arriving and his message seemed to be resonating, leaving him confused before figuring out the reason.

"You used a phrase before. New Lutherans? I wonder what you mean by that?" Jarvis asked after some silence.

"Indeed. I imagined you had heard one of the sidewalk debates. You're here because of Benjamin Mills? I only ask because it will make my explanation much simpler."

"Yes I suppose I'm here because of Benjamin Mills." Jarvis replied, realizing how tired he was, a nap would be necessary he decided.

"Well you're not the only one. Many have traveled from all over the country to hear him speak and to visit this town, myself included. He taught me in my younger days and had a very big influence on my development. Although I disagree with his brand of religiosity, which is one that dances around the divinity and the reality of Christ's presence on earth. He imagines that it's the bedrock story that's important and that Christianity gives the most accurate account of truth and how one should conduct themselves in the world. That's my interpretation of him at least. And it's captivated a generation, they all came to hear the words from his mouth. Came they did by the masses, all rightfully entranced by him. He only spoke at the bar that he manages but despite that Church attendance rose, the congregation was packed, in fact, we had run out of seats and some had to stand in back during my sermons. With every movement, though, it is inevitable that the flame will fade, and one characteristic of youthful fervor is its precociousness. One who is swayed one way can no doubt be swayed the other way just as easily. Often even, the harder one falls on a particular side the harder they will inevitably end up on the opposite side, only learning from their mistake when the passion quells and they end up in a moderate form of the initial position. But I'm getting ahead of myself. I will say this, those who were here will return here. Benjamin really did create a masterful body of work and with this generation it may have been delivered early enough to be accepted as the original position. Those young Christians in the street, although they claim otherwise, will be back."

"New Lutherans?" Jarvis reminded him, sitting forward with his elbows on his knees, eyeing Thomas.

"Oh yes. As our attendance here peaked, essays began being published by a truly immoral man named Luther. He believes in nothing and denies any meaning to life or value in it. He has written voluminously and free of adversaries for some time now. I do my best to sermonize against him but I'm afraid our seats are losing occupants daily."

"What about Benjamin Mills?" Jarvis asked.

"He manages the bar still but with an intellectual despondency. The whispers are that he's gone mad. That Luther so thoroughly trounced him that his mind snapped. It's not true of course, but this theory appears to be giving even more credence to Luther's position, inviting everyone to read it with vigor and even to switch to Luther's entirely opposite view. Those that do with a real mischievous glee call themselves, 'New Lutherans.'-"

THIRTY-FOUR

———

ALEXANDER SAT RELAXED AS LUTHER SPOKE, HIS EYES PEERING OUT the parlor room window. The neat grass gave way to a few cultivated shrubs before the chaotic and dense woods proclaimed their dominion. The darkness shone bright and acted to soothe his wandering mind. Luther had been speaking a lot lately and demanded more argument than necessary from him, no doubt to sharpen his own thoughts, although he never left the house. He maintained whole-heartedly that one should never meet anyone that they have any literary admiration for, and seeing how he had recently gained some recognition he made it his mission not to disturb it. In writing one can transcend humanity, all the author's vices and shortcomings are not forgiven but retroactively vanish. Previous writings that were potentially not up to snuff cease to exist as the reader's eyes follow the author's delicately crafted path. And arguments can be made with such sternness that they take on the character of truth, like an adventurer who discovers an ancient text might read it, with reverence. Luther wrote with a conviction that so long as it was only his arguments that were judged no fault could be found. It was approaching lunch time but Alexander was not hungry, Luther had been arguing more or less with himself for the past few hours, Alexander only interjecting occasionally when he deemed absolutely necessary to prod a particular point. He decided to go for a walk.

There was an enjoyment now, in town, for Alexander. Watching Luther's thoughts blossom in young minds before being contorted beyond recognition gratified a sense of irony that few other things roused so effectively. He now walked with an inquisitive gaze that jumped capriciously from one person to the next listening for words that he knew to be wielded aggressively in Luther's work. He remained walking with a rare smile until a subtle breeze made the hair on his arms stiffen, stopping, his heart began to race. It beat quick. His chest felt heavy. He looked around. Everyone was moving slower. Thud, thud, thud. Eliza sat on the bench outside The Dancing Sheep. Her pale skin glistened amidst the gray skies overhead. Her shoulders, nose, and cheeks were garnished red from a complexion not suited to extended sun exposure. She sat on the red bench, in a cool blue dress that hung loosely on her supple body. The wind eagerly grabbed it, pulling it tight against her and her black hair pranced eagerly. She looked relaxed in so far as she was sitting completely still but her body appeared stiff on closer inspection. He viewed from where he stood, having turned the corner and just far enough to admire her pristine profile, the rigidness of her breathing which was deep. Her shoulders moving up and down slowly, deliberately, her chest expanding to allow as much oxygen as possible to ease her wooden decorum. Thud, thud, thud. He approached slowly. Time stood still as he lingered near her and noticing that she did not notice anything but the ground in front of her, he sat down close. He tried to speak but his chest was tight and he did not possess the amount of oxygen necessary for words.

She recoiled at first, yelping as she reeled her head upwards towards his face. He maintained an anxious smile waiting for her to speak first. Observing his nervousness, she began to laugh, scooting back close to him, taking his hand in hers onto her lap.

"Oh Alexander!" Her smiling eyes scanning his face and a grin adorning her lips, she continued enthusiastically, "Would you believe that I am sitting her to regain my senses? That I was as anxious to see you as you are now? Would you believe that it has all vanished this very moment?"

He grinned in reply, "What makes you think I'm anxious?" he asked.

Eliza freed one of her hands, both being pretzeled around his, and put it to his heart. Thud, thud, thud. She laughed.

"Here feel mine." she exclaimed, taking his hand from her lap and pressing it against her chest. He blushed and noticing this her face turned pink as well.

"It's beating just as fast as mine..." he reported.

"Ah I suppose you're right. I think it will pass after we talk for a bit." she said gaily. "Where do you think you're grabbing?" she added after a moment, taking his hand, which he had given up possession of, away from her chest and returned it comfortably to her lap where her hands clasped it. "There's plenty of time for that now that I'm here... For talking I mean."

Alexander smiled, "Have you brought your belongings?" he asked.

"Yes, they are with Simon but I sent him away. I made quite the scene in my nervousness, I yelled at him you know? Everyone in the area stopped for a moment, only a split second, imperceptible to most but I have a keen eye for scenes and so I noticed. From my appraisal this town must be accustomed to dramatic scenes because everyone acted cordially and continued on pretending not to have noticed my outburst. It was helpful. Sometimes the eyes of onlookers' prod one on, invite one to be more theatric than necessary, but here I was revealed to be nothing out of the ordinary and so I did not revel in the spotlight and calmed down rather quick. Anyhow Simon is probably driving in large circles around the town and will eventually show up at your estate in the hopes that I will be there and be satisfied. I'm too mean to him I confess, but what am I to do? My occasional annoyance is temperamental and the result is that I am short with people sometimes. It's only after that I realize my mistake, sometimes not until I'm lying in bed ha ha. Am I to get up that moment, push my covers off and go apologize? No that would make it even worse. It's something that we all must live with. The proposition that we seriously offend people regularly, which isn't bad necessarily, but that we do so accidentally is the rub. An accidental insult... No, that's not exactly right is it? I arrive in the situation by my own actions so the insult results from my own activities. Unintentional is a better phrase. Unintentional can be characterized properly as, 'if I could relive the moment I would change it.'-"

"Would you mind elaborating?" Alexander asked, his stiff posture softening as he sat back comfortably, allowing Eliza's perspiring hands to grip his. "What would an accident be characterized as, what's the distinction?"

"Of course, Alexander!" a grin appearing on her face, "An accident would be unavoidable, like a bridge collapsing under one, or if you prefer a more personal touch say a carriage collision where I was the driver. I couldn't really say, 'If I could go back I never would have chosen to crash my carriage.' There's an unmistakable element of intention in one versus the other. An accident is being backed into a corner of action so to speak, having no choices available to oneself, whereas I will contend that the word unintentional as I am proposing would leave room for other outcomes, other manifestations of my will in the world. If we return to the carriage example and I am transported to moments before my carriage crashed what choices would I have? To make a drastic change of direction maybe but who's to say that would turn out better or worse, what is prompting this change of mind?" She leaned back against the bench, her shoulder touching Alexander's before continuing, "It's just occurred to me, a more interesting way to make the argument.

We can call the distinction a matter of authenticity. In the carriage example I could say for instance, that I was initially operating authentically and the crash occurred regardless. If I was transported back to the moment of the crash and asked, 'are you traveling in accordance with your self?' the question would seem comical, I'm just driving a carriage, of course I'm acting in accordance with my self! In other words, there isn't a large enough motivation pertaining to my being to render necessary a change, I'm acting enough in accordance with how I want to act that the outcome of which is not sufficient to render me in a position adequate to guiltlessly change my behavior… That was a nice sentence wasn't it Alexander? Would you believe that I came up with it just now? Anyway we could then simply say that unintentional means that the action was inauthentic and therefore subject to rectification. So unintentionality means: actions guiltlessly subject to rectification. And to speak on guilt in this sense for a moment, I would surely feel substantial guilt If I saved myself from a carriage accident only because I have some divine quality which allows me to make my choices again."

"My response would be…" Alexander began slowly, "That there is no difference at all. You initially said, 'an accident would be unavoidable,' and I contend that everything is unavoidable. Nothing in the world can be avoided in any sense whatsoever. From each event a necessary event follows and this pattern can be traced all the way back to the beginning of time. Every action we take, no other action is possible in that moment, so even if there is a feeling of avoidance it is incorrect, we are, in a sense, always avoiding the avoidable and never avoiding the unavoidable. If one was transported back, all the conditions would remain the same, all the various inputs, for instance: one's mental state, one's surroundings, one's past, etc. This would result in the same outcome every time. It's a straightforward proposition and a logical chain: if one believes that causes have necessary effects, a point that is impossible to refute, what comes next is a concession of any sense of genuine choice. It's all predetermined."

"Oh Alexander, don't think using words like logic and proposition make your argument more sound. You said, 'we have a feeling of avoidance,' and there I would agree, and then you say, 'it is incorrect,' and that I have to furrow my brow at. Incorrect on whose account? I won't accept it. If I feel like I'm avoiding something, I'm avoiding it."

"No I'm only using those words to retain consistency between your argument and mine. Avoiding? It is an incoherent concept. Unavoidable? Equally incoherent. Everything just happens along the causal chain which operates from the beginning of time until the end of time. We are not free to act however we please."

Eliza looked into his eyes, leaned towards him and, with two fingers, gently tilted his chin upwards before kissing him on the lips. Her hand lingering near his chest she clenched what she could of his shirt and with the other hand instinctually caressed his arm. His eyes closed as he reciprocated, his hands gravitating towards her hips which remained close. Her cool breath mingling with his. Satisfied after a long moment, she sat back shoulder to shoulder with him, his cheeks red. She put her hand on his chest to feel its quickened pace and took his and placed it against her chest to feel the same.

"Where do you think you're grabbing Alexander?" she said, slightly out of breath, before laughing merrily. "You've given me serious liberties with your argument you know? You have just described something beautiful to me, you've described absolute freedom. I can do whatever I like with you and we can chalk it up to destiny? Okay Alexander I'll bite; I have no freedom if it means I can kiss you whenever I like."

He sat with blushed cheeks before continuing, "And as for your second point. About authenticity…"

Being lost in each other's company neither had noticed people gathering a few feet away forming a considerable crowd taking up much of the sidewalk. Although they paid no attention to the two on the bench the crowd spoke loudly and the chatter interrupted Alexander's thoughts as he peered towards a carriage that had just arrived. Eliza's eyes followed his gaze. A figure stepped down from the carriage and walked modestly, his head tilted downward and his face painted with melancholy, towards the entrance of the establishment behind them, The Dancing Sheep. He walked resolutely without acknowledging the crowd but seeing Alexander on the bench he smiled to him and, observing Eliza next to him, he tipped his cap before returning to a solemn trudge onward into the restaurant.

"Who was that?" Eliza asked, looking at Alexander who had regained his natural state of composure.

"Benjamin Mills." he replied.

"Who?"

"Benjamin Mills.. he.."

Before he could finish she interrupted him with a sound of confusion, a partially formed 'What?' sprang from her lips before she looked down at the bench they occupied which shone red underneath them and gave one a feeling of summer among the gray that towered around them. She viewed carefully the bench that she had seen an exact replica of just a day before near an apple tree, recalling the name 'Wilbur Hamilton,' which adorned the gravestone. There was a golden plaque here, subtly on a brick underneath the bench, that read, 'In memory of Angelica Hamilton.' Confusion announced itself to her and, gasping, the signs all revealed themselves at once. She looked above to the gray sky, simultaneously noticing the unusually crowded streets. She laughed and looked into Alexander's eyes which glowed green,

"Let's go back to your estate if you don't mind, I've got some questions that would best be asked sprawled on some comfortable, quiet grass, or a nice couch perhaps."

THIRTY-FIVE

A CLANG ECHOED THROUGH THE AIR AS BENJAMIN FLUNG THE door to The Dancing Sheep open, taking a deliberate step before turning dramatically to where he had taken to sitting recently, in the corner, while avoiding the eyes of all the inhabitants, where a pile of newspapers awaited him. His friend Phillip sat there as well. He was reading intently before noticing Benjamin's arrival and folding his paper back to its typical dimensions before tossing it back on the tabletop. Benjamin sat, letting out a sigh as he did, and was immediately approached by a few younger boys, no doubt students who had recently arrived and remained unrebuked by him. As they neared and before a word could escape the open mouth of one, Benjamin began,

"Gentleman, it's lovely to have you at this establishment. If there is anything you need, anything at all please don't refrain from asking Natalie, who you will find behind the front counter." They lingered before Benjamin added, "And since you require more instruction, I will give it to you. I am unfortunately under the weather and unwilling to speak to anyone but the dearest acquaintances. Forgive me for any disappointment this may cause you. Now please leave me to my paper."

The boys turned one after another and walked away, surprisingly unaffected by the reprimand. Phillip's sidelong glance remained on the sitting Benjamin and he jeered, unable to resist, "Does that make me a dear acquaintance?"

"Unfortunately. I may have misspoken, maybe I'll go fetch those gentlemen to sit down and have a proper conversation so that you may not feel superior to them. They looked like charming boys after all but I'm in no mood to meet anyone new."

"Knowing that you won't go retrieve them, I'm flattered. I will do good things with this superiority granted me."

"Indeed, Phillip if it's one thing you're known for it's good things." Benjamin laughed.

Phillip grinned, "You know Benjamin… It's good to hear you laugh. Even if it is at my expense."

"Yes, I can't remember the last time. It's a welcome sign, I can say I honestly imagined myself incapable of any joy, I was reconciled to a life of grief. But if I can share something with you, I saw Alexander today." A smirk appeared on Benjamin's face, as if he was concealing an impulse to smile. "It's been a long time since I've seen him and so it filled me with genuine happiness. He was with a nice young lady as well. That makes me very happy."

"Did you talk to him?" Phillip asked.

"No, he hardly noticed me, in fact I felt as if my very presence was interrupting something." Benjamin laughed, "Oh to be young!"

Phillip smiled and they both picked up a paper and began reading. Drinks were brought and no one bothered them despite the lively nature of the venue. Voices clamored here and there when wrestling over a point of disagreement and when arguments became loud, Natalie, who was a long time secretary of Benjamin and for the time being in charge of The Dancing Sheep, ushered them outside to one street corner or another where the debate could take on a new volume. Afterwards they would inevitably stream back in jovially and with lighter subjects on their tongues. This was the perpetual state except during mass hours when a great portion would vanish for a while before returning with a new fervor and the process would repeat.

Benjamin having digested the stack of papers returned the pile to its position on the opposite side of the table before looking to Phillip who was taking a sip of water, looking out the window, also having read through the stack.

"You know… I don't think Wilbur's suicide was the final blow to my health. I do feel heavy and like I've aged many years and assume to now be operating from those which may be my last, whether true or not, but it isn't from the death necessarily that makes me feel this way. You are aware that it was Katherine who found him hanging? That she went out to do some gardening and came home to see his body swaying? They were supposed to be taking time off. Resting in the country where they could process Angelica's death in peace. He must have known what he was going to do and waited for his moment. My God, could you imagine what Katherine must have gone through…? Must be going through… And she's gone to stay with her father and all I can do to help is watch after The Dancing Sheep. He's really gone and all those memories we have together are extinguished. The general thing to say is that they are kept alive in me but I'm not sure that is true. Memories are shared after all."

"Katherine is in my prayers; I agree that there is no crueler fate… If I may be crude Benjamin." Philip said timidly, "A helpful standpoint to take when dealing with something of this magnitude, although it is a very hard standpoint to take, is an objective one. To view the event as stress and remember that those afflicted are the subjects of an immense amount of it. Therefore, thoughts are obviously less than ideally clear and to not take what you've discovered from this event too seriously until you've had proper time to accumulate some distance."

"Point taken Phillip, maybe this is a weakness of mine, I find myself blaming Wilbur perpetually for what he's done to Katherine, and as you can see, I level many criticisms at him, including depriving me of a substantial amount of fond memories. All my past remembrances of us are tinged with this last transgression which I view as unforgiveable." Benjamin sighed.

"Focus on today, old friend." Phillip replied, a warm smile on his lips.

"Today has been a good day." Benjamin said in a low sincere voice.

THIRTY-SIX

———

JARVIS WALKED, PATTING LUCY'S HEAD AS HE GUIDED HER BY THE reins behind Thomas who walked in front of him, leading him to a member of his flock who was situated roughly a mile away from the church in a moderate overgrowth of the town, although it still referred to itself as being Wilheimer Falls. The weather was what Jarvis had come to expect but was not entirely prepared for, having only experienced it on the days preceding his arrival, which he found dizzying. The color remained the same, no hues escaping the clouds which presented a uniform gray that only changed when the sun set; instantly it turned black like a candle being blown out. Jarvis felt constantly anxious wondering how much day light was left before the peace of darkness would finally satisfy his dread of being caught unawares in the middle of a task. He followed closely behind Thomas and prodded him to learn more about any blank spots in his own knowledge of the story of Gray Town, which despite John's primary role, he himself took a serious investigative stance towards also.

"You said that Benjamin has gone mad?" Jarvis asked.

"No, I said many take his despondent mood as going mad and that they use it as justification for the validity of Luther's work, but it's not Luther's work that is the cause. His best friend committed suicide."

"Wilbur Hamilton?" Jarvis muttered.

"Yes, how did you know?" Thomas turned, looking surprised.

"I must have heard the name mentioned somewhere."

"Well not many people know about it and it really hasn't been reported anywhere, as it happened outside of town. It absolutely devastated him. You said you came here because of Benjamin, so I'm sure you've heard of Angelica, she was the catalyst for this whole shift. When she died Benjamin gladly looked after an establishment in town called The Dancing Sheep and Wilbur and his wife left to one of Benjamin's country homes near here. After Wilbur was found everything changed, he vanished for a couple days and that's when Luther struck. It was too obvious to be coincidence but I'm still unsure how he acted so fast. Two days after Wilbur's death a lengthy essay was published by Luther which actually advocated suicide. Can you believe that anyone could be so base as to use a suicide as a sort of challenge? Luther is a persistent figure in town so he must have heard of it at some point and would definitely conclude that few would make the connection between Wilbur's death and Benjamin, so it might be said that he wrote it in the face of Benjamin. Luther's essay claims that suicide is not a problem but a reasonable solution. That life is devoid of all value and one way or another the value remains the same... In his defense he says it's not the only solution but what good does it do after an entire argument in favor of it? And so soon after Wilbur's death."

"And Benjamin hasn't responded?"

"Of course not! He's entirely debilitated, completely unaware of what's happening around him. The new movement towards nihilism that Luther is prompting. Despite my agitation, I don't mind those who think differently than myself or what conclusions people arrive at. My concern comes from people being deprived of the word. My church was full a few weeks ago and you saw it now. Whatever people may think it's still important to hear what

Jesus has to say and from there they can make their choices. It's my opinion that the word is truth after all and I only hoist it on people as a man of duty would. And if I could speak to Wilbur I would not say that what he was doing is a proper solution. I would tell him that he has a duty to live. Whatever conclusions he has come to are irrelevant in the face of those around him, whom he must accept may have come to a different realization. I would acknowledge the harshness of my words and tell him that he must bear his suffering with gritted teeth and work to nurture the beliefs of those around him. And he would live... And so I ask you Jarvis, from these two positions: one which results in death and one which results in life, which can be more appropriately called the truth? The New Lutherans are growing in number because Luther's ideas are so pervasive, his arguments solid, but they are missing something. They are missing life!"

"Has anyone responded?" Jarvis asked.

"There's no one to respond. For all the scholastics in town there aren't any of that rare variety of free thinkers. After all the very nature of the circumstance annunciates that. These thinkers, and I will include myself in this, I admittedly in the same category, traveled across the country why? Because of a fervor for another person's thoughts. I preach the word of Christ, not my own, but I am here because of an affection for Benjamin who has influenced me greatly. Many have said I remind them of him and I blush with pride at the comparison."

Jarvis, feeling tired from his journey and not sure what to say lingered in silence for a moment before answering. The road underneath him was well kept and Father Thomas led by two or so paces, angling towards Jarvis as he spoke, at a casual pace.

"I see... I'll admit that my brother is a journalist and very taken with the story of this town and his interest has rubbed off on me. Although he isn't here, I'll attest that he predicted something like this. For all his faults I have to admit he strikes me as a fortune teller with some of his predictions." Jarvis, gathering his thoughts and trying to remember what John had said paused abruptly after his sentence, continuing on only after a few moments, "I'll put it like this: how else could this situation fizzle out?"

"The same brother who had you seek me out? Yes, he seems like a smart man. I suppose if you put it like that the current circumstance strikes one as inevitable but I disagree. I came a long way to take up residence in this town not just because of Benjamin, not solely him, hearing about it from a distance, from halfway across the country there was a genuine allure. The fast pace of life in most places leaves little room for contemplation. The mostly gray weather here... it... seems to slow people down. Although obviously that isn't true in every case, every town has their business class who sees only money, but I'll say that everyone here is much more reserved. There is a humbleness. Have you seen the street side debates? The locals don't care." Thomas laughed, "They continue operating as normal, the ones who come to church come to church and the ones who go home early go home early. But to answer your question more precisely. How else could it have gone? Well I still hold out hope. The value of life is still here. The meaning that is all around us. Benjamin's life was, perhaps unknowingly, spent sowing the respect for divinity in his admirers. I came to see it through, to show them that in Christianity all things can come to fruition. That in this gray town there is light. I did not and do not expect a fizzle. I expect a revival and here is only the beginning and what a perfect place for a beginning. The New Lutherans is a phase that will pass and those that left will return with a stronger faith than before."

They turned down a modest road with a large house adorning the end. A fence guided one along, partitioning the vast but slightly overgrown fields that surrounded the building. A stream flowed some distance away cutting itself into the plain greenery and then behind the home before disappearing in a far thicket which marked the property line and the start of dense woods. Thomas turned to Jarvis and smiled.

"Anyway…" he said, "This is the home of Macey, who will be glad to have some company. She's a long-time widow but the wealth is her own, she actually has a keen eye for speculation, one would hardly expect it. She may actually be the perfect host, now that I think about it, she is a good friend and business partner of Benjamin and would probably be more than happy to answer any lingering questions you might have about him."

As they grew closer they noticed the bobbing of a woman crouched near a garden that accentuated the view from the front porch. Thomas waved, nearly beginning to skip as he saw her and shouted her name, prompting her to jump up with a smile.

"Father Thomas!" she exclaimed, removing a pair of gloves from her hands and tossing them to the ground, "How great to see you." She looked around theatrically back to her home and to the garden where she was working and then to Jarvis and smiled, a content sigh escaping her lips, "Father Thomas." she said surely, placing her hands on her hips.

"The pleasure is mine as always." Thomas replied, before gesturing his hand towards Jarvis. "This is my new friend Jarvis, he showed up to my service this morning and said, 'Whenever I'm in a new place I always go to the church first, right to the church.' and then he said, 'I need a place to stay.' and I thought of you Macey."

"Jarvis." she repeated, shaking his hand. "I would be happy to have you. And just in time too, I was digging holes you see? They are going to go all along this road. I'll be putting trees there! And won't it look splendid! Come, turn around and envision it. Yes, just like that, won't it look brilliant?"

Jarvis and Thomas both turned and agreed.

"Thank you, Macey, I'll leave you to it. It was nice to meet you Jarvis, stop by for service later and we can talk more. Now if you don't mind I will leave before Macey puts me to work." Thomas said.

"Now Father are you sure you don't want to dig a few holes? You know what they say about labor and a good day's work and all that." Macey said, putting her gloves back on.

"Tempting, but I really must return." he said, winking as the last word entered the air. Turning, he walked away waving as he left.

Jarvis looked at Macey who appeared spry and witty, observing her gracefully aged features. Inevitable wrinkles accumulated near her eyes but acted to accentuate her pristine blue irises. Her nose perked up confidently and her lips sat in a subtle smile. Her erect posture allowed her frame to appear taller and added a distinguished element to her decorum. Jarvis saw all this despite her dirty clothes and tired features.

"Jarvis. Yes, it's great to have you." she repeated, patting him on the back. "I'll go get another shovel, you can grab that one right there. See how I spaced the first few holes apart? It will go like that all the way down. I put boys to work when they visit me. You can nap after and I will make you a nice meal, but now you have to dig. Dig and then you can nap and then we can talk, I enjoy hearing about travels and you look worn from it. But now we dig."

She took Lucy by the reins and led her to a stable a short while away and made sure the horse had anything it could need. When she returned with an additional shovel in her hand she nodded and plowed it hard into the ground parallel to the side that Jarvis was digging, a few holes ahead of where she was.

"Thank you for that." Jarvis said, referring to the pleasant treatment of his beloved mare. They spent several hours working, a young girl, near his age, occasionally bringing out water for them. She would shyly gesture with a towel if Jarvis needed the sweat wiped from his forehead but he was too tired to notice. Finally reaching the end of the long driveway Macey showed him to a spare room and Jarvis threw himself on the bed, not acknowledging any features of the room he passed out instantly.

His eyes opened slowly and looking at the ceiling, his refreshed body sunken deep in the covers beneath him, he lingered for a moment trying to recollect where exactly he was. He looked around, the room was small. Simply designed wallpaper plastered the walls and a window allowed an abundance of light in. Jarvis tried to guess how long he had been asleep but couldn't due to the nature of the weather. He sat up and noticed a glass of water on a night stand next to the bed. He remembered Macey and the events of the day, he grabbed the glass and feeling the precipitation on the sides he recognized that he must have slept well. He kept his boots off but brought them in his hands to place them nearer the front door to avoid an additional trip upstairs where his room was situated. As he opened the door the smell of food annunciated itself and he hurried down the steps despite not knowing where exactly he was going. He followed his nose down a hallway and past the front door, tossing his boots down as he went, a beautiful kitchen that glowed white, pans on top of burners and a lovely sink that he admired, never having seen one so nice before.

"Oh you're awake." Macey said, turning a corner and walking into the room. "Jarvis." she added surely, "Yes, it's good that you're awake, I couldn't wait any longer I had to begin supper. You'll forgive me, I would never dream of rousing a sleeping man but I've no qualms about tempting him awake with the smell of a good meal."

Jarvis laughed, "You're too kind mam." he said, "I must have slept a while, I'm a napper, my brother has it out with me about it but it's just how I am."

"He's just jealous Jarvis! I wish I could nap but I would be up all night. My body says, 'alright you've had your sleep,' and I'm out of it for weeks! It's terrible, I often want one too. I dreamed of a hammock once upon a time. If you walk out back you'll see two trees that would be perfect for it. I haven't gotten one because I know I'd fall asleep in it and be out of it for weeks, a proper sleep schedule that is. I admire you're napping Jarvis."

Jarvis smiled.

Macey began stirring pots and moving things around to their ideal spots for the cooking process. As she hurried about the young girl who had brought them water walked in. Macey introduced her as Millie and Millie smiled at Jarvis while she helped her Aunt cook. The food was delicious and despite Jarvis's interest in learning more about Benjamin he enjoyed Macey and Millie's jovial conversation, which he reflected later, wasn't about anything in particular, so much that he reconciled to after dinner, and when Macey went to bed directly afterwards, despite the relatively early hour, she told Jarvis to, 'make himself at home,' and Jarvis told himself that the topic of Benjamin could wait.

Jarvis hadn't experienced the sensation of being at home for years and so he struggled to make himself feel it. He explored quietly where he could without opening any closed doors or prompting anything to move. The landscape around Macey's house was pleasant and he enjoyed going from open room to open room and peering out the windows. Near a fireplace, occupying a central area in a spacious room, he found a large comfortable chair next to a long couch with another chair to the side. 'This must be where she entertains,' Jarvis thought, sitting down on one of the chairs. A large window lingered opposite himself, allowing a glimpse of the expansive field behind her house. The stream he noticed in the distance when walking up the driveway earlier that day flowed close enough that one could almost hear it. Jarvis imagined that Macey had cultivated this beautiful view over a lifetime. He sat comfortably and peered out the window. The soothing grayness lending itself to slow breathing, and Jarvis sunk in his chair.

With his eyes closed he allowed the chair to engulf him as the light from the window remained distinct behind his eyelids. After a while he heard the front door open and footsteps walking from room to room until entering the room in which he sat before quickly turning around. He listened to the footsteps fade and then return and when he opened his eyelids, he saw Millie standing with a piece of wood in each hand smiling. He smiled back and she placed them in the fireplace before taking a match and lighting some kindling beneath them. The fragrance from the burning logs filled the air, the red glow emanating from its origin mingling with the dull hued picture that the window presented. She sat on the couch near him and crossed her legs watching the flame.

"Isn't it perfect?" she said, leaning back, sinking into the sofa.

"Perfect." Jarvis replied, his eyes open, watching the dance of flames, listening to the crackle that occasionally erupted from the wood.

"Father Thomas must have liked you, ya know? To have brought you here."

"Is that right?" Jarvis asked, a curious slant forming on his eyebrows.

"Yes. He's been annoyed lately, I think. All our inns and boarding houses in town are full and the tired sheriff and the mayor, who's a walking skeleton at his age, don't know what to do. The travelers have slowed down, but they do still come. It seems like it's all fallen to Father Thomas and it's been a toll for a brand-new pastor who hasn't even met his flock on proper intimate terms to ask them to act as hotels for strangers. Still, he's done it cleverly. He's split it into two camps: people who want to help can offer their homes or just their beds and the pay he demands from the occupants makes it worthwhile for the homeowners either way. So for instance if they are reluctant the owner can decide to offer just a bed and the person staying has to come in after a certain time and leave before a certain time. Or for more money they can have full access to the home. A lot of the flock including Macey have offered their homes for free but Father Thomas almost refuses to utilize those folks. But he brought you here and Macey just puts you to work gardening, which she would do to any soul that walked onto her property."

"He seems like a good man." Jarvis said, "This seems like a good town... I like Macey, a nice lady."

Millie laughed, "Yes my Aunt is nice! I stay with her during the summer when I'm not jumping between school and home. It's refreshing here."

"Do you ever get used to the weather?" he asked.

"Of course! Ya know... The sun does come out occasionally. Most people don't believe me but it does. I think they're just so preoccupied that they don't notice but you'll see, it does come out!"

Jarvis laughed in response, adding to Millie's jovial air. "I suppose it must come out eventually." He replied. "I must say I enjoyed the church, that door is spectacular. And the inside, I don't think I've ever seen such a contrast."

"Yes." Millie nodded putting a finger on her chin, "If this town can claim any fame at all, other than Benjamin Mills and the situation he has caused, it can claim that church."

"I've never heard of it before?" Jarvis announced, quizzically.

"Right. I did say, 'if any fame,' which doesn't mean too much in terms of actual esteem. I suppose maybe because I've been coming here since I was little it seems like common knowledge." She stopped for a moment before her attention shifted towards the fire, "I'll say I do take pride in it." she added, trailing off as she spoke.

"You have my interest! Tell me more!" Jarvis laughed

"Right. I forgot that the story starts in a bad way... The church is young in terms of churches, the old one burnt down. A couple died in the fire, from the smoke, they were pulled out by the returning pastor but the smoke had ruined their lungs. It was a real tragedy. Obviously anytime something like that happens, a church burning down, or people dying, it's a tragedy but the church was beautiful and the couple was wealthy and well liked. Is it wrong that it strikes me as more tragic because they were wealthy? Anyway, the man who died... his grandfather was an Archbishop in France and came when he heard of his grandson's death. He arrived much later but brought with him that marvelous door from an ancient French church. He gave sermons and revitalized the town and convinced everyone to stop construction on the church that was being built. Thankfully the process was slow, and he conscripted an architect he chose to build a new church, using the door. They tore down what had been erected so far and built what stands currently, a sort of monument recognized only by the initiated but a splendid church to the rest. It was all done for free, at the expense of the French church all thanks to the Archbishop. And when it was completed, churches from around the world sent artifacts and gifts to properly adorn it."

"What a beautiful story."

"Yes, you should ask Father Thomas for a tour! He's very fond of the church, he traveled a long way to be here and is a splendidly good speaker."

"I will!" Jarvis replied, "What happened to the Archbishop?"

"Archbishop Climicus was his name, he went back to France about a year after the incident, it all happened very fast. I don't know what's become of him now, he was apparently very old when he came."

"I see. I'll make a point to ask Father Thomas about everything." He smiled. The fire crackled in the room and Jarvis looked out the window. The landscape had turned black without him noticing and only a faint gleam from the stream could be vaguely made out. Jarvis sighed.

Millie turned sideways, lying flat along the couch, one foot lazily dangling off the edge. Jarvis remained watching the fire as it faded slowly, his eyes shutting with the dying flame.

THIRTY-SEVEN

THE GRASS OF THE FIELD WAS SOFT UNDERNEATH THOMAS'S BARE feet. Overhead the clouds had parted and the rare sun renewed its acquaintance. He stood tall, his shirt damp with sweat. He had thought briefly of Jarvis whom he had met the day before, how he was absent from morning mass, no doubt because Macey was an early riser and put him to work, but now his mind was clear. The rounders set sat beside him in a rope bag, the bases and a few extra balls occupying its contents. He held a bat in one hand, the other coiled loosely around a ball. He threw the ball high, switching to a two-handed grip onto the bat and swung hard. A loud crack announced the balls flight into the empty space normally occupied by clouds before falling a far distance away, where it sat among other balls he had hit earlier. A wide array garnished the field, some closer than others. His gaze lingered in the distance. The wide landscape painted green, blazoned with streaks of white sunshine. From his peripherals he observed Eliza drawing closer. Her image was vague in his side-long glance but to him her figure was striking enough to be identifiable anywhere. He kept his eyes forward and although his heart quickened, he maintained a composed expression. Words spun in his head, attempting to align in a useful way but failing as one sentence after another clarified itself before being deemed insufficient. She drew closer, walking quick but composedly. She lightly kicked the rope back with her foot displaying the contents, the numerous different colored balls splaying out. Thomas looked downward unsure of what to say, he turned his head towards her but his body remained forward.

"Can you believe…" she stated anxiously, "That he told me that he needs some space?" she laughed, "I only just arrived and he needs space. I really cannot make heads or tails of it. Or can I? Who knows? I've been on the road so long maybe I've forgotten the proper way to interact." She sighed, Thomas could barely hear what she was saying, his face was hot with embarrassment but he managed to appear and feel somewhat receptive despite receiving no explanation. She continued, "He spends a lot of time in his head, as do I, but I at least have the decency, while in my head, to include him. To have an image of him lingering about no matter what I'm thinking of. Maybe that's given me an unrealistic representation of our relationship."

Thomas turned his body towards her, "Everyone needs space Eliza, some more than others."

She nodded, "Even though I've just arrived?"

"Especially because you've just arrived." he answered.

After a brief silence she announced, "Your altar boy told me where I would find you and what you might be doing… I thought you would have given up the sport considering how thoroughly I beat you."

Thomas's solemn expression erupted into laughter, "You beat me?"

"Of course, weren't you keeping score? Really Thomas, it was bad…"

Thomas's muscles felt tired, sweat was dripping down his forehead and he suspected that his exhausted state had prompted Eliza to prod him into a contest. With a smile on his face he shook his head, looking down to the bat in his hand.

"I must confess I wasn't keeping track; I don't remember who performed better. Would you care to remind me Eliza?" He tossed the bat down in front of her feet.

The sun was out. A vibrant field stood in front of them. Freshly cut, it emanated the pleasant smell of earth and grass. There were no woods in sight, only a brushstroke of green along the horizon. One side was littered with balls that Thomas had hit earlier which sat at varying distances. Eliza knelt down, rubbing some grass and dirt onto the handle of the bat before taking it tight into her grip and standing tall. She turned towards a fresh expanse, free of Thomas's previous hits, and motioned him to hand her a ball from the rope bag. He obeyed, placing it delicately into her open, extended hand and observed her carefully. Looking unashamedly at her for the first time since her arrival he noticed that she looked limber. Her hair was tied back into a tight ponytail that hung into the open air, catching what breeze it could, occasionally brushing lightly onto the back of her neck. She wore tight fitting but unrestrictive clothes that would breathe should they need to and he noticed that the fabric under her armpits were dark with dampness. She had taken the bat with an air of confidence and the ball looked as if it belonged in her hand. 'Is she already warmed up?' he thought, 'So she'd planned this scenario from the start.' He eyed her, unable to conceal a tinge of affection, and she smirked, tossing the ball upwards. The sound of exertion rang from her tight lips as she twisted hard, cracking the ball convincingly as it collided with her momentous swing. The ball flew high into the sky, Thomas's eyes briefly lost its trajectory to the bright sunlight before finally tracking it to a spot far away, catching sight of it as it bounced once then thudded onto the distant ground. She had chosen this direction intentionally, Thomas decided, so that her ball could not be measured against any that he had hit previously.

She tossed the bat casually in front of his feet and put her hand to her forehead, shading the sun, and looked into the distance as if unable to see where her ball landed. Finally satisfied with her theatrics she put her hand on her hip and looked to Thomas with a grin. Picking up the bat he motioned to her and she bent over, rummaging into the bag for a ball before handing him one. He took and looked gravely towards her ball. He felt tired. Her arrival had obviously disrupted his rhythm and he was just about done anyway. The bat felt heavy in his hand. He took a moment to rally and then threw the ball high. He squeezed tight onto the bat and swung as hard as he could manage in his current state. The ball exploded from the bat and flew into the sunlight, followed eagerly by Eliza and Thomas who struggled to maintain a view of it. It landed a short distance past Eliza's ball, rolling flamboyantly as it bounced along unfettered by victory. Excitement filled him and he narrowly restrained himself from shouting with enthusiasm. He looked to Eliza who nodded merrily.

"Good hit Thomas." she said, smiling, "Although I've just arrived and had no time to warm up. Still. A good hit. Inspiring."

Thomas laughed, "I suppose you're right. Will you help me gather the balls? I really should be going back now."

"Of course."

They walked slowly into the field, their shadows close.

"You know… I did enjoy our week." Eliza said, timidly. Thomas stayed silent although his pace remained slow, with hers. She sighed. "I was on my way to see him. Alexander. And I didn't intend to remain anywhere for any extended amount of time… Ah, what am I trying to say?"

Thomas leaned over, picking up the first ball that they had arrived at and placed it into the rope bag.

Eliza started again, "I guess what I want to say is that you're a good man." She crouched down, picking up a ball nearer herself and placing it into the bag that Thomas extended towards her, she looked him in the eyes sincerely, "And I'm a wretch."

"Eliza, enough…" He stopped his movement towards the balls, "The event… You rejected me. And that is fine, honestly, it's okay.

I asked the question, for you to come with me, as much for myself as for you. In other words, I had to ask because in my soul I wholeheartedly wanted to ask, I have no control over the outcome of the question and that is something I've come to accept in my life. You rejected me and I grieved just the same as I would have rejoiced if you had indulged me. It was what I truly wanted after all but I take life seriously and find validity in all its various manifestations. I threw myself into my grief and felt the full weight of the rejection. I did not hide from it or try to justify your actions, I took the situation as it was and felt everything that I could. Your presence here is jarring and it will take me some time to work out why. I imagine it's because I had closed that door and reconciled to the probable reality that I would never see you again. It's passed. You have no reason to feel bad."

They finished gathering the balls in silence and began the walk back. Sun shining overhead, each damp with sweat. Thomas rolled his sleeves up before tossing the bag over his shoulder as they reached a wide path leading towards the church.

"Alright let's hear it then." he said, the honest compassion returning to his voice. "You said, 'he told me he needs space,' tell me about it."

Eliza's cheeks turned pink before she smiled, "Oh it's really nothing, I feel better now…" She perked up, "If you insist though, I will explain."

"Yes. Yes. I insist. Go on."

"Well I traveled across the country. The world actually if we go back far enough. For the love of my cousin Alexander. He's never left my mind. You know part of me feels bad for him because it has always seemed like he doesn't have friends, he only has conversations if that makes sense. That is why our relationship is so special, because I cut through that aspect of him. I am continuity, a figure who I know he loves although he may struggle to show it, but he has before. And he's written me letters… He would never admit to it; he probably doesn't even admit it to himself. We all have certain moods after all, where passion rings above all else and we think of that person a world away. Would we really remember writing a letter in one of those moods? But he did write and what his letters contained was beautiful. And I only imagined that what he wrote would come alive in him as it has in me, now that I'm here."

"I see. I would say give him the space he wants for now. And give him time as well. He's hasn't seen you, hasn't been in your presence. He will come around."

"Oh Thomas, I think his whole life may be dedicated to *not* coming around." She shook her head as she continued, "I came on too strong, much too strong and I've ruined our relationship. I actually… Would you listen to this? We were only just reunited and I demanded that he let me sleep in his bed. I called it proper hospitality considering how long I've been traveling. He moved to a guest room to satisfy me, leaving his bedroom for myself but I followed him. Then he moved to a couch in the living room and I followed him there as well… I slept on an adjacent chair. When I woke up we had breakfast together and I asked him what we were going to do today and it looked like he had a headache." She laughed, "Oh that face will haunt me until the end of my days. What was I thinking?"

"I can see why that could be stifling…" Thomas agreed, "But as you said, he loves you and therefore he will come around. He's simply forgotten what you're like and once he properly acclimates, he will forgive any transgressions on your part."

"What I'm like? Careful Thomas." she laughed again, "I'm only kidding, you're right I suppose, this is what I'm like and that's why I called myself a wretch. I think you're correct though in your analysis and so I thank you for the kind words. He really does rely on rationality. His conclusion will no doubt be that my excitement was unwieldy and so I acted bizarrely but will calm down once he satiates my desire for him, at least to some degree, so that my feelings are manageable. Then we can negotiate."

Thomas nodded. They neared the church, approaching from behind, and he put the items in a small shed just outside. "What will you do for the rest of the day?" he asked, "Service begins in a few hours, you're more than welcome to stay."

"I appreciate that Thomas. Or… now that we are at church I should say Father Thomas. That really has a nice ring to it I must say. Father Thomas. No thank you, I have an idea. I know we've decided to give him space but giving people space is very boring… I think Luther is on my side and they are no doubt discussing Alexander's obsession with rationality this very moment."

"Did you say Luther?" Thomas asked with a furrowed brow.

"Yes. Do you know him?"

"I know him…"

"A wonderful man! I've known him since childhood. A special individual, isn't he? I've mentioned Alexander, well Luther is the caretaker of his estate, although their estates are essentially one and the same at this point." she said, enthusiastically.

"Eliza, I don't think so… That man is trouble. He has no morals. An abominable man… You said you've known him since childhood?" he said, his voice taking on a reluctant tone.

"You're mistaken Thomas." she answered sternly.

"Have you read…? Do you know… What's going on in this town?"

She smiled but her eyes remained tense, she cleared her throat in agitation before beginning, "Thomas I am here for Alexander. All the rest is interesting but nothing more than a tourist attraction as far as I'm concerned."

"A tourist attraction…?" Thomas's posture became straighter and his eyes obtained a fieriness to them. "This town… is a battleground for meaning. The fate of everything relies on the conclusions reached here… Have you read, for instance, his piece on suicide? And my gosh, the timing of it! These aren't just empty words Eliza, they are prompting people to action."

"Maybe you're right Thomas. Father Thomas. But on the suicide piece, I've heard of it and Luther assured me yesterday that the timing was coincidental. Think about it, isn't that the first question one has to deal with when doing philosophy? Of course that would be his first announcement!"

"Is that so? Isn't that quite convenient?"

"Anything is quite convenient if you contort it to be…" her voice reaching an unflattering volume, she caught herself, finishing her sentence in a lower, more pleasant tone. "Anyway…" she continued, "You're underestimating the utility of individuals like Luther. Part of me envies those religious people, the fervent ones, who have never been challenged in the slightest or had to question what they actually believe. It's better for everyone if someone comes along and says, 'I know you've been having fun but it's time to grow up.'-"

"So, to grow up is to have no values? Come on Eliza, you believe in something don't you?" his tone matching hers and despite how heavily contested the subject felt they both retained a softness in their presentation.

"I believe in something. I would even call it God. But truthfully, I don't even know what that means. I believe in beauty, and love, and tragedy. Flowers, death, family. Marriage... I believe I would like to have children... I never said I agreed with Luther, but he is a smart man and one cannot take that away from him. Let him make his arguments. Rejoice that your faith will be all the more strengthened from them."

"And what about the people who take him too seriously? The people who kill themselves."

"I never said you can't make arguments for yourself. Contradict Luther. Convince the masses."

"Eliza that's the problem with ideas like his… They are convincing. He's no doubt spent his entire life ramming one question after another against the wall called existence and he's left with a few powerful arguments that one would need an equal amount of time to refute. That's my problem with overly philosophical types. And history stands with me on this, I believe. Someone spends their whole life establishing something and it requires the next person in line to spend their whole lives either building off of it or debunking it… I wonder how much Luther travels?… Anyway, I don't have the time, talent, or intellect to refute his arguments. It's the sad truth that I've had to accept. For every argument I made he would have a nice sounding counterpoint. And how can I, in words, explain Christianity? That it is not an argument made thousands of years ago but a mode of existence stated for today, for every age and person to rediscover. How can I explain that faith is a passion? How can I use words to explain that no words can explain, that no words can bring that passion to one's soul?"

Eliza put a hand on Thomas's shoulder. "You're a good man, Father Thomas. I don't have an answer for you… All I can say is that I prefer to view life poetically." She hugged him, "It was good seeing you."

He smiled, "Where are you off to?"

"I figured I would go speak to Benjamin Mills." she replied. Thomas decided not to question her.

The back door of the church was a few paces away, as Thomas turned towards it, it opened suddenly. Jarvis emerged and seeing Thomas looked startled.

"Oh, I was just looking for you Father. I was told you would be a bit of a walk away." He laughed, "It wasn't such a trek after all."

Hearing a familiar voice Eliza, who had begun walking, turned around. The startled expression reappearing on Jarvis's face his voice quivered as he spoke, "Oh Eliza you're here. You did say you were coming here. Who would have thought we would both be here? I've only just arrived yesterday. I'm staying with Macey! But you don't know Macey, do you? She's lovely. You've met Father Thomas?" his words came out jumbled and his face reddened as he spoke.

"Jarvis! What a wonderful surprise, it's great to see you. I thought you were going with John? Yes, I've met Father Thomas. And I do know Macey." she paused for a moment, "But I must be going!" She turned and began walking. Jarvis stepped forward awkwardly.

"Wait! Eliza. You aren't staying for the service? I thought, since you're here, we could do something."

Eliza continued walking and Thomas couldn't make out whether she had heard Jarvis or not, he looked to the confused expression painted on Jarvis's red face and concluded that he was in a similar state of perplexity. Thomas looked compassionately at him but felt guilty due to the satisfaction that pulsed uncontrollably within himself, knowing that Eliza had spoken to him at length along with her perceived willingness to continue the conversation they were having if there was anything left to say.

"Come on Jarvis, let's go inside." he finally said, putting a hand on his back and motioning towards the door.

ELIZA FOLLOWED THE SIDEWALK ON HER WAY TO THE DANCING Sheep and she was welcomed by the flow of townsfolk. Their quick pace hurried her own meandering style but she welcomed the solitude provided by the silence of her fellow travelers. They walked determinably, almost as if marching and only slight remarks symbolized that she was walking with her own kind. Eventually the quiet gave way to a clatter. Eliza knew she was close to her destination when she heard a shout in the distance. A smile grew on her face as she walked and began to be encompassed by what felt like commotion. The group around her morphed one by one from generic looking townsfolk to a more unique variety, each possessing their own flair, something to make them stand out. Sure there were a few duplicates, Eliza noticed, a few individuals who in their journey to be unique ended up at the same spot. They would stay away from each other if they made the discovery, no doubt, and thereby retain their individuality.

The crowd was larger than when she had seen it the previous day but it appeared livelier now. A young man was standing on the platform of a lamp post and hanging with one arm towards the crowd. His voice was booming and much louder than Eliza had imagined it would be from his meek appearance. She walked past and as she entered The Dancing Sheep she wondered, for a moment, how far his exclamations carried, but anxious to meet Benjamin she reconciled to finding out another time, and as the man looked somewhat familiar she assumed she had seen him before and would see him again. The door closed behind her.

She recognized Benjamin reading a paper beside another man in a distant corner. She took a moment to absorb the setting. A quant restaurant, well organized and clean. Most of the atmosphere was wood and it shone vibrantly in the mixture of candle and lamp light. The colors green, black, and red announced some items and drew one's gaze sweepingly across the restaurant. The bar had an immense selection and Eliza noted that the placement of wine was impeccable. She decided to have a glass, sitting resolutely on a high stool, she motioned to a pretty woman behind the counter who then poured the exact wine Eliza was thinking about asking for effortlessly into a cup without so much as a word, before disappearing from Eliza's mind. Eliza lingered casually, sipping as she took notice of the inhabitants around her. A distinguished countenance filled the room. Low contemplative tones echoed throughout. She saw men attained from every wrung of society, or so she assumed from the clothing and choice of accessories, yet all exuded a confidence that allowed the dwelling to emit an especially cosmopolitan charm. Looking around she expected to acquire some attention. Her beauty had developed in her certain expectations of distinct customs that applied only to her. Here she received none. No glances teetered past her. No quick peeks. She finished her wine slowly, trying to identify internally why she felt a slight pang of offense that no one had come to speak to her.

Finally, she approached Benjamin who still sat reading in the same place as when she entered. Another man sat next to him. Well dressed and similar in age to Benjamin. As she drew nearer, the man put his paper on the table and looked Eliza up and down. Although she stood in front of them Benjamin's eyes remained scanning the sheet in his hand, one of many sheets that was strewn across the table.

"The audacity…" the man said and although Eliza was confused she replied with a confident grin. "After what you did yesterday! You know… The young ones out there won't stop talking about you. It was quite the spectacle. A real display of iconoclasm. And you've come here to what? Show off to the young ones outside, they've surely seen you enter. And you've lingered so they will think you're quite special."

"Maybe I am special you old cock." Her brow furrowed as she spoke. With a condescending laugh she continued, "I've no idea what you're talking about. Besides I'm here to meet Benjamin, not you."

Benjamin remained reading as the man next to him replied, "You mean you don't know why they are all talking about you…?"

"I had no clue they were talking about me to begin with."

"The red bench." the man said, "You sat on it all morning."

Benjamin's eyes lifted from the paper.

"So what?" Eliza replied.

Benjamin turned to the man next to him and with a tone of confirmation said, "She's the one that was with Alexander."

Upon hearing Alexander's name Eliza's heart throbbed and she instinctually leaned closer to make sure she didn't miss a word.

The man laughed, "Is that right? Have you heard the fuss that they are making?"

"No, I haven't heard." Benjamin said, thoughtfully.

"What fuss?" Eliza asked to which neither of the men paid attention.

Benjamin folded his paper and stood up. Placing a hand on his chin, he maneuvered, almost pushing his way past her and began pacing slowly.

The man who remained sitting sighed. "Take a seat if you'd like." he said. She sat down across from the man who had begun shuffling the papers into a tidy pile.

"I'm Phillip," the man said, his eyes distracted as he motioned to the pretty woman behind the bar.

"Eliza." she responded.

Silence permeated between them until interrupted by the pretty woman who placed a tall glass of wine in front of Eliza and a short, nearly overflowing cup of scotch in front of Phillip. Eliza turned to look at Benjamin who seemed to be in a trance, walking back and forth with his arms folded and one hand resting against his chin, through their secluded section of the restaurant.

Phillip drank eagerly and after making a formidable dent in the contents of his cup, allowing him to maneuver it easier, he began speaking with a theatric tone, "You know the story, but apparently not all of it. It is likely that you missed something, seeing how you are unaware of your mistake. Or maybe you would have done it anyway, I'll perhaps ask that question after I tell you what happened, assuming you know enough to pick up where I start. Angel-ica Hamilton… She was the niece of Wilbur Hamilton who owned this establishment and is essentially the goddess to which the gen-eration now prays. She was a stunning beauty, good to her core, and loved by everyone. When she died it was a serious blow to the town, especially Wilbur, who took some time off to properly grieve while Benjamin took charge of The Dancing Sheep in his absence. This, as you know, caused a stir and people began flooding in. One day, when the crowds were as they are now, Wilbur, feeling better, decided to go for a walk into town. He pushed his way past and saw a boy sitting on that red bench outside, which had been dedicated to Angelica and he… In a frenzy he pushed the boy with all his ef-fort. The crowd fell silent as he surveyed the area with a disoriented cadence and all watched as he stumbled and collapsed unconscious. So you see, the crowd now puts the red bench in its proper place, that is, among the artifacts of divinity and so on."

"I see… No. I never would have sat there if I had known… Or I think not at least. I would rather not cause people pain if I can help it."

"Oh, I don't think it's pain you've caused but surely you have acquired some notoriety."

"Benjamin isn't mad? I didn't offend him?"

Benjamin sat down next to Phillip, across the table from Eliza and looked into her eyes. "It's just a bench Eliza… I'm Benjamin." He extended his hand to hers which she took comfortably. "I as-sume you're familiar with what's occurred in this town recently. Have you read Luther's essays?"

"Not many, I've heard him mention the one about suicide but we only spoke briefly."

"I imagined as much, you being acquainted with Alexander it only makes sense that you are with Luther as well. I can tell you that whatever he told you was false. A lie to make himself feel in the right and a contradiction to how he proclaims to live his life. I suppose he told you in relationship to that particular essay that it had nothing to do with timing? Why would he mention that to you if it really had nothing to do with timing? Anyone who he is personally attached to he seems to apologetically spout that false-hood but to the majority who discover the suicide slowly he allows the essay to simmer as a description of reality and the truth of his words manifesting in the world. He really timed the publication perfectly. Right before the public found out, they read this sterling inventory of suicide and then there it is! They hear about one and from an integral actor in the community."

"I'm not one to question the motives of friends…"

"Fine, fine, that's all well enough. The impact is still the detri-mental factor, even putting aside the timing which only amplified the initial reception. That's why I'm glad you're here. You're perfect to write a rebuttal!" Benjamin smiled as he finished speaking.

Eliza with a confused expression responded, "What are you talking about? Why would I write anything."

"You have notoriety Eliza." Benjamin laughed, "What better way to use it than to win over those who hate you."

"Why don't you write?"

"Luther is a smart man. I cannot take that away from him. Any-thing I put forward will be utterly torn down. I absolutely cannot be the one to respond. No matter what I wrote he would begin with, 'to my grieving friend,' and it would undermine my whole retort. He would paint me as grieving and all my points as emo-tional representations of grief, no matter how calculated they were. You on the other hand are a third party that can properly respond and who cannot be undermined so easily."

Eliza laughed, "No one even knows who I am, surely it could be said, 'who is this person who is writing.' Wouldn't that un-dermine me?"

"Of course, but everyone knows who you are! You can sign your work with, 'From the Red Bench.' It will put your image into the minds of everyone while technically remaining anonymous. A beautiful young romantic! And what's better is your image will act to tinge your words with the beauty required to contest Luther's hard logic. When someone yells at you, you do not yell back, you whisper. The contrast is what sways people. One must be warm, compassionate, and expressive to show the cold inflexibility of Luther's arguments. It is only a single response that I would require, to break the silence, invoke the fire in the souls of the readers and then I could write, myself, again."

"Yes, I suppose you're right." Eliza nodded, "The question is why would I? I only just met you after all."

"You only just met me, this is true. I will say that, although I'd review and help to refine what you write, I would never publish anything that you didn't agree with."

Eliza interrupted, "How are you so confident that I believe what you think I do?"

"I saw how you looked at Alexander and how he looked at you. You know... I'm fond of him and it makes me happy to see his eyes like that." Eliza blushed as Benjamin continued, "Eyes give a lot away."

Eliza laughed, "Fine! I've nothing else to do today."

THIRTY-EIGHT

———

"Do you really think I'm the one to talk to concerning this subject?" Luther asked, he sat comfortably leaning back in a chair in the study. Alexander walked back and forth in front of Luther's desk.

"What do you mean? You're the perfect person to talk to." he said, clearly lost in thought.

"If that's the case haven't you given yourself away already? There are two possibilities as I see it. You have come to a conclusion which you want me to help concretize. I view this as unlikely considering your current state and the fact that you have never sought my guidance per se. The other possibility is that you've come to a conclusion that you want me to disrupt, to sweep away the foundation."

Alexander laughed, "What are you on about? I've given myself away? That's not possible because I haven't thought it through, so what is there to give away? My initial sentiments? Fine, what do they matter?"

"They matter quite a good deal, but we can return to them in more detail later if you prefer."

"Fine. Fine, we can begin with them if you insist. Have at it."

"Perfect." A self-assured smile lingered on Luther's face, "We can at least use the concept as an entry point. The question would be why is it ever necessary to erode the initial sentiments? In other words, why should one not act solely on these sentiments?"

"Well it's obvious," Alexander replied, "One can assume that there will be circumstances where initial sentiment conflicts with how one wants to live. And because of this, in order to err on the side of caution, a safety mechanism of sorts is put in place, one that says, 'do not act on initial sentiments for they may contradict how you want to live.' There's no implicit rule that dictates that the final conclusion is always different from initial sentiments but there's no reason to pay attention to them. If they match up they match up. The important thing is that one's decision to act be in accordance with how they want to live."

"And how is it that you want to live?" Luther prodded.

"With an emphasis on intellectual development."

"And can you really make such a hard distinction between something called intellectual and something called sentimental? Or for our purposes can't we expand the phrasing and say emotional? Isn't that the crossroads you claim to be standing at?"

"Yes, I would accept that description as the crossroad I am standing at and tormented by. And in terms of whether or not I can make the distinction, of course I can. The criteria could be this: intellectual development would result in a more robust area of expertise. You've influenced me enough Luther that I wouldn't use the word knowledge with any real reverence but I can use the word information without guilt. Intellectual development could be described as an increase in one's ability to assimilate and contextualize new information. I don't see anything but the most insignificant role for emotion in this realm. And seeing as you are taking a more inquisitive role to start, I think I can guess what you would ask next, 'to what end?' The answer as you know is, there is no real end. Perhaps I could say the ideal, which is to possess all information but that is obviously impossible. That's what life is though isn't it? A pursuit of the unattainable. At least with something like information genuine progress can be acknowledged, must be acknowledged. An old man who has spent a lifetime dedicated to the task will be undeniably more advanced than a child who has just begun the operation. And what would we make if we explored the emotional realm? Is an old man who has dedicated his life to it any better off than a child? No... In fact, he is worse off. Our emotional peak is in childhood and we can look back with joy at it although we must retain a forwardly stern disposition and say, 'luckily I know better now.'-" Alexander sat down before continuing, crossing his legs and, looking behind Luther at a partially protruding book that briefly caught his attention, continued, "And now you, playing devil's advocate, would ask, 'and what about happiness?' I would say that only in so far as it is effortless does happiness fit into the equation. And only so long as it does not impinge upon the general task. If in brief moments we remember our past with a sense of enthusiasm, that's fine, for instance, considering we did not know any better. Those who never learn become stuck in a cycle of great effort followed by enthusiastic remembrances. They get these same brief pangs of joy, thinking back to their childhood, and attempt to relive them, to create more, hoping that at a future date the same feeling can be cashed in again. They do this until they die. Never maturing enough to acquire anything worthwhile. Why? Because all their thoughts are concerned with this happiness. The cost in most cases are too great... My current circumstance. The crossroad I see. Any possibility of fruitful thought is eroded because... How am I to think of anything else?"

Luther sighed, "This is precisely why I am the wrong person to be talking to. Love sounds manageable from a distance but it's obvious that from within it is more trouble than its worth. My honest opinion is that it should be avoided at all costs. Relationships in general actually. Words are so cumbersome that under no circumstances can we really do much more than talk past each other hoping that one word or a few sentences will stick in the dirt and properly blossom. Love manifests in the world as an eternal attempt to understand another person, but what if one has no interest in people? What is love without a willingness to attempt to understand?" he paused for a moment before continuing, "But if I may be uncharacteristically optimistic for a moment, it may be worth experimenting with, worth trying, although the outcome is obvious... I'm afraid that's as responsible an answer as I can give."

ALEXANDER SAT, FEELING THE WEIGHT OF HIS HEELS ON THE ground and observing the sensation of the grass beneath his feet. Leaning back, his hands heavy on the earth, he listened to the light patter of the stream a few yards in front of him. Growing up in Wilheimer Falls he was sensitive to the varying hues of gray and what they meant. Knowing that the last remaining light would vanish soon he reconciled to extracting every moment he could before returning home. Flashes of Angelica sprinkled his thoughts. Her features had shifted from what he remembered, and he wasn't sure that the image in his head was accurate. She had, he imagined, taken on qualities of the paintings he had seen. He had contemplated her through consistent brief pangs in his chest but never reached a definite conclusion. Images of her teetered in and out of his awareness and now she reappeared. He sat watching the stream. In his peripherals she seemed to be sitting next to him. Turning his head, he imagined her as well as he could, her blonde hair hanging lazily, reflecting the disappearing light of the sky. Smooth tan skin decorating the green landscape behind her. Blue eyes that pierced with determination. She reached out, delicately placing a hand on his face and smiled. He almost felt the warmth of her hand, and her soft words echoed through him. "You know we weren't meant to be together." she said, solemnly, "But I think... I think you can still be happy, should want to be happy..." Alexander looked forward towards the stream and she returned to a similar position. She laughed, "One touch would have been nice though." Alexander smiled looking into the distant woods which hung dark past the stream saying to her and himself, "One touch... would have been nice."

As Angelica faded his mind wandered to his childhood. The garden that his mother had cultivated came back to life. It was nice presently, as Luther had hired a master botanist to ensure its upkeep, but something about its past iteration presented a different kind of beauty. Knowing that the dirt was dug into by her hands. The image of her sampling the various scents. Once he had told her that two plants traditionally were not put together and she laughed, saying, "So what? It's our garden." He had felt guilty about that for a long time. Now it was an endearing memory despite the inflection of guilt that still accompanied it.

His mind continued to drift. Her face. Her funeral... And then to Eliza. Eliza... made it all bearable. Where had she been? Now that she was here... He was reminded. Her smile reached into the past, alleviating where it was necessary, a salve to the lingering aches. Now her image appeared beside him. Resting with her hands on her knees, a cute smile pointed at the dimming horizon. It was a look that reached into the future. Showed him the way.

In the darkness he made his way home and approaching the large white estate from the front he felt a strange sense of warmth. The closer he got the more he felt like he belonged. Opening the door, a deep breath of relief escaped his lips and he began walking towards his room. He approached the stairs that led to his bed but noticed a faint candle in the living room. He walked quietly, his light steps silent as he moved through the house, careful not to disturb the atmosphere that he now felt so welcome in. He entered and saw Eliza sleeping on the same couch she had the night before. Her pleasant white cheeks catching the slight glow of flame from the candle. Her thin lips loosely open, allowing tiny breaths to come and go like a gentle breeze. Her neat hair tucked beneath her with an occasional strand shining in solitude in front of her face. He lay on the couch next to her and fell asleep.

THIRTY-NINE

————

MILLIE LOOKED PLEASANT IN THE EARLY MORNING. MACEY SLAP-ping her hand on his back Jarvis smiled, he had never met anyone who was so energetic this early. He tried to recall if he had ever met anyone who woke up as early as him and John before but no one came to mind. They had already eaten a modest meal, enough to give them energy until they made a larger breakfast after some work. The sky was bright and Jarvis noticed that the sun peak-ed through more persistently earlier in the day or maybe it was Millie that made it seem so. Jarvis had a shovel in his hand and dug quickly. He preferred this task because it was difficult, there-fore Macey and Millie were spared, and he was proficient in it, although it didn't take much skill. He felt useful.

Macey had a greenhouse that was filled with flowers, Millie had shown it to him after he had spent the day in town previ-ously. He had walked back in a slump after Eliza had seemed to shun him. His thoughts spun after receiving what he perceived as a rejection, deciding it didn't even matter if she heard him or not, it was the way she looked at him and the way she walked away. After Simon had reprimanded him, he declared to himself that he didn't care, but after her finalization he came to the conclusion that he did care. He cared and it hurt. He felt vulnerable. Millie had taken his hand and shown him the flowers and he cried with-out knowing why but he hadn't thought of Eliza since. The flowers were beautiful and she had explained every different variety to him and he enjoyed looking from the flowers to her smiling face, back to the flowers, and so on. As he dug, his glance kept gravitating to her and the thick dress she wore blew heavily in the breeze as she worked. Handprints of dirt adorned the front of it where she had wiped them several times while transporting flowers from the greenhouse to the garden. Jarvis decided that he would ask her to show him the flowers again when he had the chance.

Once he got to work, he noticed time flew by. It was only the next moment that Millie tapped him on the shoulder and told him to come with her inside for breakfast, and that they were planning on going to the midday mass again, as was their custom. Macey had a shop to run and Millie told Jarvis how the next day it would be just them charged with making progress in the garden. She said it innocently but her eye contact lingered for a few seconds after she had said it. Jarvis smiled. At the table, breakfast was modest: bread with butter, sausage, and fruit. It was better than anything Jarvis had enjoyed on his travels and he ate eagerly. He noticed that after working so early his mind remained occupied with the progress of the garden and he yearned to return to the hole he was in the middle of digging and wanted desperately to finish transferring the small tree from a remote part of the property to the freshly made hole. The sound of silverware against plates was what generally echoed through the house at this time, all being preoccupied with whatever interrupted task remained outside.

A knock on the front door signaled the entrance of Thomas who came in carrying a bushel of apples and placed it in the center of the table before putting a friendly hand on Jarvis's shoulder and his other on Millie's who sat next to him. He patted pleasantly before crossing his arms and walking to the window to observe the progress they were making.

"Good morning!" he said, turning and smiling at them. "You're really making progress."

"Here, eat." Macey said, putting some food on a plate and bringing it over to Thomas, "Oh what am I doing, sit! Sit!" She pulled out a chair and guided Thomas to it, taking him by his sleeve.

"Alright! Alright!" he laughed, allowing her to sit him down, placing the plate in front of him.

"And to drink, Thomas, what can I get you to drink?" She pulled a cup from the cupboard and placed it in front of him.

"Oh water is fine, thank you." he replied, popping a grape into his mouth.

She nodded pouring water from the pitcher into his cup.

"I actually received a letter this morning for you Jarvis and seeing how I cannot pass up on an opportunity to visit I thought I would deliver it myself." He removed a letter from his jacket pocket and handed it to Jarvis, who took it eagerly.

"I was wondering when he would get a chance to write me," Jarvis smiled, "Thank you for bringing it over Father.

"Of course." he said, folding the buttered bread from his plate in half and taking a bite.

Macey made small talk with Thomas while they finished their meal and afterwards, while Millie and Macey returned to work, and Thomas hurried back to give his morning service, Jarvis excused himself to his room to read the letter.

To my brother Jarvis,

I arrived in the town just outside of Richmond, two days after your departure and while admitting that it initially exceeded expectation the final result is that it was a colossal failure.

My impression upon entering the town was excitement. Arriving in my customarily early fashion, I went unnoticed for a while and observed. I scouted the town and it appeared natural in the morning hours and even as people awoke. A wagon arrived carrying food and little vendors emerged as they might in older times before established shops were the norm. Normal seeming people came from all directions and a merry gathering occurred as they bartered, joked, and consumed. It began to dawn on me that I must be in the wrong town. Confused I went to what I perceived to be a tavern and was grabbed rather rough-handedly by a group of students who interrogated me. As I was beginning to dread the thought of more travel so soon, I was relieved at this detention because it confirmed that I was in the right place. I managed to talk myself into their good graces by explaining that I was a journalist enthralled by their cause and wanted to write a dedicated piece about it. Afterwards they let me roam free, I agreeing not to disturb the practices that had established themselves. This questioning had taken several hours and so it took me some effort to find the population after I returned to the heart of the town, as it was at this point completely empty.

After finally finding them in an old town hall, which I would classify as filthy, I sat in the back and observed them. They were holding a daily town meeting, the structure of which is, I think, notable. Comments, ideas, complaints, and so forth could be submitted at any time for review by the town. A board of three random individuals would decide beforehand if the notes were worth reading. The individuals were randomly chosen at the end of each session so as to be ready for the next day's undertaking. One could submit the same note a maximum of once per week and never more than four weeks in a row. After four times submitting the note is punishable before an as yet undefined time has elapsed. In other words, what I witnessed was surprisingly smooth, the town now running for a month, a lot was dealt with already. The entire town voted yay or nay on the notes and occasionally committees would be assigned for certain projects.

The real confusion came, though, when I began making serious inquiries to the inhabitants and found them all agreeable. I decided to follow one man around who was particularly affable and had invited me to his home. It was a shabby old hotel where the wallpaper was coming down. The bed was in good shape, though, and so I didn't feel especially bad for him. He didn't talk much and we sat until someone knocked at the door and he called them in. It was a lazily dressed man who appeared surprised to see me. After a proper questioning he revealed to me that he was a doctor and that he and his team had been medicating the population as they normally would be for the entire time the town has been around. The food was essentially donated at a loss that the outside vendors were accruing. His team and him were essentially undercover, the students only just recently losing interest, but before had been rabidly following the towns happenings. Pretending to be patients they gave the necessary care to the inhabitants, making sure everything ran well.

So, as you can see it was not the revelation I was hoping for. Despite the genuine establishment of the local government, everything else strikes me as a sham. I hope all has been well for you Jarvis, I look forward to seeing you when I finally arrive and yearn to hear what you have been up to.

Yours,
John

MILLIE LINGERED IN THE GARDEN LOOKING AT A PINK FLOWER THAT she had chosen because Jarvis had smiled especially bright when she showed it to him. It looked at home. She thought of Jarvis's smile. How sweat accumulated on his cheeks when he worked, how he had laughed when she had slipped on some mud. Lost with the flower, she was retrieved when Macey put a hand on her shoulder,

"Could you give me a hand with this Millie?" she asked, pointing to a decent size rock that needed to be moved.

"Of course!" She took one side and Macey took the other. On the count of three they both lifted and moved it to a pile that was beginning to accumulate from the week. Millie let out a sigh of relief when they were finished, the rock being heavier than it looked and spoke, "Aunt Macey, I think... I want. To spend the rest of the year here."

"Oh Millie! It would be a pleasure." Macey hugged her, realizing what it meant.

JARVIS SAT WITH THE LETTER REREADING IT AFFECTIONATELY. Never being away from John so long he wondered how he was faring and hoped for the best. He was startled out of contemplation when Millie knocked on his door. Opening it with a smile, she reminded him that it was time for Mass if he wanted to join them. He confirmed and got ready. Although he didn't own many clothes, he had one shirt that was less embarrassing than the rest and put it on, the dirty pants he wore now were the cleanest he had at the moment so he kept them on.

They arrived early and sat in anticipation, especially of Father Thomas's sermon which would follow the normal processions. But for now, it was quiet. Macey liked the silent church. None spoke until Macey pulled Jarvis, who was between her and Millie, close to her and whispered to him.

"I think you should stay. I think you should stay with us for a while."

Jarvis looked at Macey whose compassionate smile made him feel warm and welcome. He sat back and looked at Millie, her red face pointing forward. Although Macey had spoken softly, she was heard. Jarvis observed for a moment Millie's cute posture which had stiffened at the question and how she labored to appear normal. Attempting to stifle her breath, partly to hear better, her breathing had taken on a quick shallow pace. Her body pointed unnaturally forward and her eyes looked everywhere but the direction of him. He smiled and felt like he saw what appeared to be the beginnings of a grin on her lips.

"I would like that Macey." he replied. Millie letting out a deep exhale. Her red face returning to a more natural pink hue. Her hand which sat close by his inched little by little until their pinkies were touching.

ELIZA AWOKE. HER EYES OPENED SLOWLY, LIGHT PENETRATING THE room only vaguely, just enough to signal to her that night was over. She felt well rested. The blanket nestled around her retained her warmth, reapplying it generously to her traveled body. A liberating soreness conveyed itself from her muscles. It was the soreness one feels when motion has stopped, when one finally has time to recover. Her eyes lingered on the window, observing the distant green of trees. Watching branches adorned with leaves swaying slightly. She smiled. Her gaze drifted to the couch next to her where Alexander slept soundly. Her smile acquired a new element of emotion, straightening for a moment while she gently bit her lip, tears gathering in her eyes. Here his boyhood was preserved, this Alexander she recognized fully, here he revealed how he felt. 'Maybe he's had a nice dream,' she thought, acknowledging that a change had occurred. She remained laying, content. His chest rose slowly where it remained momentarily before a descent accompanied by the pleasant sound of his exhale. His mouth hung slightly open, his breath deep and prolonged. 'Even in his sleep he looks clever.' She giggled to herself at the thought.

As she watched, her stomach growled. Falling asleep early the night before, she had deprived herself of a satisfying dinner. Fearing that she would wake Alexander up, and knowing herself well enough to understand that she would be distraught if his sleep was disturbed, she quietly maneuvered and went to the kitchen where she met Luther who was huddled over a bowl of oatmeal. He nodded as she entered. She sat across from him taking an apple from a fruit bowl which occupied the center of the table.

"Simon's still asleep?" she asked, taking a bite of her apple.

"Yes, he's a hardworking man." Luther laughed, "we cleared an entire thicket yesterday. Out behind the stable."

"Is that so? I hoped he would relax for a while."

"To men like him Eliza, there is no better relaxation. Labor in the benefit of one's own home. This is home after all."

"Yes." Eliza smiled, "This is home."

"It's good to see you again Eliza."

"You as well Luther." she replied sincerely, "Did you read what I wrote?"

"Yes, I read it."

"My provocation?"

Luther laughed, "Yes, it was a very clever response. I know not to underestimate Benjamin but employing you was a smart move. Still those who prefer logic and reason will not be affected. Because of this I have no reservations in complimenting the beauty of your composition." Luther grinned.

Eliza laughed in response, "That's good, I simply could not resist. Benjamin is a charming man after all, how could I refuse."

"Indeed." Luther agreed.

DESPITE WANTING TO WATCH THE PALPITATING MOVEMENT OF AL-exander's chest and the soft sound of his breath she decided to, despite the anguish it would cause her, go sit on the porch instead, allowing him to make contact whenever he chose.

After a decent duration, the sky fully alight, he emerged from the screen door that separated them. Eliza smiled noticing that he wore the same clothes that he had slept in, which declared to her the importance he attached to seeing her.

"I didn't mean to send you away yesterday…" he said, sitting next to her. "I was thinking about you, I missed you." He sighed.

She looked at him, their eyes meeting. She remained for a moment looking into them before replying. "It's okay Alexander."

FOURTY

———

Days had passed, Benjamin satisfied with the tone that Eliza's essay had conveyed was in good spirits. 'She's something, that's for sure.' he thought, taking keys from his pocket and unlocking the front door of The Dancing Sheep. He grabbed a stack of papers that had been delivered by someone who was an even earlier riser than himself and entered the restaurant, pouring himself a glass of water and sitting with the papers in a secluded corner. After an hour or so Natalie, who took care of the actual operations of the establishment, entered. And slowly in Benjamin's peripherals the place came to life. He read the stack and looked up, the day was bright and The Dancing Sheep was busy. It's regular crowd was joined by a reinvigorated assortment of youths, who had gained the courage to enter sensing the merry mood of everyone, Benjamin included. He looked next to him and saw that Phillip sat in his normal seat sipping a glass of scotch and reading the papers that he had discarded earlier.

"Good Morning Phillip." he said, peeking outside the window and observing the commotion that he had come to expect. Outside the window, in the cut grass yard that expanded out from the building, a group sat in a circle. They looked cheery and awake, lips moving slowly, opening just enough to let words escape. Benjamin could almost hear their quiet timbre. Across the road was where the debates occurred. One individual usually hung from the light post which had a generous platform that one could comfortably stand on, and the other took a competitive stance on a plain bench that sat outside of the nearby bank. They looked lively as well. Benjamin smiled. "You know I avoid listening to the reception, but… how has it been? From the Red Bench."

Phillip put his paper down and followed Benjamin's gaze outside to the group that sat in the grass. "It's nice don't you think? That they just sit there, by the flowers and talk. No debates, just talking. In my old age I prefer that group." He then looked to the crowd huddled around the light post and bench, "Although there is something special about a good spar, actually exposing your ideas to the chopping block." He stacked the papers in front of him neatly, almost being dramatic on purpose, but such was his style. He continued, "In Church I heard a whisper, 'it was about God without ever mentioning God,' that is what the low voice said and I imagine that is what they are talking about now. The reception has been what you probably expected. That group sitting out in a circle was not there when I arrived several weeks ago, it only just materialized. The essay was just what was needed, the feeling in the town was becoming stale and combative. If I'm honest I think the movement is passing, the students are being called back to their universities. And you obviously expected that as well, which is why I imagine you were secretly so eager to find a way to respond to Luther. Summer is coming to a close and Eliza's letter from the red bench was a perfect conclusion, it energized them and now I expect they will return to their parts of the country with a serious sentimentality. Another great awakening."

Benjamin smiled, his eyes remaining on the group that sat in a circle. "Is that so? It turned out okay then?"

"Yes Benjamin, this all turned out okay."

Benjamin sighed, "And the New Lutherans?"

"Luther is a smart man and will continue to write forever. Those who want to live in accordance with the most convincing logical proof will follow what he says. Is that really so bad though?"

"No, it's not so bad, as long as they are shown the alternative. I feel better now… Now that they've seen it."

Benjamin walked to the crowd of young gentlemen who had, in good spirits, entered the restaurant. He spoke with them extensively and asked each of their names before heading outside. He sat in the circle and spoke in a low tone, careful not to claim more time than anyone else. Afterwards he went and stood on the platform of a light post, joining a debate on some obscure theological point. He went home happy, laid in bed, fell asleep, and never woke up.

FOURTY-ONE

WILHEIMER FALLS WAS EMPTY. THE STOREFRONTS GLOWED IN THE absence of the townsfolk who were normally detained by the beautiful hues that emanated. All had gathered for the memorial. The field was large. It needed to be to accommodate everyone. The gray sky overhead felt right. It was the last days of summer and the travelers who had been ready to leave extended their trip for a few days. Despite the high attendance the field was silent. None spoke. A stage was set up for those who wanted to say something but it was understood, without words, that those who were supposed to speak, knew so. Phillip spoke, then his childhood friend Katherine, Macey's strength showed as she spoke. And lastly, Alexander.

What he said wasn't wordy. He spoke of what he knew. He spoke of Angelica. He spoke of Wilbur. He spoke of his time with Benjamin. And when he was finished summer was over. All returned home feeling the weight of an undeniable truth, that life is short.